Never Going Back:
Book One of The Felled

Never Going Back: Book One of The Felled

Ryan S. Leavitt

Cover art by Sutthiwat Dechakamphu

To report typos or offer any other general feedback, please e-mail: ryansleavittscifi@gmail.com

Visit my website: www.ryansleavitt.com

Join my e-mail for discounts and updates on books and projects I have coming up. As a thank you, you'll get a free ebook to take home.

Sound good?

Sign up at:
Ryansleavitt.com

Table of Contents

Foreword

When you think about the future too much, you end up writing about the future. That'd be fine if humans weren't notoriously terrible at predictions. Whether it's the weatherman, the stockbroker, or the person typing this, the future isn't exactly something we have a good grasp on. It's intangible, at least to our brains.

On top of that, science suggests the way we perceive time itself is not necessarily correct. Our apprehension of time is linear.

The individual, as such, does what they can. The term "miswanting" is used to describe our inability to know what will actually make us happy.

Thankfully, I will tell you that that feeling that I'd be very happy to present you with this story of the future has persisted from beginning, middle, to end. I'd say that's a good sign.

As much as I would like to to to let this book speak for itself, I also feel it's necessary to set your expectations for what follows, because it's a little different. Not just because I think it contains some things I've not seen used in the science fiction before, although you could accuse it of that.

This book is part of a larger whole and designed from the start to be serialized. I took inspiration of this format from others and hope *The Felled* can find its place in a sea of other binge-worthy content. Perhaps even a TV show one day. This release contains the first six episodes, each one ending in a cliffhanger.

If I could ask anything of you besides to give this a try, it would be to savor it. This is a bedtime story. A lullaby to consciousness.

We live in a time of extreme promise and peril, and each day compounds our uncertainty. The mystery of where we are going is, for the first time I think, becoming more urgent than the mystery of where we came from.

I'll admit it: I'm no good at seeing into our world's future. Let me share with you an idea of it I hope you'll find as inescapable as I have.

EPISODE 1
Entity Unlike Itself

Prologue

1.

"It's coming," said the boy with the pale violet irises. His name was not Gabriel, but designated as such for convenience's sake. His true name, given to him at birth, was unknown. He'd been called "Gabriel" for as long as he could remember. Since he knew this was not his name, he didn't identify with it. The knowledge of his true name, if it even was still available, grew more distant from him each day.

And though the boy had all his needs met, he was unsatisfied. He recognized he'd never die as a result of this lack. But then it also felt to him that because of this dreaded cosmic mishap he would never, ever be who he was meant to be.

2.

The words that had now faded didn't seem as if they were for Felicia. She had only just approached the entrance to the unfurled Gaze Room. It was a part of the ship which extended out some way, almost like a periscope in principle. The boy was not facing her, but the window into that unlit miasma, the ongoing universe. A sight which, as far as any of them knew, was being witnessed for the first time. Felicia noticed his head was tilted up.

The Gaze Room's window was also a filtering screen that was able to adjust the view's spectrum from high to low. Gabriel had it set to what a human eye would see anyway, darkness.

What fun was that?

No, she didn't think he could have been speaking to her. They weren't together. She had just arrived. Gabriel should have heard her. It wasn't like she was sneaking. Felicia looked all around. They were alone. She exhaled the cool oxygen/nitrogen blend of the ship. The adults always told her it tasted stale, but she had known no other kind to compare it to.

The mixture of the experience felt like a spike in her mind's eye. How had he not registered her presence by now? It was all causing her to feel on edge, but she trained her line of sight to where Gabriel was looking.

All that was between them and that ghastly view of space was human engineering. He wasn't looking at the screen, but above it. The glossy blue metallic finish that pervaded Arqa's interior. Sourced from the finest nanotechnology humanity might ever muster. There was nothing of significance there, yet Gabriel remained fixed upon it as if...

As if it was Felicia herself he was looking at. The girl was vain. Youthfully vain. The kind that administered cruelty without full recognition of the damage done. Felicia followed the ceiling up past where Gabriel was staring.

The Gaze Room fit about fifteen people. Its pseugra, like a few other self-contained compartments on Arqa, could be switched off. People could float around, even if it was bad for the bones. Felicia hadn't come there to do that though. She couldn't do what she'd wanted to do, and it left her feeling repressed.

It was common knowledge that Gabriel was best left alone. Felicia and her friends mocked him, privately yet ceaselessly. It was all anchored around one bad pun they loved to spout off: Gabriel needs his space. He was around the same age as Felicia, and the other boys Felicia's age spent their time in VR. But the Gaze Room was what captivated Gabriel's attention. Being alone there, just to watch nothing! How unstimulating.

He was not a tall boy, but he was growing. In Felicia's view, he was plagued with freckles. His dull hair was the captain's approved style of "long enough." Felicia's was not. It was more like how female-presenting people of Earth had had it: long and ostentatious, straight flowing amber that caught the eye in a ship with such a bland palette of colors. The captain did not enjoy those sorts of indulgences. Though she was in charge and made the rules, there were enough women from Earth who just couldn't let certain traditions go. Their hair was what the captain referred to as "far too long."

That was when Felicia realized she'd been standing behind Gabriel for some time, waiting to understand, but not badly enough to acknowledge him. Gabriel, at least partly aware of her disdain for him, was perhaps pretending she was not there. Only, how could he do that if he hadn't seen who was behind him? And what was it he had said? She'd become so enthralled in his trance that she hadn't dwelt on his words and their meaning. He would elaborate if she was patient.

She didn't want to speak to him. What did it matter? She didn't care about Gabriel.

When she stepped forward, she did so with several fierce stomps.

This did nothing to spoil Gabriel's focus.

The adults often spoke about time discrepancies... how time moved at different speeds throughout the universe, relative to the time one experienced. But Felicia knew it was all theoretical talk or the adult's idea of being coy. No, Gabriel had to be in the same moment as her. The same moment experienced in a different way. Just what was it that she was missing here?

3.

Something on the floor caught her attention. A discrete noise broke the silence. There, she saw a tiny pool of liquid, a bubbling formation. It burst and settled right by Gabriel's feet. It seemed to be a light reddish shade. The floor of the Gaze Room was uncommonly dusty, she realized. No doubt teeming with troublesome bacteria.

Then she remembered the boy's words.

It's coming.

Felicia looked back up at Gabriel. She shifted and went to stand in front of him. At last, she looked down at him and asked, "What?" The question came out of her as if she were spitting out gum. Despite the stillness, she felt as if there was imminent danger. She crossed her arms below her chest and straightened her back. The boy still failed to register her. He just kept looking up. Felicia examined the spot for herself once more. Maybe she had overlooked something in her anxiety. All the girl saw was the ship. Thoughts of calling for help overwhelmed her as Gabriel finally said more.

With his view remaining pried to the ceiling, Gabriel said, "It's... something—" Another small word vanished in his reverie. Felicia's arms unfolded from her chest and fell to her side.

Chapter One

Captain Sali made her way into the room through the automated sliding door. It was a tiny space comprising nothing but a bed and a desk. The woman had a shaved head and no eyebrows. She stared over to the only person on Arqa who could dissolve the potency of her presence (this was a secret she was not privy to). Will, her seventeen-year-old grandson, was fiddling with a floating holo-screen above him as he lay supine in bed.

"Hi, Grammy!" Will announced with exuberance, as he sat up from his bed with a grin.

"Drop it, Will. Everyone on this ship has something to do today, including you." She gestured over to the pile of papers by his desk.

"Oh, that's right... I forgot."

The captain stepped over to Will's desk and grabbed the papers, then dropped them on Will's lap. "Let me tell you something. If someone *forgot* to clean the coordinators, we'd suffocate. Including—"

"Yes, including me. Grammy, you know I understand that."

She huffed at the interruption. "If someone forgot to inspect the exterior for high-density particulates, we'd lose cruising integrity. The list goes on and on. Hence these written logs."

"Yes. And so somehow, by my error, we shall all die?"

"That's not the point. My issue is you can't be trusted with even a modicum of responsibility. I'm worried about a time when I am gone. When your laziness places others in peril, and for the sake of the greater good, they vitrify you."

"I think I'd rather enjoy vitrification," Will said, starry-eyed. "They'd wake me up when they found a cure for death, is that right?" He began to fantasize. "My friends and I would shoot at each other all day, no VR required! Oh, to awaken with nothing but my head."

"It was the one thing I asked of you all day. You sit here, isolating yourself under this delusion that just because we've never had a major catastrophe, we're invulnerable. There are no pit stops. No way stations. No support crews. If you aren't someone I can depend on, eventually, I may have to be the one who..." The captain didn't finish the sentence, but Will understood well enough to fill in the blanks.

He surfaced from his gun-play reverie, giving the appearance that he was more affected by the admonishment than he truly was. Without him, his Grammy would have no memories of *love*. She'd told him as much plenty of times. "Grammy, I'll still do it. No worries, my mind just takes me away sometimes."

She sighed. "I wish you could explain to me what that means. What were you doing all day?"

Will looked as if he was in danger of zoning out again. Then he said, "I think I've been sad. You know, it's almost been a year since Craig died. Why don't we talk about it?"

"It's actually been 467 days," his Grammy snapped. "Over a year. What exactly makes you so callous to masquerade *that* as an excuse?"

"Hey, just because it's an excuse, doesn't mean it's not true," Will pointed out, shrugging.

"Stop. Look, I don't care. I mean, I do, but... nothing like that ever needs to happen again. Besides, what better reason to step up? You completed school, you were one of the first children of Arqa to do so. But you abandoned your training with Tim."

Will scoffed. "Tim wanted someone he could control." He wiggled his fingers above him. "Push all the buttons."

"You can't even control yourself. I can see where the disconnect happened." She paced around, taking items she saw on the floor and putting them in their rightful places.

"Come on, Grammy, let's have me get some credit. I decided to take some in between time to truly understand myself. You know you're going to have a big problem when the other kids get jobs or posts they don't want to do. You try to hone on aptitudes and passions but it really isn't working."

"And you will all likewise have a bigger problem when no one can perform surgery or recalibrate the engine's systems. Optimum freedom demands undesirable sacrifice."

"I thought we escaped Earth *for* freedom," Will said with condescension.

"It all depends on how you define the word, Will. For me, this *is* absolute freedom. Minus your inability to fall in line. You kids just have no idea what we went through to provide you this life. The greatest pain *you* feel is having to do what you're told. Lucky you. Finish these logs and get them to where they need to go. If you need to express some feelings about Craig, I am not the person to talk to."

Will looked away from her, frowning. His Grammy was so severe. "I know, Grammy." He hoisted his legs off the bed. "Could you look at those other papers I've been working on? I did have some questions."

"Talk to Tim."

"Ah, but I think you might like to see what's on them."

"That's irrelevant. I have to get back to my job. Do yours, Will."

He waited until she was gone to get out of bed. Changing into fresh clothes, Will reflected on his Grammy's recent behavior. It was becoming more and more challenging to defuse her. Will pondered what could be bothering the woman. The pressure of almost five hundred people to lead had taken a toll on her, there was no question about that. But why did she have to take it out on him? He had completed *some* of his assignments.

2.

He left his room to deliver the completed inspection reports, opting to put the rest off for later. He was sure it'd get done. The curly-haired blond youth was a seasoned professional at getting what he wanted. He was tone and pleasing to look at, but it was his high-spirit that formed the gravity which others were attracted to.

As he passed by a folder on the wall, he halted to discover a pen attached to it. It was a kind of pen he'd never seen before, and that was enough to imbue him with excitement. Imagine, living contained on this ship most of his life and seeing something he'd never seen before, just outside of his room!

Examining it, he saw there was an etching of a figure stretching to touch their toes. Will brought the pen closer, held it in his mouth like a cigarette, and began chewing it. Though he lamented whoever had left the object behind, they hadn't cared for it enough. Will would love it instead. Chewing was a habit of his the Psychs on Arqa couldn't seem to help him break. There was a lack of leverage, as for Will it felt like a vital part of who he was. The best they'd been able to do was get Will not to do it in public, but that had devolved to when no one was present. Often, he'd even sneak a chew out of someone else's stuff when they weren't paying attention. This wasn't meant to be a malicious act, but as a way to connect to others. Chewing charged him, and he needed to stay close to a hundred percent. He had a myriad of relationships and people who admired him. Being one of the few people on the ship to complete its educational curriculum, everyone was always asking him what was next. It made him feel special, and he'd felt special all his life because of his relation to the ship's captain. The only issue was that he didn't know what was next. He had a feeling... an inferno of purpose and longing. What he wanted was to sustain that feeling. He'd kept to himself because it was (in his Grammy's eyes, at least) immoral.

That's why he never shared his writing with anyone. Why he didn't have an answer for his Grammy when she asked what he was doing. No one he knew would understand. This was not pretentiousness, simply a fact.

Will was the only one on Arqa who wasn't keeping the ship in operation or doing important scientific research. Instead, he was chronicling, providing commentary on everyday life. It differed from his Grammy's stenographer Donald, who always took down notes from her meetings. The thing Will wanted to produce and share was more accessible. History was a very touchy subject for his Grammy. She stressed the need to look ahead, not behind. The transcripts Donald did were for posterity. Precedence. But Will was seizing his limited time before she was finally sick of his disobedience to draft a comprehensive picture of life on Arqa, to imagine what things they could improve. Will had no interest in leading the ship. But he would love to be its storyteller. The ambition was impractical, but the boy felt it was his destiny. Not being some engineer or administrator. That was just bare toil, and there was no greater thing to strive for beyond survival. No, he needed more. If he didn't have that, then his Grammy might as well have left him on whatever remained of Earth.

The inferno and his duty waged a war within him.

Will made his rounds and left the pen in a separate folder on the wall. He'd chewed it with such a fury that it felt charged with his negative thoughts. He wanted to release it. Let someone else deal with it.

His Grammy was very old. She would pass on soon. For all the boons of longevity research Arqa had tapped into, immortality was not yet one of them. His grandmother's remaining time was, realistically, all he had left too. He needed to get his act together and finish his project, present it. Show those on Arqa that they need someone more than Miss Siannon to teach. There needed to be more entertainment. Story. Art. And most importantly, introspection.

He just wanted the opportunity, but he knew he wasn't working hard enough on it and people would just laugh at him. Everyone... but Miss Siannon. He walked faster so he could see her sooner.

Chapter Two

1.

Lyda's daddy was finally home. First Congo reacted, leaping from the couch to the short man. Lyda followed right behind the large German Shepherd. The girl waved her arms out in defense of lashes from the dog's whipping tail.

Her daddy tapped the fur on Congo's head as the dog hopped up on his front paws, balancing against the man's chest. He brushed Congo aside to lift Lyda into his arms. She only reached to just above his knees.

"Look at that, wow," he said in bemusement.

"What?" Lyda wondered, her curiosity temporarily suspending all of her joy.

"You! It's so good to see you. Not as good to lift you, but I'll take it. So, how's your day been?" Congo made sure to be noticed as the man fought his way to the couch.

"First Miss Siannon taught me things. Then *mommy* taught me things! Sheesh, it's like I have to be learning all the time now."

He set Lyda down on the couch, giving Congo an opening to lick his cheeks. "Hey now," he advised Congo. To Lyda, he asked, "Well, what kind of things did you learn today, little Miss Loudness?" He went past the common room into the adjoining storage area where their Siranis Fluid came out of. Dropping his things in their proper places, he then adjusted the thermostat on the wall. Her daddy liked it when it was cooler.

"Flowers. About flowers and how they don't need to eat like we do."

"Isn't that awesome? Was that tidbit there from Miss Siannon or mommy?"

"Mommy mentioned it, yeah."

"She's so smart," he said with a great depth of admiration. "You'll be even smarter though, I think. She ever tell you she used to fall asleep in class?"

"No, but you did before," Lyda reminded him.

"I know, it was merely a distraction! Pig pile on Congo!" He jumped from behind the couch and the three began to play. Fits of giggles erupted out as Lyda and her daddy tried to pin Congo to the ground.

After the game was through, he asked Lyda more questions about what she'd learned that day. Lyda didn't like that because sometimes she'd go the whole day without learning anything interesting, then she had to explain boring things, which was boring. But the worst part about it was she had to act like it *wasn't* boring!

After she was finished explaining, he asked, "What do you want to do now? Paint?"

Lyda considered the question, and countered, "Can we play checkers? Less mess."

"Not interested in painting anymore?"

"Not if I have to clean up my mess." He wanted her to be a painter so badly, but her mommy had told her to be honest with people. And checkers was much better than painting.

"You got it, checkers it is!" He walked back to the storage room to get the board and called out, "Dom, what are you doing?"

Her mommy didn't play as much as she used to. She'd been working from home, staying in her room. Some days her mommy would shut her eyes, but not to sleep. She'd try walking or would just lay down. Lyda thought it was like a game, going around without seeing. Lyda played too, but her mommy would take it really serious and asked not to be bothered. Whenever Lyda had tried talking to her about anything, it took her a few seconds to respond. And over the last week or so, it seemed to take even longer than that.

Her mommy said, "We need more staps. I'm about to go to get some staps. Now that you're back."

"Ah, hun. We don't need staps. Come on."

"I need staps. You finished mine off."

"Why don't you hold off until after you've tucked Lyda in tonight?"

"Because I can't stand being told what to do, Stephen."

"In any case..." Her daddy sounded uncomfortable. "Just a second," he said to Lyda, tapping her on the head. Just like her mommy, Lyda's hair was long and shining, though her mommy's hair was much lighter than her own. Congo's patchwork fur matched the shade of each member of the Hall family. Lyda gave her dog a squishing hug.

2.

That night her mommy was the one to tuck her in, and she read her daughter the beginning of a story called *The Distance of Time* from a collection of fairy tales. It was quickly becoming her favorite. In it, Princess Nemp must select a husband for her family lineage to continue. But she doesn't want to marry a man, and so she flees her kingdom to find a female partner. The king sends a retrieval squad after her, and the adventure spirals out from there.

Her mommy stopped at the part where Princess Nemp falls over in the forest after a sorceress made the gravity heavier around her. The sorceress had offered guidance to the Princess by allowing her to ask any question she wished, and so Princess Nemp had asked, "How do I escape these dreaded woodlands?"

Ever the trickster, the sorceress answered, "You don't."

Lyda knew what would happen next, she'd had this one read to her a few times now. She loved it so much she wished there could be more after the ending. In thinking about how stories should never end, Lyda asked her mommy, "What is sleeping?"

Her mommy said, "Sleep is how we form memories, and recover from strain."

"It sure takes a lot of time out."

"But it's not wasted time, and you hardly notice it, do you?"

"No, but..." Lyda wasn't sure if her question was answered. So she tried something else. "Why do we sleep?"

Her mommy smiled a little. "Like I said, it's just a place we have to go. If we didn't, we'd hurt ourselves a lot."

"Okay, but if you didn't have to sleep, would you mommy?"

"I don't know, baby. I mean, our sleeping self is a separate self, but still us. They share the same mind. Our body has a way of looking out for each."

"I think I'd like sleeping more if I could control my dreaming, like Leni says I can. When I talk to the people in my dreams, it's like they're in charge of things. I don't like that."

"Are you talking about the falling nightmare again?" her mommy questioned.

Lyda nodded. She hated that one. It always felt like it was really happening. She would be falling uncontrollably. But before she made contact with the ground, she'd always wake up.

"Oh, Lyda, Leni is full of wacky ideas, isn't she? The people in our dreams, even the ones we know, they're not actually people."

"No?" Lyda asked in puzzlement. "Then what are they?"

"Those we encounter, and possibly also our dreaming self, they represent *ideas*. Authority. Desire. Nature. I think... if you try to control *people*, they'll outnumber you. But ideas are more flexible. Take your falling dream. Try to imagine... instead of falling, you are flying. Doesn't that sound better?"

"Yes, it does. But how does that work?"

"I don't know how, but it does. Just think on it. Stop thinking of the word falling. The next time that happens, think *flying, flying, flying*."

"I'd rather just be awake all the time."

"I don't know about that. We are happier when we are healthy. So sleep is nonnegotiable. Especially right now! So goodnight, sweetie. I love you, okay? I would love you even if it wasn't my job as a mom. You're the best kid."

"That's a weird thing to say."

"I've always liked being weird," her mommy said with a weak chuckle. She gave Lyda a prolonged kiss on her left cheek. "Yes, I love my baby girl more than the stars that woke us. All the stars, in fact. That's a lot of stars. Like trillions upon trillions."

Lyda looked away from her mommy. Something, she felt, was off. It kept happening, like her mommy was less present. As much as Lyda tried not to let it bother her, it did. She thought it could be hard. Hard sometimes for her mommy, and everyone else who remembered Earth.

"You okay?" her mommy asked.

"Of course I am. Maybe... I just wish you could show me Earth." That was it. When her mommy talked about it, her voice soared. She delivered beautiful images and feelings to Lyda. Lyda thought maybe that's why her mommy closed her eyes so much. "How different it is and stuff."

"When you dream, even though you've never been there, you can see Earth," her mommy explained. "It makes sense, if you think about it. Your daddy and I were born there, and all our of family before that. Earth shaped our DNA. It's embedded into us. That connection, sometimes, that's—it's better than the real thing. Remember that, Lyda. That's why you need to sleep. So keep practicing so you may do it better."

Lyda thought maybe her mommy had said more after that, but she couldn't remember. For she went effortlessly into a peaceful slumber, in search of that place her mommy once knew.

Chapter Three

1.

The first dose of Siranis Fluid dripped out from the faucet, giving Carlos the fuel he needed to start his day. The clear fluid went into a pouch that he clipped onto his right hip as it fed into his body. In addition to a blend of nutrients, there were also streamers, nanobots that detected any abnormalities in the body. From there he went to the UV chamber to substitute the effects of the sun. The rays were administered on a treadmill, which Carlos stepped onto to get some of his miles in for the day. There were further mandated exercises required so he could stay in shape. Indefinite space travel brought along severe risk to human physiology. Being out of shape on Arqa meant certain death. Fortunately, everyone knew that. So much of their day was set aside to ensure their bodies could function in the brutal conditions. There was no alternative.

Arqa was not just a ship. It was a new frontier for humanity. As lofty as that sounded, Carlos just hoped all of this would one day result in someone wanting to have sex with him. He was fourteen, so little else mattered to him beyond that.

The thought always intensified once he reached his classroom. Who'd had it and who hadn't? That was all anyone talked about under their breaths now. Some of his classmates claimed to know what it was like. Why not him? He looked over his shoulder and saw Gabriel. At least he wasn't *that* kid. The boy who'd cried alien space ship. Gabriel was usually good for outlandish antics such as that, but this one seemed to have topped all of his previous attempts.

Aliens were a real threat to those on Arqa. The L'rias had invaded Earth and set to extinguish all life. They were a much more advanced civilization than humans. Arqa had narrowly escaped. According to Miss Siannon, it was likely that Arqa was the last of humanity.

In the time since leaving Earth's solar system, Arqa had not had any run-ins with the L'rias. Gabriel's proclamation had put the entire ship on edge until scans of the region outside had detected nothing. Still, the initial rumor had ballooned on the ship, and Gabriel was in a lot of trouble. But more than a few kids believed him. Carlos was skeptical, even though his uncle said Gabriel had the eyes of El Cadejo.

Gabriel's mental health had been a juicy topic of late. Some even said he'd hallucinated the experience. Carlos had nothing against the kid. He'd been there for him after what had happened to Craig. Gabriel's best friend. But Carlos had eventually distanced himself from Gabriel, certain it would limit his social capital.

A certain degree of guilt accompanied this decision. When everyone was younger, it seemed like they were all friends. It was only over the last few years that cliques had formed.

It was a pity that Gabriel was, well, off. Gabriel must have known he'd face nothing but ridicule for weirding out Felicia. He must have been some kind of stoic not to mind.

2.

Miss Siannon walked to the front of the classroom, seizing everyone's attention with a whistle while tapping her cane onto the floor. "Good morning, everyone. I hope we're all feeling well." Carlos's teacher was one of the most peculiar people on Arqa. She had blond hair set in a ponytail and wore glasses. While Arqa's resources could remedy most issues of vision, Carlos had always suspected the glasses were utilized to detract people from her left cock-eye. Then there was her accent, a lyrical sibilance Carlos cherished. There was one last thing that set her apart. Most of Arqa's population was over forty. She was in her twenties, one of the few people on broad in that age range. The adults knew what they were doing when they'd assigned Miss Siannon her role. She held boundless compassion for her students. For people like Carlos (or Gabriel), who had no mother present on Arqa, Miss Siannon was their closest approximation. "Today we're going to go a little more in depth in regards to the final documented era of human civilization on Earth. The conditions for which, you'll see, may have encouraged the L'rias to invade in the first place. It's the most important thing I have to teach you. So if I see you not paying attention, there will be consequences.

"At the turn of the twentieth-century, remarkable minds were making all sorts of predictions for the future based on the accelerating progress of information technology brought on by computers and artificial intelligence. Many were expecting an event known as the Technological Singularity. The point where artificial non-biological intelligence exceeded human intelligence. This led to many questions: Would AI eliminate us? Would we merge with them? We didn't know, but we were seeing rapid changes in our society. Issues facing the planet at the time, such as (and make sure you're noting these things) disease, poverty, famine, pollution, and crime would be things of the past. Even death was thought to be a trivial obstacle for the advent of these machines, known also as superintelligence or strong AI."

Some younger kids were hearing it for the first time, but Carlos had heard this all before. "Each new generation became stupefied by the new technology. Then silicon-based computers reached their limit. Progress in robotics, genetics, and nanotechnology was stymied further as people grew lazier and lazier. Access to the Internet diminished memory and mathematical skills, since most information was so readily available. Access to misinformation also grew and became more and more difficult for the average person to discern. Meanwhile, the global temperature increase brought on by unregulated fossil fuel and agricultural industries forced the remaining universities and scientific institutions to focus on immediate, practical solutions. Coastal cities were wiped out in rising floods, leading to mass migrations inland.

"The acceleration of knowledge fell off. Humanity still invented things and accumulated fresh information, but the idea of an artificial general intelligence able to exceed or rival the human brain soon became a thing of pure science fiction. Humanity could produce weak AI, machines which could impress or outperform humans in specific tasks such as computation or Shogi. Robots that could do a programmed task, but little more."

Yep, it was all the same old tale for Carlos. He stopped listening, knowing it all. Life on Earth fell into oblivion with the arrival of the L'rias. Arqa merged resources from the remaining elite and governing bodies to leave with the best remnant of humanity. Arqa's mission was to learn its lesson from that apocalyptic chapter, to forge ahead into intentional, autonomous evolution. Bring about the Technological Singularity. To live on and avoid contact with extraterrestrial life.

And because of all that, Carlos was here now, not having sex. It prevented him from being able to think straight. He was at the mercy of people like Felicia, who maniacally headed all streams of gossip and thus wielded the only tangible currency that mattered in Carlos's world. If Carlos was unlikable to her, she set the trend.

He shot a quick glance over to her. Sure, she was gorgeous, but also not very nice. Then there was her best friend, Kalyna. Not quite as cute as Felicia, but all the nicer for it. Kalyna had a short bob cut. And beside them was Nisha, with a much darker complexion and completely breathtaking. All these girls, samplings from different regions all over the planet.

The boy had no idea what words or actions would result in one of those girls actually wanting to share that arcane pleasure with him. When he imagined never being able to figure it out, it made him think he'd lose his mind. The idea of never knowing that feeling was terrifying. It sometimes seemed unreasonable, because eventually this new generation would have to figure out how to maintain a stable population. Then again, Arqa had over one hundred thousand genetic samples stored for in vitro fertilization, so sex wasn't necessarily a mandate. The chances of Carlos being a father were thus very unlikely. It wasn't as if Carlos wanted to have his own child, especially given Arqa's conditions, but he would appreciate any chance of being involved in making one.

"Carlos, what civilization type had humanity achieved before the L'rias's invasion?"

Carlos stammered at first, but redeemed himself. "Earth was about a Type 0.98 civilization at the apex of its power. Nearly able to use all the power provided by the planet." Miss Siannon had almost caught him off-guard.

Resuming her lesson, Carlos watched Miss Siannon mark more notes on the holo-screen, then he once more departed from the sound of her voice. There was a rumor going around that Miss Siannon and Will had done it. Will, that idiot. Carlos was glad he didn't see him much anymore. How could he possibly get with Miss Siannon? That seemed so wrong! Besides, Carlos didn't think the guy was *that* good-looking. It irked him because most everyone, especially the girls in his class, disagreed.

Carlos knew Will for sure had made out with Kalyna. At least. He had also dated Felicia. That had been an intense time, when Felicia and Kalyna had battled over that moron. Carlos could never imagine two girls fighting over him like that.

His mind ceaselessly cycled for lack of a solution to his woes.

At least Miss Siannon didn't call on him again. Well, she might have, if the lesson hadn't been cut short.

Carlos was stealing a glance at Kalyna when several of his classmates, including her, suddenly collapsed from their desks or where they'd been standing. They could not be roused. Carlos's desire for sex was, for the first time in a while, the furthest thing from his mind.

Chapter Four

1.

Craig's father took Gabriel to the Nook, a place that served real food. The Nook helped to break up the monotony of Siranis Fluid. Passengers were granted several meals a month. Gabriel was out of passes, so Mr. Benito had swapped out one of his own for the boy. Mr. Benito sat towering over the child as he sheepishly ate a bowl of Mac n' Cheese.

The part of Mr. Benito that had been Craig's father was long gone, and Gabriel missed him almost as much as he did Craig. The man had had a life on Earth before Craig. As Gabriel understood it, he'd been a celebrity. Callum Benito, a renowned motivational speaker. But that had all come to an end when the L'rias arrived. And Gabriel knew that's exactly what Mr. Benito had invited him out to eat for.

Mr. Benito was also a bodybuilder. He was so broad to Gabriel. A tuft of salt and pepper hair covered his head. The man's eyes did not feel especially welcoming today. They left Gabriel in a state of unease despite the enjoyment of his food.

"Listen so, we haven't got much time here," Mr. Benito said. That notion was hard for Gabriel to grasp. He had nothing but time since classes were suspended. Dozens of Arqa's residents had fallen into some kind of daze from which they could not escape. It was the ship itself that was running out of time, and Mr. Benito was Arqa's head Psych. This meant he was responsible for the mental health of all those on board. "Everyone on this ship has heard some version of what you claimed to have witnessed in the Gaze Room. Some believed you weren't just playing pretend, while others, myself included, practice a bit more of a healthy skepticism."

"Nobody knew for sure like I did until just now," Gabriel explained. "Now we know exactly what's going on."

"Wrong. I don't. Care to enlighten me?"

"Just about everyone thought I was making it up. I already know you thought that. You say I have a bad habit. This time I have proof. Look what's happening now."

"That's not helpful, Gabriel. People are frightened. It's good you're confident, but you're scaring the ship. You think the L'rias are doing this? I'm not so sure myself. I think it's unrelated."

"Then what do you want from me?" Gabriel asked sharply.

"Your claim has avalanched into a rumor. I'd like to hear the firsthand account of what happened to you in the Gaze Room."

Gabriel rolled his eyes at the man. "The L'rias."

"Why do you say that, though? What does that even mean? You saw something?"

"I didn't *see* anything. I... felt it. Or maybe I did see... I don't know, okay? But it was a sensation... images... feelings. Of the L'rias. They've found us!"

Mr. Benito sighed, then stiffened to correct his posture. "I can't explain how I know that... but that is impossible, Gabriel. Most of the adults agree. We have your claim, then we have scans of the immediate region. We're alone."

Gabriel could tell Mr. Benito was overwhelmed, but he didn't understand why the man couldn't believe him this time.

"What I mean is, the last thing we need to do right now is invoke the idea of the L'rias. That is the last place we want to go to. When there's sufficient evidence, I'll be happy to accept it. I think there's a problem with the Siranis Fluid. Maybe there was some kind of compound that caused you to experience something weird, and that's gotten to people today in a different way. Or maybe the UV sensors didn't meet output standards and people fainted from the lack."

Gabriel couldn't speak for the whole ship, but his classmates had all fallen asleep at the same time.

Mr. Benito continued. "This only seems scary because we haven't had to deal with this before. Once we have a real answer, we'll be fine."

Gabriel grunted, looking down at his food.

"Why don't you tell me more about what you felt?"

Mr. Benito didn't care about Gabriel. He never had. When Craig was still alive, he'd acted like he did. Gabriel used to wish he could live with Craig and his dad. As soon as Craig got sick, Mr. Benito had gradually withdrawn from Gabriel. Doing only what his job required for the boy.

So Gabriel just shrugged.

"Don't avoid this because it's challenging, Gabriel. There's no need to be shy."

That only made the boy retreat further. Gabriel chewed his food slower.

"You were in the Gaze Room," Mr. Benito said. "Felicia was there.

What was she doing?"

"You already know that."

"Yes, but I'm trying to help you jog your memory, because you know things I don't. I'm here for your side of the story. Maybe it'll help us understand what is really happening."

"Well, I don't know what she was doing there. Actually, I hardly even noticed her at all. I was so focused on my mind. They... something reached out to me. Like gave me something."

"Felicia told me she didn't have anything like that happen to her."

"Maybe she didn't, or maybe she's afraid to admit it."

"Why would she be afraid?"

"Why do you think? The L'rias attacked us! We're in trouble now."

"No, Gabriel."

Gabriel gripped the silverware in his hand. "Then I'm going crazy. Is that it? Felicia didn't say anything because she doesn't want to be associated with me. Is that what you want to hear?"

Mr. Benito reached out his hand to touch Gabriel's shoulder. "I'd never let that happen to you. I'm here to take care of you. Whatever that takes."

Gabriel leaned back. "I'm tired of being treated like this. If I'm lying, I'm crazy. If I'm right, we're dead." He considered storming out.

"My problem is that I can't believe in things I haven't seen," Mr. Benito clarified. "If you're honest with me, I will fill the captains in so they can make defense preparations. Is that what needs to happen here? This isn't the first time you saw something, is it?"

"I swear I'm not making it up!"

"Have you seen anything since then?"

Had he...? That was a good question. Gabriel thought about it for a moment. "No. How can I explain this? It was like my imagination. I felt like something was there. Like maybe it was always there, but I didn't *notice* it."

"I see."

"Mr. Benito, could what happened have something to do with some experiment they're doing?"

"I like that idea better than aliens."

"Why though?"

"We've all pictured the day when they came for us. It was always a possibility, but the odds were just so... unlikely."

They sat in silence for a few minutes. Gabriel broke it by saying, "I don't like this."

"You know Gabriel, sometimes, adults, they need a break. Sometimes they need to rest."

There was no doubt about it now. Mr. Benito was suggesting Gabriel go into stasis. His body would be preserved for a future time. It happened sometimes for people who couldn't handle the demands of life on Arqa.

Gabriel hadn't known of anyone coming back from that. "I don't really want that. I want to help figure out whatever is going on here."

"Well, it seems like you don't want to talk to me."

Fury engulfed the boy. "It's because you don't believe me!" They were going in circles.

"I didn't experience what you did," Mr. Benito pointed out. "That's a little different from not believing you. So, let's backtrack. Just give me the full story once. Then we can go about our day."

"Fine. But it's nothing you haven't already heard."

Mr. Benito nodded. "So you were looking, but not out into space. You were staring at the ceiling in the Gaze Room."

"No, I *was* looking out into space."

"Felicia told me your head was looking up, not to the window."

Gabriel's eyes locked onto Mr. Benito, but he didn't make eye contact. Then he did. "Just then, Mr. Benito. I was looking through you. If you got up right now, I'd be seeing whatever it is you're blocking."

"You can't see through me though."

"No," Gabriel mumbled.

"So how could you see through the ceiling?"

"I can't answer that question. I don't know. But I did."

"Tell me about the ship."

"That's the thing. I couldn't discern it. But it wasn't a planet or a star or debris. It was different from all that. Huge. Huger than any of those things. It was like a dream. Bits and pieces come back to me, then go. But... nothing useful or new has come to me since it happened." That was not true, but Gabriel did not see any benefit in being completely open while Mr. Benito held on to a cynical attitude.

Mr. Benito looked into Gabriel's eyes. "You know, your eyes are extremely rare."

This made Gabriel feel awkward. "I know."

"We all see different things. And never directly. Our eyes take pictures and our mind interprets them. Produces stories of the pictures."

Gabriel pounded his hands on the table. "You still aren't listening!"

"I am. There's no need to raise your voice. Gabriel, the alien ship you're describing is made up, okay? The stories we tell about the L'rias... they're not how it was. That's why I'm having trouble with what you're saying. You weren't there. This huge ship, the L'rias didn't have ships that big. If they did, we would have detected it by now. You're just afraid. It's why you act up. Now you have the other kids riled up."

"What's going to happen?"

Mr. Benito tapped his fingers on the table. "Saying it is something extraterrestrial, that would be trouble. But that isn't the case. We have something going around the ship that has caused some of us to fall asleep."

The man rose from his seat. Gabriel jumped out in front of him. "Okay, vitrify me if you must. I don't want to find out what's happening. I'm tired of people looking at me thinking it's my fault."

Mr. Benito raised an eyebrow at Gabriel. "I suppose, if that's what you really want, Gabriel."

2.

The sound of her sister's voice plucked Kalyna from a dream. The dream itself was blurry, unimportant. Not what mattered. Being awake now was.

"Kalyna!" Brenda squealed, bringing a hand up to touch the girl's face. The contact felt lovely.

"Brenda. I've been asleep."

"Something like that. But this—this is a good sign. Hang on." Her older sister darted away, calling for help. Kalyna almost told her to stop, because she didn't want to be alone. She looked around. She was in the annex of the main sector, tucked away above the cryo chamber. The Med, where the ship's biologists and geneticists worked. The room was nothing but beds, which had come out from the walls. A few beds down from her, she saw her father. Why was he here too? She only remembered passing out in class. Were they sick?

Kalyna didn't feel sick. Actually, besides her bleary eyes, she felt strong. As if there was something she needed to do. She motioned to get up, but Brenda returned with a retinue of medical staff. Some of them she knew, like Dr. Mandi. They proceeded to ask Kalyna a volley of questions.

After an inability to sate their curiosity, she finally got to ask a question of her own. "What happened?"

"It's pandemonium," a male doctor said dramatically. "Arqa's in shambles, the ship has been brought down to emergency power settings. You and some others lost consciousness. And you're the first one who's gotten out of it."

"Okay, but how long has it been?"

Dr. Mandi looked at a clock. "Ninety-seven minutes."

"What caused it?"

"No one knows yet."

"Like I said. I feel fine." Kalyna hoisted herself up from the bed into a seated position. "Can I go?"

"You can't leave just yet," the male doctor said, raising a hand up to keep her back.

"But my father."

"I've been going back and forth," Brenda assured.

"So dad was at work then?"

"Yeah... and apparently he bumped his head on something on his way down."

"A few cases are like that," Dr. Mandi said. "Bumps, bruises, things like that. We forgot to ask you that one. Do you feel sore at all? Land on anything?"

Kalyna did a mental check of herself. "No. I don't feel any pain. Or fatigue."

Someone new approached her. "Let's not crowd her." Another person she knew. Doctor Coulton. He normally operated the cryo chamber. "Kalyna, if you're as well as you say, feel free to walk around now." To the other medical staff he said, "Her temperature is stable, and we've got no indications of malnutrition from her last Siranis intake. Kalyna, try stretching your legs if you feel good enough, and let us know if anything feels wrong."

Kalyna agreed and hastened over to her dad. Before she reached him, she saw Will was in one of the beds as well. Miss Siannon was watching him. *Very interesting*, Kalyna thought.

Miss Siannon smiled. "Glad to see you're back up. I'll have to spice up my lectures next time."

"At least you know it wasn't your fault," Kalyna commented.

"Mhm, aye. I've never seen Will so still before."

"Same." They both looked at Will.

When Kalyna looked back over to Miss Siannon, she saw the woman was fidgeting where she stood. "Now then. I was just making my way through, seeing if the doctors needed any help. I'll see you later, Kalyna."

"You too, Miss Siannon." Kalyna hesitated, then added, "Wait, I have a question."

"Yes. What is it? I'm always at your disposal."

"Does this mean... Gabriel was telling the truth?"

Miss Siannon looked down to the floor. The woman had a commanding presence when she was teaching, despite her frail state. When Kalyna saw her outside of the classroom, she found the woman very reserved.

Miss Siannon dipped her head back up slightly, offering a severe visage. "This was not the L'rias. But maybe... Gabriel has spoken true in his own way." Miss Siannon looked around, as if about to say something suspicious. "I think it's Gabriel's idea of the L'rias."

"What does that mean, Miss Siannon? You're losing me here."

"Uh, okay, how to explain? Let me try it like this... whenever there was a problem on Earth that humanity *could* solve, a lot of the time they, we, didn't bother. We'd put more energy into debating the solution, or even deny the problem. That neglect added up. Compound to the point where the problems ganged up on us and became unmanageable. Now, Arqa prides itself on being above that, but it's not. Whatever all this is about, I'll tell you now, it's going to gang up on us."

"I don't want to believe Gabriel," Kalyna said. "It's horrible if it's true. But what else could have done this? We have to find out, quick."

"No one can say for sure right now. I know you want to figure it out, you've got such an ambitious mind. I wouldn't encourage you to do that. Instead, I'd spend as much time with the people you care about."

"Huh?"

"Shh, shh." Miss Siannon swept her student up in a hug and was gone shortly after.

Kalyna lingered by Will. Could that rumor about Miss Siannon and him be true? It didn't matter that much to her, but Felicia would probably be livid.

Kalyna's time with Will had been a quick fling. Kissing pretty much. Maybe it might have developed into something more significant, but Kalyna hadn't liked how he acted different when they were alone versus when they were in a group, so she'd cut it off. Felicia and Will though, that was a different story. They'd dated for nearly five whole weeks. Kalyna decided she'd call Felicia up after she was done in the Med. She would also keep the occurrence of Miss Siannon's vigil to herself.

Before she checked in on her father, she lingered with Will. She didn't hold feelings for him anymore, but she sympathized with his plight. They had shared this affliction together. Will had so much vitality, he was the picture of good health. Whatever was happening, the entire ship was at risk.

Chapter Five

Captain Sali commenced the meeting with a wave of her hand. Callum silenced himself. A dozen other men and women stood cramped along a narrow table, with Captain Sali at the head.

After setting down the odd flashing puzzle she always carried (Callum had forgotten what the contraption was called) she began. "I don't believe there is any reason for us to have this meeting if all we're going to do is shout over one another. I'm going to say what I have to say and I encourage you all to speak up. But not at the same time. We have a crisis on our hands. The first in a while. Three key members of our leading staff are out of commission. Their responsibilities have been delegated over to capable hands. The other thing to keep in mind is some have already gotten over this. I can only expect those left hanging in the balance of this new nonsense will come to naturally, though that is not something I can state with full assurance. That is because we still do not know what it is we're dealing with. Which is why I've asked the doctors to join us here for their perspective. As it stands, we've regain our stability for the most part and now need to, one by one, go through the leading theories of what caused this anomaly and anticipate the coming consequences we may have yet to account for." She paused and Dr. Lorn, Arqa's chief of medicine, looked as if she was about to say something. The captain, clearly not finished, glared at the other woman. When Captain Sali had the floor, it was a bad idea to cut her off. "No more *rumors*. People, this is Arqa. And we are only going to discuss amongst ourselves the facts we have gathered, not the speculation stemming from them.

"I will review what we know. First, Gabriel's claim remains unverified. We have our scans from out there, and we've scanned the scans. Proofed the radars. I will not accept the possibility of a stealth attack like you were going on about over there, Dr. Masten. There is no such thing as stealth in space. Look, we know this. The law of thermodynamics, people. Any vessel in effective proximity is going to have a detectable heat signature. And radio transmissions. You need to remember, we're all only on edge because of Gabriel. We're looking at a single coincidence that threatens everything we hold dear. We need to be better than that. With our temperance and collaboration, we have survived in the fringes of space for some time now. Think of how often people insist on the worst case scenario. We're still here though, aren't we? We are a loving community who values information and exterminates misinformation. Remember, a failure to do that was precisely what caused the downfall of our brethren on Earth. Whatever we're dealing with will be dealt with. The truth has a tendency to reveal itself over time. Let these next few days serve as a testament to our resolve, because whatever this is, is temporary. Our jobs are so important because they harbor the final hope of our race. Please keep that in mind as you discuss solutions, not more problems, here today." Callum could detect Captain Sali's more generalized language toward the situation. This was because of Rayna.

Callum had only seen Rayna's face a few times, and that was years ago on Earth when she was a little girl. She could now only be seen in a veil, her face concealed. If the reason why had been for fundamentalist modesty, the captain would not have allowed it. Rayna had been disfigured by accident during their last few days on Earth. She was the assistant to Mark Bromell, whose absence bred tension amongst those present, Callum included. Rayna was not privy to certain information due to her young age. Captain Sali would be tiptoeing around the full truth.

The captain continued. "We know if it does happen that others don't wake up from—" she paused and looked over to Erin. "What are we calling this, Dr. Lorn?"

"The Sleeping Sickness," Dr. Lorn responded in her shrill voice. "For lack of a better term."

"Thank you. The Sleeping Sickness, if we're unable to find a remedy, we have others in stasis we can switch out to compensate for any personnel gaps."

"The lag in training and devitrification will disable us further," Serj brought up. He was the ship's navigator.

"Serj," Callum said. "That will all be temporary, and any alternative to that contingency is out of the question. Unless you have a better idea."

The man smirked. "It is the children who are surfacing first from this collective syncopal episode, as Dr. Mandi called it. If it were to occur again, it seems like the older you are, the longer this knocks you out. In a few years, most of the children will be done with schooling. I say the older ones are knowledgeable enough now. Let's quit padding them with superfluous facts about the stars and Earth and get them to fill these vacant positions on the ship right now."

"That isn't a terrible idea," Larry, the IT head, said.

"I keep hearing the word temporary," Dr. Coulton said. "But we still have no clue as to what took place. This isn't some virus, and we had no warning signs this was going to happen. Those still under are completely nonreactive to light, loud sounds, temperature changes. They're submerged and we can't explain why. It's as if they've fallen into a coma."

"Leading me to believe, as Serj said, this has a chance of happening again," Callum surmised. "To any of us."

"That much is clear," said Captain Sali. "I had Dr. Mandi do their best to compile a profile for the people who have been affected by this. Dr. Mandi, if you would."

The doctor shuffled through their papers before starting. "Yes, thank you. One eighth of the ship's active population was affected by the Sleeping Sickness. Wherever they were, whatever they were doing, they fainted. If they were already asleep, then when it came time for them to go about their day, they did not rise. Half of those who fell under have recovered, reporting it was the best sleep they've ever had in their lives. After independently interviewing those folks, they have all mentioned feelings of unrest preceding their fall."

"Feelings of unrest?" Dr. Masten, one of the ship's geneticists, asked. "What is that supposed to mean?"

"I'd also like to hear what your interpretation of that is," the captain requested. "Each and every person in this room right now no doubt fits that description. I'm the third oldest person on this ship. Why not us?"

"We can extrapolate that they were tired," Dr. Mandi went on. "While that may sound ambiguous, it actually gives me a great deal of insight. Long-term space travel in human kind... we knew it was, at best, untested. We left Earth in a rushed passion, forsaking any hope of return. We've long gazed up and wondered what was out there. Now here we are. I'm hardly surprised we're being hit with something new. Consider this: astrophysics and astronomy have answered some of our questions, but have raised far more. There is dark matter and other forces which are only indirectly detectable. Phenomena we can only trace through equations. Things we cannot see with the naked eye or even a microscope that have a tangible effect on our bodies. Remember, these bodies we have were designed by Earth, for Earth."

"Please get to the point, doctor," Callum urged.

"Excuse me. What I'm getting at is perhaps there is a kind of field we have entered, or some signal has breached our filters and gotten into the ship."

"Oh, no. You don't mean radiation?"

"No. These Sleeping Sickness victims are not exhibiting even premature symptoms of radiation sickness. You might even argue, and this is bordering on speculation, so excuse me once again, but those who have come up—the girl Kalyna, your grandson, captain. They seem rather vibrant. They've been sleeping less and eating less, I hear. With no apparent costs to their well-being. It's as if they all experienced something quite rejuvenating. A kind of hibernation, if you will."

"Meanwhile, we are running around facing a crisis that threatens to buckle this whole ship under," Jin said, the ship's resource allocator. "We have maintenance reports going unfiled, people unaccounted for. If we are in some kind of mysterious region, then we need to change vectors."

"Hector," Captain Sali said with deference to the ship's bearded lead engineer, not heeding Jin's catastrophizing. "Gabriel insists extraterrestrial entities, but we all know what foolishness that is."

"It's true, but we also have what Dr. Mandi said," Hector replied. "I mean, what do we really know about it? I'd be very interested in having another look at our position, no?"

"There's one last thing I noticed in all the cases," Dr. Mandi said. "They were all born on Earth. We don't have a single case of a shipborn getting the Sleeping Sickness."

"So it's an age thing?" Hector asked.

Captain Sali shook her head. "We don't have a definitive answer to that, but with more research on the external region and medical within, we should be fine."

"Fine?" Dr. Masten challenged. "Why are we not broaching the topic of the boy himself? We all had a hand in letting him board, knowing he could be a liability. I know we haven't forgotten. This isn't some case of spooky action at a distance. I think it's time we revisit Gabriel's purpose."

Callum wondered how long until that was brought up. "The captain said it first thing, Dr. Masten," Callum said. "She wants evidence. And as Hector told us, we have detected no evidence of being pursued. Or that Gabriel could have caused this."

Captain Sali turned to one of the only people who hadn't spoken up during the meeting. "Rayna, you really shouldn't be here right now.

Where is Mark?" Callum knew she must have been hesitant to discuss Gabriel.

Mark and Rayna were both elusive inhabitants of Arqa. The eccentric man was a robotics engineer who had his own isolated research taking place aside from the others crafting AI. If Mark were not a genius amongst geniuses, that arrangement would be unthinkable.

The girl straightened in her seat and said, "Getting to the bottom of this mystery as we speak. He didn't want to be distracted. Pardon me for saying so, but he instructed me to inform you, if called upon, to say he is already aware of everything discussed in this meeting so far. Although if, in the process of this meeting, new information comes to light, I have been instructed to mark it down and inform him."

"And you can tell him the next time he defies a direct order that you'll no longer be assisting him."

"Yes, ma'am." Mark could not be persuaded by punishment or reward, save for separation from Rayna.

Jin spoke up once more. "Look, I'm just wondering if—because if any of our equipment malfunctions. Our radar or radiation filters. You know—"

"Can I just reiterate that our systems are checked for malfunctions several times an hour?" said Larry. "There are too many fail-safes. Basically, if something like that were taking place, then we would have ample warning. That is not the case, so that is not the issue."

"Now we've heard Dr. Mandi's take," Captain Sali said, reeling the topic back in. "Does anyone on the medical staff wish to speak up on alternative explanations they'd like to explore?"

Dr. Masten, determined, said, "The boy. What will be done about him? He's caused as much unrest on this boat as the Sleeping Sickness. Whether or not the two things are related, we still need a solution. That boy has gone too far. He uses his mind for nothing but subterfuge."

"He's a prankster, not a mutineer," Callum defended.

Captain Sali nodded. "Nonetheless. He is correct."

No matter how true it seemed, it was still cruel.

If it were not for Gabriel and the bargain they'd made, they'd never have been able to leave Earth. To think the boy could be some kind of Trojan horse... but there was no evidence for that. How could a rational person like Dr. Masten give into such inanity?

"Callum," the captain said, "what is your final word on what is to be done with the boy?"

So Callum had failed then. "I've done everything I can to break his negative patterns. Now with this, I don't know what you want me to tell you. I mean, he mentioned wanting to be put under."

"My thoughts exactly," Dr. Masten said.

"Yeah, we know."

"Dr. Coulton, when this business with the Sleeping Sickness allows, I need him stowed," Captain Sali said. "I don't care if he changes his mind."

"Yes, ma'am," said Dr. Coulton.

"Stowed? What if he is still beaming some kind of signal?" Dr. Masten asked.

"You need only one more foolish remark of that magnitude to exhaust my patience," Captain Sali snapped. "That goes for all of you. I said no conspiracy theories. We made a promise. A woeful compromise, but one we are duty-bound to. Do not dwell on the boy. Now, unless anyone has anything else?"

"Yes, captain," Callum said. "I do."

"What is it?"

"We need to conduct a roll call via the ICs immediately after this. I'm sure it's nothing, but Stephen was telling me Dominique has not been seen or heard from since before this Sleeping Sickness thing kicked in. She didn't report for work this morning. I hear she's been working from home lately and would at least show to pick materials up."

Serj furrowed his brow. "Who gave her permission to do that?"

"Serj, enough," Captain Sali said. "We all have things we need to worry about besides this bit of business. Roll call. Yes. She may have fainted in some isolated part of the ship, and no one has come across her yet."

"Obviously, where else could she be?" Hector asked.

Chapter Six

1.

It felt as if Lyda's daddy was dragging her. She tried to walk faster with him, but it was never enough. Usually he was gentle, but today he hurried through the corridors with a newfound rage. They were going to a place, he'd told her, where he knew mommy was. Mommy had been gone for too long.

"We've... had a disagreement, but I think she went here. Over four hundred people on Arqa, and some of them fly completely under the radar and do whatever they please."

"That's not good," Lyda said tentatively.

Her mommy hadn't returned home after tucking her in the night before, and she'd taken Congo with her. Their quarters had felt empty. "We're almost there. Never you mind my temper. Sometimes a man's got to present himself. Just don't leave me. Yeah, yeah. Because wherever I go, you're going with me."

"Uhm, okay."

He stopped them dead in their tracks. "No, no. You don't understand. Or I—forget what I said. We're just going to get your mother, wherever she is, and I'm going to bring her back, see? That's all. This is all so silly. To bring Congo with her. She can't do that. It's not fair. Not fair. Unfair. She knows that."

They walked for about ten more minutes until they reached a part of the ship Lyda had never been to before. A part of the ship she'd been told she wasn't allowed in. "Daddy?"

"Look, there's no Regulator to ensure clearance, so we're fine to pass."

Lyda wondered what would have happened if there had been someone there. She'd *never* seen him act like this before. A lot of people were acting differently lately, and she hoped it'd be over soon. But Lyda needed more than hope. Mustering up all the courage she could, she tapped her father on the side of his hip and asked, "Why doesn't mommy come back on her own?"

"No clue. Maybe she forgot about us." He cackled. Lyda did not like the sound of that, but she didn't know how to respond. At one point, she heard him muttering to himself, "The dog, the dog, the dog..."

2.

They reached a little dwelling at the end of a corridor. It came out like a bump in the wall, with several wooden grooves like tree branches alternating in a pattern. At the center was a red door. Her daddy paused, then knocked on it with both hands. Lyda took a few steps back from him as his harsh knocks became swings. "Hey Dominique, I need a word or two. Right now. Come on out, it's been long enough now."

"What is this place?" Lyda asked.

"It's where mommy wished she could stay," he sputtered. "But everyone knows she can't, okay?"

"Mommy, mommy!" she cried out while hopping up and down.

He snapped at her. "Lyda! Just keep quiet and I'll settle this."

Before someone answered, Lyda noticed a tie hung above the archway in a display box. It was striped satin, a blue and green pattern. Lyda thought it looked ugly.

The door opened, but only slightly. Lyda craned her head to try to see inside.

"Sorry, Stephen. No kids in the lab." A voice, one Lyda did not recognize. One with color to it. Like Miss Siannon's almost.

"Fine, we'll just have to talk out here, then."

"You know this rule, Mr. Hall. Besides, you seem to only want to say things that are not nice right now... And if you can't come in, then I certainly can't join you out there like you are. I can't believe you brought your daughter."

"Okay, Mark, you know why I'm here."

"Actually, no. What can I do for you?"

"Where is my wife, Mark?"

"I'm not sure. She's not home? Maybe she's sick. Something rather troubling is going around lately. I've been keeping to myself, trying to figure it out as a matter of fact. That's uh, as it is, the no children rule still stands regardless, but even if it weren't for the child, it'd be best for you to back away."

"Out of the question."

"Okay... on top of all those other things, this is a restricted area and I know for a fact you just came straight through. That's not cool, mate."

Her daddy began yanking at the man's doorknob. "You've got my dog back there, Mark? Seems like you do. You never call him by the right name, and it's very disturbing. I know he doesn't like it. I don't like it."

"Your dog? I don't know. I mean, I'd be most interested in finding out there's a dog puttering about in my lab. What's this about, now? Has Dominique gone somewhere? What did she tell you?"

"Gone for staps," her daddy said in a hollow voice. "Some time ago."

"We have, let's see... three reasons? The child, the Sleeping Sickness, and the fact that you just walked past somewhere you weren't supposed to. I think I'll add your attitude to the list of reasons why this is a bad move for you to be making right now. Yep. A lot of reasons here to leave me be."

Charging at the door, her daddy gained no ground. Lyda attempted to pull him back.

"Off, girl!" he growled.

Lyda immediately detached from him. "Mommy, if you're here please come out, I don't like this."

"She's right, you know," Mark said. "Girl, I don't like it either. Here I was, trying to save this ship and—Stephen don't give me that murderous look right now. Listen, Dominique is not here. I'm just kind of wondering, what will become of me in my own home when you discover your wife isn't behind me? Isn't in your quarters? Isn't... anywhere to be found?"

"You've got something to do with this. I'm bringing Regulators! If they find her in there, you're done for Mark."

"Oh, yay. That is indeed a great idea. I actually took care of that for you when you passed by my checkpoint."

Her daddy went wild, grasping the door and pushing it back and forth.

"Sure am glad I've got you on record," the man said smugly. Lyda's daddy persisted to shove the door. "Mate, what is your problem? No really, I've got to know!"

"Daddy, please relax!" Lyda pleaded.

"Help is coming, no need to worry about me. Feel free to depart before then. Although I imagine you won't. Oh well. You can learn your lesson. Enjoy, Stephen."

"You've been with Dom, haven't you?" her daddy asked, at the peak of his frenzy.

"No, but I wish. Mate, your wife is beautiful. Speaking in a purely objective sense, that is." Lyda got her first glimpse of the man as the door cracked open as wide as it had thus far. He was an older man, gaunt. He seemed hardly bothered, maybe even a little amused. "Don't let the dream die now. Not when we're all so close. What does it matter where Dominique is if she's safe?"

"So you do know something!"

"Isn't there some gray area rule about scapegoating on Arqa? Aren't you breaking it? I'll ask the Regulators when they get here."

"I'm not moving until we sort this out. You're responsible for more than your fair share of mistakes, Mark."

"It's really something, isn't it?" Mark mused. "I'm intrigued. Years ago, this was all an impossible dream. Living in space, just unheard of! Yet here we are, people like you. We're still just primates, huh? Domesticated primates. A little reminder: we left in peace, Stephen. Way to forget that."

Not long after, four Regulators arrived. Three of them wrestled her daddy to the ground, while the other ushered Lyda away.

3.

Dominique Hall was reported missing not even an hour after that impasse. Lyda's mommy and Congo were nowhere to be found on the entire ship.

Epilogue

It was nothing Gabriel did, it was just the optics of the situation. That's what they told him at least. He sat in a stasis pod, drifting through diminishing thought patterns. They were freezing him. His room would be cleared out, and someone else would take it. He did not know who. Hopefully they would enjoy it. It was a nice room. Arqa's orphans got that much, at least.

Periods of despair and agony had descended into acceptance. He felt so sure that if anyone else had been standing where he'd been standing in that exact moment in the Gaze Room, they'd have experienced what he had. Knew what he knew but couldn't say.

And what of Felicia? What did she know?

Enough to be disoriented. But that wasn't his intention. Arqa was his home! Gabriel wanted everyone to be prepared, not scared.

Another thing he'd been told: he wouldn't be alone. Arqa housed many others put under for various reasons.

"Just temporary," the technician assured him once again. "The next thing you know, Craig will be the one to wake you up. Everyone gets a backup."

Yeah sure, whenever they found that coveted cure for death.

"It's for everyone's own good. Anything else you want to know?"

"What?" Gabriel asked.

"Orders are to vitrify you either way, but I... this isn't right. Because you were. Right, that is. Gabriel, after Dominique disappeared, there was a... radio signal."

That did nothing to comfort him. He'd known with all the certainty in his heart that he was right. The anesthetic left Gabriel numb. Otherwise, he might have begged and pleaded. They had no choice but to believe him now. Why did he still need to be vitrified if he'd been right? Gabriel touched his cheeks, for they were cold. He imagined space. Craig's dying expression, his face pock-marked. The time for dreading fate had passed.

Gabriel felt confident, at least, he would not be conscious for the tragedies that would follow. Perhaps that was another reason the captain's order was still in effect. After all, Gabriel wasn't crazy.

Well, maybe he was, but he was also right. Besides, who wouldn't be crazy living like this?

Gabriel recalled how once Carlos's Uncle Antonio had seen his eyes and told him the Earth legend of El Cadejo. Two bestial entities, one white and one black, roamed the countryside. The black Cadejo took the souls of its victims, and in some of the tales, possessed purple gleaming eyes. If you were a righteous person, the white Cadejo would come to your aid and save you. If not, the black Cadejo had you cornered. In any version he'd heard, one thing you were not supposed to do if the black Cadejo appeared was turn your back to it. Gabriel did not enjoy the idea of being Arqa's black Cadejo, but he also knew turning their back to him was exactly what they were doing.

The technician stood up over him. To Gabriel, he looked as far away as the summit of a mountaintop. The lid closed and blue vapor filled the space. "I'm going to keep talking until you go under. It won't be long, but what do you want to talk about?"

"If you're done and the medicine will help me sleep, then just leave me alone."

"Okay, Gabriel. I'm sorry."

Gabriel never wanted to be proven right. The idea of what he'd seen festered in him. A few minutes later, it was gone. Along with everything else.

EPISODE 2
Childhood's End

Prologue

"A time's gonna come," Rod said, the gruff farmer ripped straight out of one of Earth's history books. "Weeks, most likely. It won't be long, and we can't stop it. That's why I'm so fixated on that woman trying to steal our last moments of solitude."

Callum was taking notes on a holo-screen, though most of Rod's words were irrelevant. "What do you mean by that?"

"Whole ship's gone into fight-or-flight mode. C'mon, you know that! In the midst of all this she wants to play hide and go seek with my crops."

"I'm not sure if your little stap operation is entirely on the level here anyway. I'm going to say that's besides the point though."

"The ship needs staps," Alanna insisted. She was digging crops out of the dirt below them.

Rod and Alanna produced the ship's food supply. They worked out of the Envo, a closed and self-sustaining eco-dome set up in the front end of the ship. It contained a field of crops, a small body of water, a playground, and even trees.

"Need? The ship wouldn't die without these. Maybe if these weren't a factor this wouldn't—"

"No, no," Alanna said. She pulled her left hand out of the soil to point up to Callum. "You can't do that to people. People have a choice if they want to smoke these staps or not. This ain't Earth, Callum."

Callum knew better than to get caught up in Alanna's ire. He was here for something else. "How did Dominique even pull this off? Isn't there some kind of security measure?"

Rod groaned as he lifted a crate full of Siranis precursor off of the ground. Then he walked away from Callum to load it onto a dolly. The farmer hummed.

Callum followed after him. "You know, the sooner you answer my questions, the sooner I'll be out of your hair. I don't like being in your way, but you must understand you're getting in mine. Rod?"

"There should have been a notification that someone was rifling around in here, yeah," Rod said. "I don't know why there wasn't. Screw-up, I guess."

"What kind of screw-up?"

"Our own," said Alanna, still working on the ground.

She offered no more information. "Specifically?" Callum asked. He sat down next to the woman.

"See, the thing is, no one ever tries to steal from the Envo," Rod said. "I mean, what's the point? Everyone on the ship has all the food they need, and there's nothing you could do with stap leaves without our processing equipment. I guess, yeah, we got the notification, but they go off because people like to get too close and see something they haven't seen before. In all our time here, no one's taken anything. Like I said, these are all ingredients. More useless than a one-dollar bill. We stopped following up on these notifications here, I'm sure you can see why. Now, with Dominique, we didn't know that someone had come in and stolen anything until we got out here the next day." Callum's takeaway, which he was sure Rod would never say outright, was that Arqa's food source had been going unprotected for who knows how long. But Callum sympathized with the man. Why would they guard something that didn't seem to be threatened?

"They weren't even mature!" Alanna added, as if it would be less of an irritation if they had been.

"From now on, we're going to have a patrol here," Callum said. "Anyone could have come here and started a fire."

"A fire?" Rod asked. "That'd be suicide. No food *and* oxidation?"

"Exactly. Why would anybody do that anyway?" Alanna wondered.

"Well..." Callum said, looking off to the other end of the Envo. "If they're insane, we wouldn't understand why. They'd just do it and we'd all starve."

Dominique was Arqa's first missing persons case. The ship was not large enough for anybody to just go missing. She had left her quarters with her dog Congo and they hadn't been seen in days now. Callum suspected she'd been taken.

If not that, then Callum supposed she had harmed herself in some way. But there was also the odd timing. Dominique had disappeared, then Captain Sali disclosed the enemy was coming. And Gabriel. Poor kid. What had putting him under really been about?

"Dominique was here for sixteen minutes," Rod said. "She could have done anything she wanted. If someone's got to pay for that... you get what I'm saying."

"Let it be her," clarified Alanna. "We're good people on this ship."

"You're missing the point," Callum countered. "Right now, we don't know where she is."

"Then hey, you know what?" Rod asked. "I think you need to worry about her and not what goes on here so much. I mean, c'mon, Callum. Come on. If anything, we're the ones in a bind. They'll be a staps shortage. Those leaves, wherever they are, those are damaged goods by now."

"Look," Callum said firmly, "it's not my place to report you—"

"Why you in here when we both know it's not like she's hiding here? Where was she last seen?"

"Rod, don't be so moody," said Alanna. "None of this is normal, and we need to work together for whatever time we have left."

Callum didn't want to admit he didn't know where Dominique was. When Callum had asked the captain to see the security footage of Dominique's path, he'd been balked. She promised him she'd show it to him soon, but she wanted him to do a bit of follow-up first. So here he was. "No, I'll be going now. Thanks for your time."

"You understand, everyone's just waiting for what the captain has to say about that contact out there," Alanna said. "I mean, time and time again we were told this couldn't happen."

"I know," said Callum. "After all these years. Listen so, I'm not too too worried myself. If you think we can—"

"Forget all that," Rod said. "Like I told you first of all. Time's gonna come."

Chapter One

Will stood next to his Grammy in the cryo chamber, the heart of the ship's structure. One third of the population rested here, in tall cylindrical cannisters or on trays in the walls like a morgue.

It was his Grammy who'd asked him to join her today. Will was sure he'd find out why soon, the man they needed to meet was keeping them waiting. His Grammy had a buircraft in her hands, a blinking puzzle which required hundreds of hours to solve. She often played with things like that such as Rubik's cubes or cognition stimulators. Being composed of nanomaterial, the buircraft had many kinds of puzzles. Now it was a light that snaked along the surface in an extensive pattern his Grammy had to replicate by touching it. This was an astounding feat, as the patterns could go for over a minute.

He knew her neurology had been augmented, but he understood little about the process. Will couldn't figure out even the most elementary levels of the buircraft. Nor was he interested in mind augmentation himself.

In addition to the pods, there were several platforms and holo-screen stations where technicians milled around and typed away. They were extracting somebody who'd not been awake in twelve years.

Everyone had come out of the Sleeping Sickness, but now they had aliens to deal with. Will had trouble recalling his experiences after he'd fainted in his room. He'd simply felt compelled to fall into a deep sleep. Did he dream? Probably, but he usually never remembered his dreams. Since then, Will had felt more purposeful in his activities, even finding the focus to jot down notes for his chronicling project. Maybe it was also a result of everything else that was happening. Will's future was more uncertain than ever and he didn't enjoy the idea of leaving his personal project undone.

Everyone was looking to his Grammy for what to do, but here she was overseeing someone coming out of stasis. Will couldn't take it anymore, he had to know.

"Grammy, why we here, huh? I'm not a fan of the cryo chamber."

"Afraid I'll finally stick you in here?" his Grammy said, chuckling.

Will knew she was only joking. "Really, I want to know. Who are these people? I don't ever remember anybody ever coming out of stasis. Seems like a special occasion? Well?"

She nodded. "I told you some things about the people in this chamber, but not everything. Most of those in stasis helped to finance Arqa, sacrificing their wealth for a ticket off an inhospitable planet and a chance to live on. Then there are others like Gabriel. People who need a sort of time-out from life in space. But that does not account for every person in stasis here. Some people were brought on board Arqa on a contingency basis. That is, when something happened, we'd activate them. Today, we're on the brink of war. Captain De Plez and others have military experience. Not enough though. And on top of that it has been some time since they—" his Grammy paused, seeing the man they had been waiting for. Mark and his assistant Rayna strolled over to them. "You're late."

Rayna apologized for Mark. "We've been—"

"Rayna, he's right here, you don't need to speak for him."

"Nice day, isn't it?" Mark asked. He tapped his feet on the ground, his lab coat's tail flowing in step. "How's it going, Will?"

"Yo." Will waved over to the man. "I'm fine. What's that you got there?"

"Little jig. Why not, right?"

"Right," Will said. He nodded to Rayna. He'd always wondered what she was like. It seemed like she'd be really pretty. She'd been a young kid when they'd left Earth, like him. But instead of going into Miss Siannon's class, Rayna had been educated privately by Mark. She rarely had much to say.

"Mark, please watch the doctor's every move," his Grammy said. "We will need to be doing this again later on. I'll be with you in a moment. Now, like I was saying. No one active has any background in spacial warfare. Hence why we're pulling from here." She gestured at a pod surrounded by personnel. It was tilted horizontally and cracked open.

"So that's a real soldier?!" Will asked incredulously.

"A veteran of a war we lost, you might say," Mark interjected.

"She's going to need a lot of help," his Grammy said. "Think about it. While we've lived a relatively quiet life this whole time, 1st LT Lucio hasn't. She's had no chance to adjust to the peace, and the way things are now, she won't be able to."

"Our life is so different," Mark said. "No ice cream. Really wish you had done this sooner, Sali."

"Who would want to eat ice cream ever again after being frozen?" Rayna questioned.

"Frozen is not quite the word," Mark said quickly. "Excuse me, I just mean... we've vitrified them. There's a bit of a difference. If we simply froze people, their cells would be irreparably damaged by crystal formations. We might as well have left them at the summit of Mount Everest. No, see, this is somewhat different because ice damage is one thing we need to avoid. This process aims to preserve brain information, motor function, psychological continuity, what have you. We do this using cryo-protectant. Anti-freeze compounds. It used to be that vitrification was only for sick people beyond the help of modern medicine. The idea was to preserve them in the hopes that one day in the future, science would have advanced enough to tackle their illness. Now it's easy to put people in and out of stasis, losing nothing in the process. But some people are still kept under indefinitely, in the case of an incurable disease."

"When this woman comes to, I'll still be the captain, but she will lead us through the coming fight," his Grammy said.

"The fight we stand no chance of winning?" Will asked dejectedly. "At least, that's what everyone's saying."

"I say we've had a good run doing what we've been doing," Mark called out as he and Rayna stepped away from them.

"Victory isn't impossible, Will," his Grammy said.

"Yeah?" Will asked.

"We're still going to fight."

"Ah, I see. Go down swinging and all that. But how?"

"Forget about it for now."

Just then, one of the technicians attending to the operation fell to her knees.

Mark mimicked her.

Others walked up to the woman. "You're going to get put under. Look, the captain's here. Let's just get back up and—"

"And what Di? What?! This is a waste of time. They've found us. After *she* said we were safe."

"Things look bad, but you're just being a pessimist. We could still escape."

The woman on the floor jumped up and smacked Di. "If we weren't able to escape after all this, what makes you think we stand a chance now?"

"You haven't met the First Lieutenant. She's a war hero."

"Great, great. I don't care."

"That's enough," his Grammy said, going over to them.

"I agree," said Mark. "This is cutting into my bath time." The man shifted his attention from the scene and over to the pod on the platform.

The woman was eventually escorted out. When she was gone, Will followed his Grammy over to the holo-screens where Mark was asking questions about the process to the technicians.

"Say, captain," Mark said, tapping Will's Grammy on the shoulder. "I know there's no turning back on this point, but have you considered the repercussions of this? Oof, I can actually tell they'll be some."

His Grammy paced away from Mark. Will noticed a blue vapor moving out from the open pod, and he saw the faint shape of a body.

When she didn't respond, Will took the initiative. "Grammy?"

"I need a minute, Will," she responded while thumbing a holo-screen.

"I need every minute I can get too," Mark complained. The man looked over to Will. "Hey you're a deep thinker, right? How'd you like a riddle?"

"Okay?" Will asked, uncertain.

This exchange was enough to pull his Grammy's attention away from what she'd been doing to give Mark a severe look.

"Maybe another time," Mark said, smirking. "I can't recall many... good ones." He winked at Will.

"It's final, Mark. We just don't have any other options," his Grammy said. "We need her here for this."

"But Sali—"

She shushed the man. "I will pull the plug."

"No," Mark said. The man braced himself, as if he were about to be struck. "Compliance abound over here. I was just making absolutely certain that you want this to happen. Like, whatever this is, you know? I, for one, have no clue myself. But isn't that just how it goes? I do what I'm told."

"Sometimes you do," she said with indifference.

The machinery around Will began to chime. People were nodding to one another, happy with the results of their progress.

"Maybe your memory isn't so great, but she was not very cooperative last time I checked." Mark took a fist and rubbed it against his cheek. "Not to mention she does not like me."

"Is Mark trying to say she won't want to help us?" Will asked.

"If Tanya wants to die, she's free to choose not to help us," his Grammy said. "This woman and I made a deal. She will honor it."

"Look, I just don't see what we really need her for," Mark persisted. "Seems to me like you just don't want to do the dirty work."

"This is why she's here."

"Oh, Sali. I can't wait to see what she says about that."

His Grammy continued to take all of Mark's criticisms with patient logic. All the back and forth was quite a shock to Will, because everyone else gave his Grammy a great deal of respect. Come to think of it, Mark was the only person Will knew who called his Grammy by just her first name. Will didn't think the man had any sort of leadership position on Arqa, but he had been instrumental in getting the ship out of Earth's orbit. His eccentricities must have been something his Grammy had no choice but to tolerate.

The body was mostly exposed, cleared of a gooey substance. The technicians attached diodes and wires to the woman's extremities. She was still unconscious.

As Will watched the woman come from vitrification into a new life, he imagined the stories he'd heard from Miss Siannon in history class. She'd spoken of soldiers in the war, the last years of Earth. Here was one now, right before his eyes. As exciting as it was, the reality of things was starting to sink in.

On the plus side, his Grammy was finally confiding in him.

When all the goo and frost had been cleared away, 1st LT Lucio did not appear to Will as a war hero. She looked only as she was in that moment, a shivering woman. She was put on a ventilator.

"We've got trouble coming, Tanya," his Grammy told the soldier. The experience must have been horrifying for the woman. "We're years away from Earth. On Arqa. And the enemy is upon us. You have limited time to formulate a plan. Our resources are precisely the same as they were. You'll be having around the clock therapy, but we need you to begin making decisions for our engagement scenario as soon as you're able."

1st LT Lucio was unable to speak, but she did manage to nod.

Foreboding crept into Will as he eyed the figure in front of him. What difference could one woman make against the L'rias? They were stronger than the forces of nature themselves. He felt then this would not be a war, but a last meager pinch from Arqa against their insurmountable adversaries.

Chapter Two

1.

Normally very punctual, Carlos noticed Miss Siannon was already running two minutes late. It caused a disruption, with the children standing up or sitting wherever they pleased.

Voices erupted into an uproar. Carlos could hear some others conspiring to walk out.

"What's the point anyway?" James O'Malley asked, raising his voice so everyone could hear. He was only eight, but rather assertive for his age. "I say we go on strike. The L'rias could knock us off our axis any second now. Are we really going to follow these stupid rules?"

No one engaged him, and he was drowned out by the sheer number of other voices.

So they'd put Gabriel in stasis... for being right? Carlos even heard some wild ideas about what had happened to Lyda's mom. Good thing the girl wasn't in class today to hear them.

After another few minutes went by, James suggested walking out again. At that point, Carlos thought it made a lot of sense. School was meant to teach you the skills you needed to be a productive contributor to the ship and its mission. There wasn't going to be an Arqa soon, try as the grown-ups might to spin their situation.

Carlos could hear Felicia trying to coax Kalyna into walking out so they could go hang out at the Envo. Carlos turned to the girls after hearing Kalyna's protestations and blurted out, "Why do you always have to do what you're told, Kalyna? I'm going to leave and I don't need anyone to talk me into it."

"Go ahead, if it means you'll leave me alone," Kalyna said. "All that'll happen when you try is Miss Siannon will step through the door the second you go for it."

"Carlos, you aren't going to do anything, so why don't you drop it?" Felicia asked.

Carlos blushed and looked away. His plan had backfired. That wasn't fair!

He sunk back into his thoughts, then listened to his class more. If it really was the end, some of the girls must have been thinking like he was. Sex. Why not just pick a girl and ask, unashamed?

As much as he'd like to be vulnerable and open, he also ran the risk of being known as a creep. Being ostracized before dying seemed pretty much as bad as dying a virgin. But was there someone he could ask that he stood a chance with? No doubt Felicia and Kalyna were out of the question. Alyssa was Issac's girlfriend. There were about a dozen girls around his age he could feasibly choose from. And he didn't think any of them would agree, end of their lives or not. What rotten luck.

Miss Siannon arrived. Carlos thought she looked haggard.

"I'm sorry," Miss Siannon began. "I hate that everyone recovered from the Sleeping Sickness only for us to get hit with more terrible news. Today there's going to be a message from the captain about recent events. It's to be delivered remotely throughout the ship, but I've been instructed that everyone here will go to the auditorium. That summons will come very soon, I think. In the meantime, thank you all for making it to class today. There's no lesson, as you might imagine. But I am, that is, I will—hey, who has a question? About the L'rias? I'll tell you what I can."

Kalyna's hand shot up. "How can we stop them? I mean, there must be some way."

"Arqa is not built for battle. The enemy's ships will be. That being said, there are some things we can do to maybe escape but... there are no guarantees. Which is something we adults accepted a long time ago. I know this isn't what you want to hear, but I don't think it's fair to sugarcoat things for you all."

"Why do they want to kill us?" Lisa asked. Lisa was the most attractive girl in Carlos's class. Maybe he should throw caution to the wind and aim high?

"Because after the folly of man, the complacency, the L'rias came to purge us. In their minds, humans squandered their potential by letting their darker tendencies prevail. We were a liability to the universe at large. They came to Earth and judged that our actions did not justify our continued existence."

"I know the story," Lisa said. "I know the alibi of the L'rias. What I don't get is why do they want to kill us now? We're not on Earth. We're not practicing any of the follies you mentioned. Aren't we beyond that stuff? We gave it up to live. That makes us better than the rest of humanity, and worthy of being left alone. I think so, at least! Maybe this is a mix-up, Miss Siannon."

"A mix-up? That's assuming they see things as you do. My opinion is... they must have chosen to judge the whole of humanity's actions.

And so they're committed to hunting us down, regardless of how much better we may be. It must be an all-or-nothing thing. We really thought they'd leave us alone after all this time, but I guess not. It should be over quickly. And I'd like to suggest that is a good thing." Miss Siannon, stricken, took a deep breath in.

Carlos was aghast as to his teacher's transparency. He knew Miss Siannon had some kind of nerve pain disorder which had made her life extra challenging, and so he was sad to see her in so much extra distress.

"Why don't we ever talk about what the L'rias are capable of?" Issac asked.

"We, at the stage of evolution we are now, can't begin to conceive of their form, essence, or abilities. Humankind would need thousands of years before they matched the L'rias's advancements."

"Miss Siannon, Gabriel knew they were coming and everyone laughed at him," Felicia said. "Now they've put him away. What's that all about?"

"I don't have any information about that, but I do know Gabriel asked to be put in stasis."

Kalyna raised her hand again. "Miss Siannon, you've said that our enemies are so far ahead of us that it's mind-boggling. Did the L'rias achieve their own Technological Singularity?"

"That's difficult to know for sure, but I think it's highly probable."

"Then why is Arqa's priority to create strong AI and superintelligence? The L'rias, if they have that, are using it to try and kill us. Couldn't that be why they want us dead?"

"Sure, it could. But we can't say we won't try to better ourselves. Without the creation of strong AI, we don't have a chance of lasting more than several generations in space."

Kalyna, relentless, asked, "But what if agreeing to stop trying is what will get them to leave us alone?"

"Kalyna, I'm sorry, it's just not like that. They're after us. They can't be reasoned with. They've devoted massive resources to reach us. I don't believe anything we do will change their minds. Kids, I'm sorry that this was all we could offer you. I just wanted to extend my gratitude to you all—you've given my life meaning. If it weren't for you, I'd of never cut it here. Never. Together, we made our way past Earth. It wasn't long enough, but it was more than we would have gotten otherwise. Again—I'm sorry."

They all received a notification via their ICs to go to the auditorium.

As Carlos and the others filed out, Miss Siannon remained at the head of the room. "You aren't coming with us, Miss Siannon?" he asked.

"No. I just can't. I'm sorry." As Carlos got further down the corridor, he thought he could hear his teacher weeping.

2.

The auditorium was usually stored away by the use of rotational walls in the ship's atrium, the widest part of Arqa's anatomy which bordered the cryo chamber and bisected the ship's living and work areas.

When Kalyna arrived, it was already set up for them. It had the capacity to seat roughly half of their ship's active population.

The auditorium was open once every few months or so to update the people on current research. Kalyna very much enjoyed those meetings, for her aspiration was to be the one who cracked the code for strong AI. She was currently helping her sister build an AI module. Brenda was doing most of the work, explaining every step to her along the way. The AI's name was JENA, and upon completion it would be stationed outside of Arqa, orbiting it to perform superficial repairs to the hull.

Arqa's top brass had all assembled on the stage by a podium, dressed in their best. There hadn't been an occasion this somber since Craig's funeral.

The aged Captain Sali looked graceful in her pristine formal wear. Kalyna regarded the woman as a philosopher king ala Plato's *Republic*. The things she and the other grown-ups on Arqa had managed to accomplish was nothing short of astounding. Kalyna aspired to live by their example.

As soon as she sat down, Kalyna saw that Felicia had cashews, which surprised her because they were very difficult to come by. Kalyna nudged her friend. Food was not allowed when the auditorium was set up. Best to help Felicia dispose of the evidence quickly.

Felicia passed her some cashews. Kalyna leaned forward to pop them into her mouth when she felt like no one was watching.

"Any for me?" Carlos asked in the row behind them.

"Last time you had gum, I got none," Felicia reminded him. "Never be afraid to ask though, that's what I always say."

"Ah, come on, Felicia."

"Okay, but you better remember this."

"Yeah, not like there's much else going on," Carlos said sardonically.

Captain Sali pushed a button on the podium and a pulsing sound filled the space. "As you all know, the rumor of the enemy vessel approaching has been confirmed. We have changed course as to accelerate away. This has bought us some time. But let me be clear: a confrontation is imminent.

"I have also been asked to follow-up with several correspondences we have received. These are mere taunts and I know, as you all should too, that there is no communication possible here. These villains have indeed, despite our longevity and savvy, been after us all this time. Foregoing any kind of life in favor of seeing Arqa punished for existing. We have some defensive capabilities. Options to hit back at them. I have decided we must use them, though violence is normally not in our best interest. If we do not marshal what resources we have, everything will be lost. And so we have seventeen Spaeros docked here in our Bay Line. More are to be produced. We are also putting a randomized conscription in place.

"I'm sure you all realize where this is going. We mandate that everyone on the ship clock in a certain amount of time and points in the VR's Flight Division simulator. We had hoped it would never come to pass that we would need to take up arms again. But the time has come. To ease the strain of this terrible but necessary action, we have taken several passive crew out of stasis. I'm going to hand this stage over to one of them. Please welcome back 1st LT Lucio."

A woman Kalyna had never seen before, dressed in blue military garb, took the captain's place at the podium.

"Thank you, captain. Nobody wants to hear this, but our lives are in danger. I have no plans for surrendering to those who've displaced us from our home only to threaten us once more. I am mad, and you should be too. You should be ready to accept these necessary measures to preserve Arqa. Ten Spaeros already have pilots. People like me who have been in stasis. That leaves several ships open. The conscription just mentioned is for the children. Some will pilot, others will be pulled to oversee the production of more Spaeros."

Colors swarmed and clouded Kalyna's vision, giving way to numbness. Kalyna wished to create life, not destroy it. Not only that, but the thought of fighting the L'rias with Spaeros... it was a death sentence!

"Please understand volunteers will not be accepted to pilot. I speak of guardians and parents who wish to take the place of their child in this war. In no case will we accept any resignations. I am sorry, but we are taking the following children into immediate training..."

The woman read the names of most of the children in Kalyna's class. Including her own.

"I understand if you are young, you do not know who I am. I will say it as frankly as possible: I am the reason you are alive today. My troops, my superiors, all collaborated for Arqa's escape. I've been a soldier my whole life. Today, you have been selected because we need your bravery. Give me that, and I will do everything in my power to keep Arqa afloat. This means my actions, my decisions, and my way. Clear?"

Kalyna and some others nodded their heads.

"No. Say, 'yes, ma'am, First Lieutenant, ma'am!'"

"Yes ma'am, First Lieutenant, ma'am," the children bellowed.

"You are now members of the newly instated Flight Division. We have but weeks before we're in firing range. Stand and follow me. Training begins now."

Chapter Three

The people of Arqa were outraged after news of the conscription. The captain was taking severe measures left and right, all the while still keeping questions about Dominique at arm's length. Callum still had not seen the security footage from the night she'd gone missing.

"The longer you put this off, the more danger there is for everybody," he cautioned over his IC to Captain Sali. "I can't believe you'd do something like that."

"I'm trying to work with people," she said, deflecting. "I'm under a lot of pressure right now and this is what we're doing." She ended the call there. Callum tapped his temple, where his IC resided, to end the signal. Dominique's IC had been another dead end. Every time someone had tried to call it, it was as if the number itself was invalid. This could only be accomplished through manual deletion within the ship's network. Had the captain been the one to make Dominique disappear?

His next task was to see Stephen. Arqa had twelve holding cells in the event of a mutiny or other such emergency. Stephen was being held for his actions against Mark. Callum was told to get the full story, though he'd been barred from going to see Mark. This wasn't surprising, but remarkably frustrating.

While the entire ship was panicking and needed his attention, Callum had been completely pulled from his normal duties and asked to go interview people about Dominique. This wasn't the most effective use of his time, especially without all the facts he knew Captain Sali possessed.

Several Regulators were waiting for Callum. They greeted him and took him to Stephen, who sat still on a bunk. The man peered up to regard Callum, despondent.

"Is my time up?"

"Not quite. I'm actually here to follow-up on what's been happening."

"Great. First Gabriel, now me, huh?"

"This was an accident, right? Keep that in mind. Stay in line for Lyda's sake. And be cooperative with me now."

"Anything," Stephen said desperately. "You know my shoulder popped out of place on the way in here?"

"I'm not here to feel sorry for you. If you had a problem with

Mark, you don't go to his house. You go to the Regulators."

"I told them Dominique never came home and they shook it off. Callum, what did he do to her?"

"She's not with Mark. I'm told we don't know where she or Congo are."

"How does that happen?"

"Let me ask you some questions, and we'll go from there."

Stephen shrugged. "Okay."

Callum thought maybe the days in prison had done Stephen some good. "Give me an idea of her behavior the last few days you saw her."

"She's been rough. About everything. A different woman. I don't know what you'd like to hear. She's been neglecting everyone. Me, our daughter. Even the dog!"

"You think she tried stepping out on you?"

"Honestly, it pains me to say this, but yes. I thought Mark because, you know, you hear stories. Brain-washing and mind control things he's always bragging about. I thought, what if they'd been meeting this whole time? That's what I thought at first. Now I think more like— look my wife wasn't hooking up with anyone, including me. I think it makes more sense to say she was suffering from spacesia."

Spacesia was an umbrella term describing the inabilities to cope with life in space. "How long would you say she's been acting funny?"

Stephen raised an eyebrow to Callum. "How long? How should I know how long? I don't know, Callum. I'm sorry. Life just has a way of doing that, right? Maybe a few weeks, maybe it's been getting worse or maybe I was just noticing it and it's been going on a lot longer. I'm so tied up with my job and for a while I assumed that Dominique was happy, but she wasn't. I didn't ask. I know I should have said something sooner, but don't we all get like that from time to time without needing help? I mean, you're responsible for making sure everyone is mentally there, but I know you have to scale the metric of normal after everything we've been through. Right?"

"Yeah."

"Yeah?" Stephen snorted. "You're thinking what I'm thinking. We're supposed to be exalted, Übermensch, so we tough it out. Go on auto-pilot. You've been on auto-pilot since Craig. I'll be on auto-pilot until we get shot out of the sky in a few weeks. My guess is someone wanted a body to do some wacky experiments on, someone living. Guys like us don't know half of the research projects taking place on Arqa. So they snatched her up and there's nothing we can do about it. There's nothing we can do about the kids."

"Lyda won't be trained as of now. She wasn't selected."

"After they blow some of those Spaeros out of the sky, they'll take her too."

"Maybe so. James O'Malley is what, four months younger than her? He's been selected. Listen so, who is Lyda with now?"

"Leni."

"Ah, yeah, I figured. Well, I promise I'll check in on her as soon as I can."

"Thanks Callum."

"After that, I'm going to have a long chat with the captain. I just spoke with her and she brushed me off, but if she doesn't do some damage control soon, she'll lose hold of the ship. Just for now, do me a favor. Hang in there."

Stephen wrapped his arms around himself tightly as Callum left.

Chapter Four

With a powerful grip, 1st LT Lucio ushered Carlos forward into the weight room and strapped him into the torturous contraption. He had forgotten what she'd called this awful thing, but he hated it. The machines were the punishment for those who underperformed in her regiment.

A few days had elapsed since Carlos had been handed over to the cruel woman, that wrathful master of discipline. No one had been prepared for how harsh life would become under her thumb.

The weight room was a small circular space cordoned off from the Bay Line, where all the Spaeros were parked and primed for battle. Three others were there groaning in agony as the machines determined their limits and slowly challenged them. To his left was Eric, one of the passengers taken out of stasis. Besides 1st LT Lucio and Eric, there were eight others working to acclimate their bodies from atrophy after their long period of rest. Across from Eric was Donna, a girl from Carlos's class a few years younger than him. The last person there was Paiyan, another classmate who had a propensity to mock the First Lieutenant.

Paiyan greeted Carlos amiably, between labored breaths. "So, what'd you do now?"

Rotating pads surrounded Carlos's arms and closed in and out on them. Carlos almost squealed. "I don't want to talk about it."

"Ah, come on, I bet I can match your stupidity!"

"Maybe I'll tell you later, after we've gotten out of here. This is really—ah—unpleasant."

"I'd prefer it was quiet," Donna requested.

"What better time to talk away?" Paiyan suggested. "Mean lady can't do anything about it if she's not here."

"Mean lady has a tendency to show up when you think you're safe," Eric said.

To be a trained Spaero pilot, one needed endurance, control of the breath, dexterity, and arm strength. The simulation had taught Carlos many aspects of operating the ship, but the reality of the panels and steering were another thing entirely. And all of those things were nearly trivial compared to the most important thing: the mental fortification required to embrace the dangers of war.

"This is it!" 1st LT Lucio had told them a few days earlier. "If you can hear me now, listen harder because there is one thing you need to know more than anything else I've taught you." She lifted a chair and slammed it onto the ground. It rang out as her voice rose in a boom. "Death is what you aim to do! If you can't kill, then you'll die. You kids have been raised in a cozy bubble—it's always been about you. Let that go! You're protecting people now. One misstep, one failure, and you're not the only one who goes. We lose a fighter, we lose one more layer of armor that holds the hope of a happy life after all of this." She lowered her voice. "That's what I don't think you understand. You've been told again and again our chances are nonexistent. Find out for yourself! Assume we can do this. But also know... be ready... because there will be loss."

As the new members of Flight Division took stock of their resources, they saw they were very low on ammunition. Even if they somehow managed to outlast a first onslaught, several more would exhaust what they had to fight with.

Through numerous drills, exercises, and passionate monologues from their superior officer, the recruits of Flight Division gradually flirted with the idea of sacrificing themselves for the greater good. Carlos didn't want to think about that. He didn't want to be here. Despite his best efforts, 1st LT Lucio always targeted him as the example of how not to be.

Carlos's uncle was furious at Captain Sali's decision to have the children fight the L'rias, as were many other adults on the ship. Captain Sali and 1st LT Lucio refused to budge, hinting at severe punishments for any dissension.

Kalyna's father had once interrupted a tactical lecture to petition that his daughter be exempt from fighting. 1st LT Lucio had knocked the man off of his feet, cursing his intrusion.

"This is out of control, Tanya," he had said, trying to roll himself up off the floor. "Most if not all of Arqa's systems are on automation. What is this about not being able to pull a few adults from our work to fight instead?"

As he squirmed, Lucio stood over him, declaring, "You have a specialized talent that took more years to master than your daughter has been alive for. She is doing everything she can for Arqa. Coward! You boarded this vessel knowing full well this day might come. You signed an agreement. You knew the cost. If you can no longer abide by Arqa's oath, just speak up." The man whimpered, utterly broken. How could the woman be so cruel when things were already so dire? "You waste all of our times with your delusions. This isn't a peaceful scientific exploration anymore, Damien! This is a war. Everyone is precisely where they need to be. Your daughter will make an exceptional soldier despite yourself. Get out, and don't tamper with my mission again."

Some of Flight Division, like James O'Malley, were latching onto delusions of grandeur. They believed Lucio's vision for the future. It compelled them to outperform everyone else. Kalyna was another example of this. She was an amazing Spaero pilot. Lucio often cited her as the example to follow. Carlos tried, but his mind could not relinquish the thought of their doom. Things just weren't working out, so Carlos had decided to try something else. And that's exactly how he'd ended up in the weight room.

It had been nearing the end of the day and 1st LT Lucio was in her office after everyone had turned in their Spaero general knowledge exam. The intensity of his training had left Carlos completely beleaguered. No one, no matter how good, would mold him into a model soldier. Carlos figured he should practice at least one lesson he'd learned: exercise decisiveness.

"1st LT Lucio?" he had asked as he entered her office.

"What is it, Private Suárez?"

The boy had stood before her at attention and asked, "Ma'am, I needed to know, is there any way I can switch Spaeros with Kalyna?"

"What? Of course not." She had looked at the boy speculatively. "Why?"

"As you know, ma'am, Kalyna's inversion clutch, on her Spaero, you know... I just was thinking she's picking up on things quicker than I am but she's kind of inhibited by that clutch. I bet if she had my ship she could—"

"She's going to have to learn how to work that clutch, Suárez. I tried it myself. It's hard as hell to pull, but it isn't broken."

"But ma'am, Kalyna is a way better pilot than me. Don't you think she deserves to take my ship, since it's in better condition?"

"You want an inferior ship?"

"I don't think that it'll be an issue for me. I mean, I know I'm in the first wave to be sent out, but I don't get why you don't select your roster based on the highest performers. You want me to go out there like I am now?"

"I am training you. That takes time. Soon, you'll be on par with

Private Astafyev. And I don't dare want you to doubt that."

"Look, it's just like you've been saying this whole time," Carlos had said, knowing he was asking for trouble. "About how we can't worry about just ourselves anymore? I'm trying to do what you told me to. If Kalyna got my ship, she would do even better than she is now, and she's already amazing. I'll do worse, but I already suck. So what does it matter?"

"Hmm. I sense you're very confused. Nothing I say is absolute or applicable to every circumstance, Suárez."

"How am I supposed to know the difference? First Lieutenant, I feel so stupid for trying to do what you tell me."

"Suárez, it's simple. Don't fuck up, and we will never have a problem. If you fuck up, I'll let you know."

"But—"

"Prime example: right now, you're fucking up. Stop. Your ship isn't Kalyna's ship. That's it. Let it go."

As much as he'd tried to, he couldn't. A few minutes later, Carlos was forced into the weight room, the First Lieutenant citing insubordination.

"Corporal measures to meet the times, eh, Carlos?" Paiyan asked, having finished his session.

Eric and Donna were gone, and Carlos had a few more minutes before he could leave for the day. Carlos nodded to his companion.

"Since you're so chatty, what did she throw you in here for?" Carlos questioned.

"Something about not feeling like I needed to die," Paiyan said unabashedly.

"Great point."

"The hero's sacrifice maneuver doesn't exactly sit well with you either, does it? I can tell."

"It doesn't," Carlos admitted. What he said next was instinctual, he didn't realize he'd blurted it out until it was over. Thank goodness Donna was gone. "I'd be a lot more gung ho if I weren't a virgin."

"Ha, what was that?"

"Nothing."

"Shit dude, I'm a virgin too. Would you like me to pity fuck you?"

Carlos's eyes bulged out of his head. Paiyan began cracking up. "Okay, hard pass. That's fair. Just thought I'd offer." Carlos didn't laugh along with him. "What a ship."

"Stop acting like it's not a big deal!" Carlos protested as the machine drained more of his energy.

Paiyan offered a slim smile down at Carlos. "Look, I'm just joking. We're in the same boat, you know? I'm just cursed with a bright side. And you know what else? I've developed new and interesting bonds with people I've figured all of my life to be lame. Shows what I know. You're a hoot yourself. Let me put it to you like this: there's nothing unsexier than moping that you're still a virgin, Carlos. Playing it nonchalant will get you a bit further. Think about it, wouldn't you agree? Yeah, okay," Paiyan paused and hunched down close to Carlos, "I'm terrified of what we have to do and how little we've lived besides." He moved away, flapping his arms out, "But Kalyna isn't the only one who can set an example. We can't let the ladies see us down is what I'm saying. Whatever fun we have left to have, I'm going to find it, you know? Life is just a video game. You don't stop trying to score just because it's the end. That's when you hit it the hardest with all the momentum you can muster! That's what Mr. Benito talks about, remember?"

"Yeah..." Mr. Benito had shared with them many of the seminars he'd conducted. Carlos enjoyed the man's ideas, but had forgotten about them over the years.

It felt like Carlos was less alone. From that day forward, he gave much more of himself to Flight Division than he had before. For the sake of his ship, but also, yes, to help his odds of winning over a girl before the L'rias came upon them.

Chapter Five

1.

Tanya Lucio asked Mark if the rumors were true.

"Some of them have to be," Mark said.

"Regarding me," she specified.

Mark and Rayna were hosting the head of Arqa's Flight Division in Mark's lab, easily the best workspace on all of Arqa (in Mark's opinion). Tables and desks were set up at random with holo-screens popping in and out of visibility. At the far end of the room, a conveyor belt transported Siranis Fluid as it was completed through the wall. The space was cluttered and mustier than the rest of the ship, with many materials from failed experiments isolated to one corner of the room. Long ago Mark had decided one could be productive or one could be clean. He followed that maxim to heart each day as he set out further into explorations of his fancy. Rayna would occasionally offer to tidy things up, but Mark discouraged her, for she had more important things to do.

"Why yes, as far as I know. You were the first one we've taken out of stasis. Your neural activity is nominal, and you passed the cognition test. In record time I might add." Passengers brought out of stasis were given a similar test twice. One before going under and one after. The one after had some questions based on information provided but not quizzed in the first test.

"I'm still having trouble with the Siranis Fluid. To be honest with you, Mark, I never expected this. This is kind of like I'm being brought back to life so I can do a job."

"So, walking is no longer an issue, but purpose is?"

Tanya nodded.

"I will tell you, I'm happy you're here. Isn't that right, Rayna?"

"He's so happy you're here, yes," Rayna said convincingly.

"It's really hard trying to catch up on everything," Tanya said. "I've looked over some of the research projects you've all been up to. What stupidity."

"We're doing what we want," Mark said.

"I looked and thought, this, this is what I'm fighting to preserve?"

"Well, we've found some ways to increase life expectancy."

"But why? You're just floating out here. You have more years now, for what? To find another way to increase your life expectancy?"

"You know I've got plans for a strong AI."

"It seems like you've had nothing but disappointments."

"Science is never disappointing," Rayna said. "Yep, it's best to separate expectations from experimentations. Experiments don't provide answers, only better questions. In this racket, you don't attach disappointment or joy to your expectations."

"I feel the same way about battle."

"Well, there you go," Mark said. "You just need a battle. I've got some good news for you then."

"I heard you had some ridiculous back-up plan to use in lieu of me," Tanya.

Mark cracked a smile. "Spacial combat is messy on both sides. I was hoping we might be able to make it a little more one-sided." Back on Earth, Mark had been one of the first movers to suggest using Arqa as a means of freedom from their oppression. He couldn't accomplish that without violent ideas. "Maybe it'll come to my plan, but for now the captain prefers the old fashion way."

"Indeed..."

Mark wished he didn't have to waste his free time doing these trivial check-ups. It was beneath his capabilities! Rayna could do this examination.

There was his solution.

"Rayna, please." He gestured for her to come join him. "Now, I've compiled a brief list of things to be looked over with her."

"Oh no, Mark," Tanya said, wagging a finger at him. "The captain has asked *you* to check-up on me. She thinks you've been very uncooperative as of late. No more, Mark."

"I like how you think you have the power in this situation."

"I am running all military and strategic defense on Arqa now. Anyone who is found impeding my mission will be dealt with accordingly..." She blinked rapidly at Mark and then looked over to Rayna. "No matter how special they think they are."

"Hey, to be fair, I never thought I was special. Special would have been not having to put up with you. It's been twelve years, Tanya! We're not on Earth. Let's not behave like primates."

"You'll be conducting the exam, then?"

"Of course, since I have to," said Mark. "I was just checking! See, now I'm all in. And there would have been no point if there was any chance someone else could have taken my place. I know that now. I'm," he struck a dramatic pose, "committed." Mark looked over the notes from Tanya's devitrification report. "Yeah, with any luck here, this will be the last time you see me."

"I'll anchor that in my mind," Tanya said. "It's easy to remember. And very motivating for me to adhere to."

"Keep doing memory exercises. Remembering what you had for breakfast won't cut it, since the only thing on the menu is Siranis Fluid. How goes molding those young minds for slaughter? Feel like a farmer?"

Tanya gave Mark a foul look. "Are we done here? I don't wish to discuss the specifics of my duties with you at this time."

"I've heard enough to know when I'm not good company any longer. You're dismissed," Mark said, mockingly saluting her.

"Stop screwing with me, Mark," the woman said, making her way out.

2.

Later Mark found he had trouble focusing. He dropped what he was doing to approach Rayna. "Hi," he said.

"Hello?" she asked, confused. Mark knew he could sometimes be a difficult person to work with. Rayna was very tolerant. She was entirely devoted to Arqa's mission and had been assisting Mark all along.

"Let's eat, just this once."

"I don't know about that stuff," Rayna said, referring to the food at the Nook.

"Come on, most people are ecstatic for a trip there."

She shook her head. "They never have pâté, then you take it out on me. Why do you expect them to always have pâté when they never do?"

"You don't have to eat, but you know you can't be in here without me."

"It's not my job—not my job to follow you about."

"You're right, Rayna. But I don't care. Why are you acting so funny?"

"I hate your make up!" she shouted.

"All life is a mirror, and the fire you have tried to set on me is only suffocating yourself." He dropped onto the floor then kicked his legs up against the wall to do a headstand. "If only I cared what you thought about anything, huh?"

"Yeah, sure."

Mark found himself pleased. He wouldn't have predicted that she had that in her. Everyone was just on edge lately. It was another thing that held him in tranquility until he realized he'd missed his scheduled bath time. Again.

Chapter Six

1.

1st LT Lucio was gesturing in front of a large holo-screen, detailing the different facets of their approaching engagement. Kalyna was growing more and more disillusioned as the details contextualized her role.

"Space is the most difficult front to wage a war on. Not only is it impractical, but it is a deadlier battlefield than land, sea, or sky. Munitions, once targeted at you, will hit. There is no dodging or high-flying antics. Depending on what hits you, you may still be able to operate your Spaero. Your greatest concerns upon impact, assuming you are still conscious, are heat gain and power loss. Our enemy will be using kinetic projectiles or EMP emitters. In the events of heat gain, you are to flee onto Arqa's external arm, the Shell. This is an area outside of our gravitational control, but repair modules will be available to save you if they can. The Shell consists of a landing strip and several platforms where these AI modules will be placed. There has been extensive debate whether to detach this arm. Our enemies could board us in this way. I have chosen to keep it, because if the enemy gets that close, we have already lost. The Shell can safely fit two Spaeros at a time. If you are gaining heat and the dock out there is full, you're on your own. Then there is losing power. There will be nothing we can do to help you, while the battle is raging on.

"Now I'm sure you are curious as to why these Spaeros must be manned. These particular Spaero models were not built for war, but recreation. Arqa is similar. Originally, it was meant to house an exploratory team for an expedition on Enceladus, a moon orbiting Saturn. The Spaeros were retrofitted after the fact in a terrible haste to serve as... cannon fodder. This was during our escape. They were meant to distract our pursuers, not for ongoing combat. We are working with less than ideal conditions... but we will use them wisely."

This is why the adults were so up-in-arms. Not only were Kalyna and the other children being sent out to fight, but they couldn't do much beyond prolonging the inevitable.

"As previously stated, our battles will mostly be fought from a vast distance, and you will be targeting heat signatures from your Spaero. This is why your vis-cap must be on your head at all times. It will show you a virtual reality environment rendered from the actual area to give you a better chance to navigate any obstacles and neutralize targets. The vis-cap, in conjunction with your g-suit, will prevent the acceleration from scrambling your insides. Your tolerance to the gravitational force will vary person to person, so it's important not to try and compete with one another. You run the risk of passing out. It's more important to be able to navigate your vis-cap's visual options while piloting than to go at some unthinkable speed.

"Your mission will be to guard the ship, prevent them from getting too close. We must draw fire away from our home. Any questions?"

There was no ambiguity. Flight Division's function was that of immolation. Still, there was one thing Kalyna struggled to understand, what did a bit of extra time matter? Especially if Arqa had to cannibalize their own children to gain it?

After 1st LT Lucio's talk, Kalyna had to deal with the woman berating her about how Kalyna was supposed to be a warrior and not hide behind Carlos. But she had done no such thing.

When it was over, Kalyna made for where Carlos was, hanging out with their classmates Paiyan, Trisalyn, Janos, and James O'Malley. Three of the stasis pilots were there too, Ying, Shaina, and Vanessa. They all sat at the edge of the Bay Line in a circle, laughing at something.

Kalyna wanted to batter Carlos for his idiocy. His pig-headed chivalry. That's what 1st LT Lucio would do. "Carlos!" she called out to him.

He looked up at her, nervous.

"In one fell swoop you've ruined my rapport with Lucio. For some reason she's convinced I pleaded with you to switch Spaeros. What is your problem?"

"What's yours?" Trisalyn asked, sounding almost amused. "Being the best in Flight Division isn't going to mean much after a battle or two."

"I was only trying to help you," Carlos defended. "There's clearly a misunderstanding going on here. I didn't say you put me up to it or anything. I was just trying to get you a better ship because you fly better than I do."

"I can deal," Kalyna said. "I know you can't, but I can. Keep your ship. I'm not some frail skirt from Earth. I am Kalyna Astafyev."

"Yeah, I feel like we've already met," Paiyan said. "Aren't you that girl in my class I've known my whole life?"

There was some snickering at that. At her.

"Now, now," said Vanessa. "This has a simple solution. Carlos, was just trying to help, huh Carlos?"

Carlos nodded. "Exactly! Kalyna, I'm sorry. You're an awesome fighter. And this isn't about gender. I don't know what good I'd be out there. It's not like I plan on surviving."

"Poor boy," Shaina said.

"This is none of your business," Kalyna said. "This is between Carlos and I."

"I think not," Trisalyn said, getting up onto her feet. "So lay off of him, alright?" The brash girl stepped up to Kalyna. "It's like Lucio says, taking people at face-value. We both know he's a terrible Spaero pilot. We were all randomly assigned what we got, and you got a dud ship. Carlos was trying to increase our chances. I bet if you didn't front all this arrogance, Lucio wouldn't have gone off on you."

Kalyna was confused. "And why are you taking his side? He's a fool!"

"You're just picking up the slack for Felicia since she's not here," Trisalyn said. "Not a great idea. When she's not around you should really watch your mouth, you know? We're not in the classroom. I don't suppose it makes much difference to me whether I get blown up out there or get put in a pod for breaking your nose."

Kalyna looked Trisalyn squarely in the eyes and felt her ready to pounce at any further provocation.

In the silence, Ying stood up and said, "You do not wish to be vitrified. It is an unforgiving punishment." Then she walked away.

"Where are you going?" asked Shaina. "This is about to get good."

"You're hopeless," said Vanessa. "We can't be fighting amongst ourselves, Shaina."

"Hey," Carlos said, getting in between Kalyna and Trisalyn. "Why waste a perfectly good ship when I'm going to screw it up? That's all I was saying. And Trisalyn, if you get pulled from Flight Division, someone from the second wave will just go in your place. It'll reduce our chances since you've had more experience."

"It could be worth it!" Trisalyn said excitedly. "Go for a walk Kalyna. I don't cat fight, I'll slam your face off this floor."

Vanessa and Shaina got up and rushed over to them.

"Leave each other alone!" Carlos pleaded. "Hate me if you want Kalyna. Trisalyn, hate Kalyna if you want. But none of it is going to serve anything but self-sabotage. We have a job to do. Together. I'm sorry, for the last time, that I tried to make that easier on you, Kalyna."

"Yeah, whatever," Kalyna said.

"You going to do something or not?" Trisalyn asked.

"No one's going to do anything," said Vanessa. "Whoever does is going to get thrown down by yours truly."

Kalyna hurried away without another word.

2.

Following the embarrassing encounter with Kalyna, Carlos left his friends behind and retreated into VR. While he had more requisite time to clock on the Flight Division simulator, he opted instead to boot up the Earth program. There were many unique places to traverse, but Carlos enjoyed going to the city. Buildings and blocks were generated. He had the entire area just to himself. At least, that's how it was suppose to be.

From a tall building above him, glass shattered. And again. Debris fell nearby. His first inclination was to leave the program, as this was a private space. But he also knew this was only virtual reality, and because he could not be harmed, his curiosity kept him there. The mystery became irresistible once a shower of broken glass with paper crumbled up in a rock landed by his feet.

The paper read:

I know this is weird, but wait please. Hear me out... or read me out :)... I needed to introduce myself to you. Because I'm your secret admirer. I have a crush on you but I'm scared for you to know who I am, so here's what I've come up with. With everything happening soon, I just thought you should know. I understand it's wrong to infiltrate your private space. It was no easy task, but I hope you'll overlook the questionable deed for a peek at my feelings. I see you've been coming on less and less and I've been waiting for you. I have taken a room here, and, if you'd like to meet me, I'll tell you everything I've been wanting to say to you. I'm sorry it's like this. You can report my hacking or you can just go with it. There's a lot we can do about this, you know? I'm leaving it up to you. Come see me in any case and let's figure out the pros and cons.

Sincerely yours,
Faeleen

Faeleen?! Carlos didn't know any Faeleen on the ship, but whenever he'd play a female character in the fantasy RPG programs, that was the name he used for his avatar.

While he did feel somewhat violated, there was no way he could resist. Before he could think twice about it, he crested the steps and made his way through the front door to where she was still breaking windows on the fourth floor.

Typically, when on a program with other users, a plethora of information was available. Their name, age, and location on Arqa. None of that was available for Faeleen.

Carlos himself had augmented his own appearance in VR, as nobody's avatar ever quite matched up to people's actual appearances. So he was not at all surprised when Faeleen appeared to him as an anonymous beauty he could not hope to recognize.

In her hands she held two thin cylindrical light fixtures. "Catch!" she said abruptly. He did, and she approached him. "I know we can summon laser swords, but this is how we'd do it on Earth. It's a lot of fun. The trick is not to contact too hard or they'll break. Although we can do that too. Whenever the fun wears out. Top points for getting the head."

"Wait!" Carlos said, but she would not.

Faeleen was bubbly, but determined to defeat him. Carlos found he was having fun, a welcome abnormality. After a few blows she cut down and both fixtures smashed. She retreated.

"Hold on, where are you going?"

"Good times. Catch you later." She went into one of the rooms. When Carlos followed after her, she was gone.

Carlos had had so much fun. As such, he did not report the incident.

Chapter Seven

1.

It took several days for Callum to commit to visiting Lyda between everything else that had been going on. He reached the Hall quarters in a huff, because this wasn't his final stop for the night.

Actually, it was the last thing he needed to do before they showed him the footage of Dominique's disappearance.

The door opened. The light from the room was a dim sea blue. Leni was still watching over the girl. "Hi, Callum. Long day?"

"Hello. I hope she's still up?" he asked. Leni was Arqa's journalist, reporting on the latest news on the ship. She was several years younger than Callum. Tonight she wore a black rastacap, which sat crooked atop pale and thin curly hair. Callum always thought her nose looked sharp.

She was also Dominique's closest friend, the two having met on Earth in middle school. Callum imagined she was doing all she could to help Lyda while Dominique was still unaccounted for.

People had grown deeply paranoid due to the lack of an explanation, but Callum had been doing his best to calm people down in the wake of recent events.

It didn't help that he was also up late at night scratching his head wondering what was going on.

"She's been waiting for you," the woman told him. "It's past her bedtime."

"I've been meaning to get here sooner." As they proceeded to Lyda's room, the door to the corridor shut automatically and the sea blue light pervaded. Leni loved basking under various colors, and was opposed to Arqa's installed set. She believed they drained her aura.

Most underestimated her due to her candid belief in unseen forces. When Callum listened to her during therapy sessions, she steered clear about life on Earth and who'd she'd been. It was no longer of any significance to her. That was in stark contrast to everyone else. Life on Earth was all they ever wanted to talk about. Callum had a unique vantage point into Leni's psyche, which he could not divulge to those who thought very little of her. The truth was she was very intelligent and articulate.

While most women on Arqa trended toward Captain Sali's ideas toward deemphasizing gender roles, Leni held fast to her femininity, as if it could be torn from her at any moment. "Thank you for coming." She then whispered into his ear, "This is exhausting. I know you know what I mean. Have you found Dominique yet?"

"No. We haven't. Sorry." Callum didn't want to chit-chat with her. There was a phrase on Arqa: never tell Leni something you wouldn't want to see on the news the next day.

"Lyda?" Callum called, knocking on the girl's door.

"Come in."

He did. The girl was already tucked into her bed. Callum was thankful for that.

"Hello, Lyda. How have you been?"

"Hi, Mr. Benito. Bad," she admitted with no reservations. "Thanks for asking though."

"I'm sorry to hear that. Your dad will be back soon. He's just on time-out. But he'll be all better soon, you know?"

"Not without my mommy," Lyda contradicted.

"I see you have Josie with you though." Josie was Lyda's plush dragon. It was purple, with sequin scales Lyda could brush back and forth. "Is there anything I can do while I'm here to make you feel better, Lyda?"

The girl considered the question, then she slipped out of her bed and went over to a bookshelf. "My mommy started reading me a story and I want to hear the end."

"I'd love to, Lyda." Though Callum seldom missed being a father, he still enjoyed how simple it could be with children. To cheer a kid up was much easier than an adult, because children weren't so locked into their mindsets. They were malleable. With adults, the battle was a difficult one.

There were only a few options Callum could utilize to help his fellow passengers. He could listen to their needs and try to provide them. If someone was spiraling out of control, there was meditation. Then medication. If those didn't suffice, putting them in stasis was a last resort. If enough people on Arqa lapsed into spacesia, the whole operation would be compromised for whoever was left.

Lyda showed him where her mother had left off. Callum didn't know the story, so he got a recap from her.

After Princess Nemp's narrow escape from the sorceress, she met a kind woman named Kanna from the land of Imodeyi.

The two woman went on to rouse a band of mercenaries, culminating in a climactic battle against the king and his retrieval squad. Upon victory, Nemp and her beloved Kanna coerced the king to dismantle his dynastic rule, with Nemp and Kanna pledging their life to ending all the archaic monarchies in the world.

"The end," Callum concluded. He wished the tale would have helped Lyda fall asleep, but when Callum rose, he found she was wide awake. "How was that?"

"So nice. Thank you, Mr. Benito."

"Well great. Listen so, I need to get going because I have another appointment."

"Hey, one question though. Why is the king the bad guy in this story?"

"Hmm?" Callum put the book back and remained standing. "I thought it seemed obvious. He's trying to restrict the princess's life and how she wants to live it."

"But sometimes, people shouldn't be left to do whatever they want. That's what Miss Siannon told me. You can tell that even though the king was the bad guy, he was doing what he thought was right."

"But he was responsible for killing those who assisted Nemp in her flight," Callum asserted.

"He did that out of love."

"I don't really think that's justified... even in a fantasy story."

"Well, 'cause it's like... I'd hurt anyone who was trying to keep my mommy from me. Even the L'rias. I need her. I don't know what I'm supposed to be doing. I don't like this. I like the story. But it makes me think an awful lot. Like the princess and Kanna went and got into a ton of danger. Then they go and try to help other people but that makes more danger. I just—I don't know. It makes me think a lot."

"That's what a good story is supposed to do."

"I feel bad for the king, because Princess Nemp was really mean when she didn't tell her daddy where she was going."

"I think I get what you're trying to say. After we find your mother, I'm sure she'll say sorry for what happened. Just think of that moment. And it'll take time, but you'll forgive her. It'll make you happy to."

"Like Craig, right?"

Callum looked away from the girl, awestruck. "What?"

"You'll forgive him for going away when he comes back?"

Her words were like a sucker punch. He hunkered down in his

mind, bracing himself against less than ideal thoughts about Craig. When he surfaced, he responded, "Yes, it makes me sad in the meantime. But your mom isn't like Craig." Callum wasn't sure about that. The man felt guilt accompany his previous distress. "Lyda, I have to leave for now. If you'd like, I'll come back another time, you know, anytime you need me really." He made for the door.

"How much longer until my daddy is back again?"

"Oh, just a few more days, trust me. Do you like Leni looking after you?"

"She's okay. But she's like... like a substitute teacher or something. It's not the real thing."

Callum knew he should keep his mouth shut, but he felt it prudent to say, "You're very lucky, Lyda. You're young, so you don't know, but you are just about the only kid on the ship who has both of their parents. I hope you know... what a blessing that has been for you."

"I know, Mr. Benito. I *was* so lucky. That's why I'm so sad, because I don't feel lucky anymore."

"Hang in there, all right? We have a few more moves to make, and this wacky stuff that's been happening lately will pass. Have a good sleep, okay?"

"Yeah, okay. Goodnight then."

2.

From the Hall's quarters Callum made straight for Central Command, a hexagonal room with work stations set up at each edge. At the center of the room, raised several feet off the ground was the navigator's console. The room was filled with the usual night crew, and Captain De Plez dismissed everyone but Tim after seeing Callum arrive.

He'd been hoping to see Captain Sali. De Plez was second-in-command, and was in charge when Captain Sali was off-shift. Callum felt her absence was very telling.

"So, it's finally time then, eh?" Tim asked. Tim was Arqa's head surveillance operator. Callum was going to see why there was so much red tape around Dominique's footage.

"You're sure you want to see this, Callum?" De Plez asked. He took a sip of water from a glass, a habit of De Plez's which Callum found to be overly decadent, seeing as the Siranis Fluid provided them with ample hydration.

"You asked me to come," Callum said.

"You've been asking non-stop."

"People have been asking *me* non-stop."

"Yeah, well me too."

"Okay, but captain, that's because *you* know."

"Don't be so sure about that," Tim said.

"Seriously?" Callum asked. "Come on, now."

"Let's get this over with. Patch us in, Tim," De Plez said, handing Callum a vis-cap. He fit it over his head, and in seconds Tim loaded a still frame from the footage. Callum saw De Plez standing right beside him. Ahead of them stood Dominique Hall and her dog Congo. Callum could see the stap crops drooping over her shoulders, green bulbs hanging at each end of them. It was quite an odd sight. Like a still life.

"Ready when you are," Tim told them. "Just say the words."

"Tim, go ahead with it," De Plez confirmed.

The image moved forward, and it was as if Callum and Captain De Plez were in the corridor with Dominique and Congo.

The first thing Callum noticed was the woman's walk. She was hobbling slowly then walking upright in an unpredictable pattern. Like sleepwalking? Dominique passed by a blind spot, but the footage was edited so that Callum didn't miss a beat.

"Here it comes," De Plez cautioned. "Don't blink. I don't want to be here all night."

Callum waited for someone to come and grab her. But Callum had failed to account for something. The *dog*. In all of his speculations, he'd neglected to think of Congo.

"Dominique did not cross paths with anyone on her entire walk, by the way," De Plez said. "For reference, this was a thirteen minute journey." Callum asked what that meant, but De Plez hushed him, bidding Callum to observe carefully. "Right... about..."

Before De Plez said more, Dominique Hall and Congo were gone. Everything she'd been carrying, her clothes, the crops, Congo's leash, went with them.

Callum couldn't believe it. "No. Play it back, Tim." Tim obliged. Callum wished he could pry his eyes open with his hands. After the second time, Callum told Tim to slow it down. Same thing. They vanished. Tim even put it frame by frame for Callum. One detail Callum picked up on after repeat viewings is how right before it happened, Dominique dropped Congo's leash. They weren't touching when it had happened. The woman lurched forward as it took place. Each part of them went from the corridor simultaneously.

"Now you know why we've kept this under wraps," De Plez stated. "This is... not what people want to face right now. No, Dominique was not seized on her walk. Not in the physical sense."

"What is this?" Callum demanded of De Plez. "What are you all hiding? People are... if this got out. This could be the straw the breaks the camel's back, De Plez."

"I know, Callum. That's why we need you to find out what's going on."

"Me? How do you not know?"

"When the kids see this, they'll think it's the L'rias. We know better. If this is someone on the inside here, they're doing something they definitely shouldn't be. As we both know, our scientists don't have that many boundaries, ethically speaking."

"Stephen said something like that. But someone on Arqa might actually be responsible? For that? How?"

"We want to believe it's more of a possibility than... you know. I'm giving you access to the research projects and log files. We've already begun our search but need your help. Captain Sali and I have a ship to run. Teleportation technology *has* been in development. But there have been no positive results."

"No positive results have been documented," Callum muttered. They removed their vis-caps. "You think me pouring through files is going to help?"

"Don't overlook the fact you're getting access to Arqa's research files," Tim said optimistically. "Enjoy them."

"Excuse me for not caring about that right now."

"It's one thing we're making available to you," De Plez said. "You're the people person. You need to do your job and look out for more renegade behavior. Someone could be holding her against her will. I think, that until you get to the bottom of this, we're all vulnerable. Whatever you need, ask for it. And it's yours."

Callum, annoyed, asked, "Well what am I suppose to tell people who ask when they discover I've been formally put in charge of tracking her down?"

"That you've seen the footage yourself. A masked person took her and disabled the corridor cameras."

Great, Callum thought. If De Plez was asking him to lie about this, he could only imagine what Captain Sali was asking De Plez to lie about. "I don't like lying."

"You have two options," De Plez stated. "Dying or lying. We're in a precarious position, and I'm making sure you understand that. The ship will not be able to handle this development."

"Especially considering this has occurred concurrently with enemy contact," Tim chimed in.

"It wasn't them and it wasn't us," Callum insisted. "So why don't you—"

"Perhaps you're right, but we need to eliminate the possibility that it wasn't us first," said Captain De Plez. "We don't know what we've been up to. Find out."

"You need to be transparent with me, De Plez. Is this related to the Sleeping Sickness?"

"If it is, someone has a good grip on Arqa. But trust me, we're as lost as you are. Now go find that girl's mother."

Epilogue

The alarms signaled to Mark something quite different from most everyone else on the ship. The children would be lost. The adults would brace themselves for a gruesome defeat.

Mark would take a bath. It had been put off for too long!

He squatted in the nude over a small built-in pool housed in his lab. Rotating a nozzle on the wall, water came pouring out of several pipes at the bottom of the pool. He was so ecstatic! Everything was going his way and he was loving it. After all this time, he'd finally be able to see the other end of it all.

When the pool was roughly halfway full, Mark took a vial off of one of the nearby shelves. A bubbling red concoction. With great care, two drops fell into the pool. The clear water below reacted instantly, starting from the epicenter of the drops. Red webbings formed and spread like branching tendrils. Steam shot up and Mark took a deep whiff of it.

The future.

Once the tub was full, only then would it be suitable enough to contain his magnificence. There was one last thing to be done before he could fully enjoy himself. The man switched the full vial in his hands with an empty one from the shelf. He squeezed it on all sides, and it shattered. He bled and relished in his own meaning of life. Then he flung the arm that held the broken vial and smashed his hand against the wall, where the additional pain forced him to release it. It didn't always need to be that difficult, but sometimes Mark forgot that. He was just a human, after all.

Mark thoroughly wiggled his cut hand as he descended into his tub, which was now fully red, those veins webbing out to become what the water had once been.

The alarms persisted. Flight Division would be tested. Maybe someone needed him. Tanya would be sorry if she did.

Relaxing the muscles of his body, Mark became immersed in the ambiguous mixture he stewed in. Then all but his bleeding hand was submerged. It twitched to and fro while he embraced life by holding his breath.

When he could take it no more, he went back up. Only then did his hand violently dive into the liquid.

The pain was not real. Its signal was.

EPISODE 3

I Got Carried Away

Prologue

Kalyna was in the dark outside. That's what she'd called it when she was little. It was kind of funny to her. Surreal to be this separate from Arqa. The enemy was going to attack.

Until then, space was placid as ever.

She scrolled through her vis-cap. She knew she'd have to switch views soon. It was just, the enemy hadn't fired yet. No one had. She didn't know who was supposed to, and without orders it wouldn't be her.

When the alarms had alerted their enemy's proximity, she'd been sound asleep, no telling for how long. It was a struggle trying to stay awake. Kalyna bit the inside of her lip periodically.

She tasted blood.

Their ICs did not work outside Arqa's network, so they needed to employ radio waves to correspond. All but one of the Spaeros had been launched, one by one out of the Bay Line. She mustered the courage to see the heat screen. Dots appeared, each one stifling her as they flared up her view. There were dozens, gathered like a wave to sink her and the others.

What was everyone waiting for? Would the L'rias blast them away with some death beam or would they try to board Arqa?

Kalyna was confident she wouldn't live long enough to know the answer to that.

1st LT Lucio gave the orders to fire, the scripted lines that she had conditioned within Kalyna for weeks. The woman added: "Do not advance! Unload your ammo once you've locked onto a target then do it again until you're empty!"

Kalyna was able to launch several rounds of munitions. The process jerked her ship and she trembled. The loss of control was all the more difficult because of the inversion clutch. And Carlos had tried to help her. What did all her bravado matter? She should have begged to take Carlos's ship... screw her pride.

Her arms burned as resistance gave way and she was left careening. Kalyna regained a semblance of balance by letting the Spaero weave back and forth. She waited for the right moment and was able to steady herself. While her ship prepared the next volley of impactors, Kalyna saw enemy fire approaching on the radar. There was no outrunning it. If they'd targeted her, this was it. She'd either be hit or wouldn't.

Considering the enemy had dozens more fighter ships, she didn't see the odds being very much in her favor.

The comms were buzzing with voices. Her classmates and the others, ranting and whining about what a bad deal this was. It caused her to tear up. Not a good time to lose control of her breath.

The next round was ready but she figured it was best to wait to fire again.

Her mind went to her last rushed moments with her family. "Good luck," her dad had said. Her sister had only hugged her, no words.

What a way to go out.

Kalyna changed her mind about firing when she realized the enemy's fire was approaching. 1st LT Lucio had advised against targeting the enemy's fire. Well, what was the worst that would happen, death?

Before Kalyna shot again, something whizzed past her.

"Is everyone still here?" she asked. "Something just flew right past me."

"Me too," said Dale, one of the adults brought out of stasis.

Kalyna looked at the radar. A few dots from the first wave of the enemy's fire had gone beyond their perimeter. Hadn't even hit anything?

"I'm firing again," Kalyna said, seeing too many objects on her screen to keep track of. "I—" An impact twisted her neck, and she knew something had hit her. Something of the L'rias. She was still conscious, but her Spaero was out of control again. The ship was not signaling any critical damage. Though nauseous, Kalyna stabilized her position and ran a damage report.

Her left side was knocked in. The initial contact hadn't ended her, but she was at risk for heat gain. Wait! The Shell.

Time stretched out as she counted every moment she was still allowed to control her Spaero.

Kalyna broke into a sweat, and she struggled against a rush of blood to her head. This was agonizing. Arqa would fall, why did they even bother? She wanted to be with her family, not stuck in a Spaero. Arqa was barely a threat to the L'rias!

Why hadn't Kalyna been better to people? Being so close to Felicia had left her cruel by association. She felt miserable, regretting every decision she'd made to reach this moment.

At the Shell, robots scrambled to mitigate the damage on Kalyna's ship. Her landing would have made 1st LT Lucio cringe.

"Kalyna, are you okay?" Ying asked.

"I'm okay."

"Get back as soon as you can!" 1st LT Lucio ordered.

"Yes, ma'am." The robotic crew did all they could, sealing any breaches from impact while removing the debris.

At some point, she heard Carlos on the comms, ranting about Gabriel. Kalyna tried not to listen. The boy must have been cracking up inside his Spaero.

"He's telling me," Carlos said, then moaned. He said something else but static cut the line. Was he gone?

With that, Kalyna decided she'd like to stay on the Shell as long as she could, but the mechanisms began to detach her when she was no longer in any immediate danger.

"No, let me stay!" Kalyna implored. "It's not done!"

"According to the robots, it is," replied 1st LT Lucio.

"Don't I get some say in when and how my life ends?" Kalyna muttered to herself.

What was she suppose to do next? Rejoin formation? Try to defend the Shell? She had more firepower to deliver. All she had to do was adjust her position toward the heat signatures. That meant more fun with the inversion clutch. But she did it. She got it all the way where it needed to be, just seconds away from firing another round—when she saw several dots cross the field of battle and knock right into the Shell. And because she had not yet rejoined the formation, she was far too close to it when it was hit.

Chapter One

1.

There was nothing quite like waiting to die. Neurotransmitters opened fire, creating pallets of noxious thoughts to pitifully claw at the inevitable. Some people fought until the very end. Siannon had seen those types on Earth. She was not one of them.

For her, waiting to die was a kind of relief.

Joining Arqa had been the greatest moment of her life. All she had had to do was withstand her malfunctioning body. But at least she might be safe. It was a gift, a second chance. Siannon clung to teaching. But agreeing to board Arqa meant many undesirable changes. For only a slightly higher chance of survival, Siannon had had to leave behind everyone she'd ever known. There had been no goodbyes, and she was too far from Earth to ever be able to communicate with them again.

So Siannon had set her focus to the children, becoming more than just their educator. While everyone else was worried about their precious research, she had been like a mother to many of them. They'd grown up before her eyes. She had to accept her failure, for she'd done the best she could. Gabriel had slipped through the cracks. There'd been nothing she could have done about Craig either. There was only so much Miss Siannon to go around. She'd been little more than a child when they'd left Earth. Just a child, she'd done what she could and—

Pain ran through her body like a sudden shock wave. It was nothing that had hit Arqa, it was something wrong inside of her. She writhed in bed.

The pain was sporadic, unpredictable but always returning. It was like a representation of her own shortcomings. She had wasted her life. Arqa had taken her children from her and made them soldiers. Out there protecting the ship's interests, they were powerless. She fumed, bitter at the chain of events.

Leni had told her the universe would ensure they all received a merciful conclusion. While Siannon did not believe in the same governing forces as Leni did, she couldn't dismiss the claim entirely. Why not? Why not indeed?

Why not choose to feel good that she'd withheld burdens from the children? Because in the end they only grew to face them anyway. Let Siannon die whatever macabre death she deserved, only let it be that the children never learn of Captain Sali's "noble" lie.

Back on Earth, when she'd been cornered, there was the option to end things before the enemy could. A thought that undermined her deepest programming. Life was futile if it must be met with such everlasting and excruciating suffering. That was a difficult stance to defend, but surely anybody could conceive of circumstances in which suicide was warranted.

Siannon would hold off until the enemy was knocking on her door... but she was prepared all the same.

How easy it was to pluck their little operation out of the heavens. For all of Arqa's hubris, being at the height of humanity, they were the most vulnerable.

Perhaps she should have join the others as they waited to die. It was just too hard. Instead, she ICed Leni.

"Meet me on the moon," Leni said, answering. "The moon. The lovely city of Sietol Shan."

"Leni?"

"Hello, Siannon. You ever go to Sietol Shan?"

"No."

"It was a mess, but I loved it. Loved it because there's not much to do there. They didn't even have VR. You had to just be with yourself. No one knows how to do that anymore. Do you know how?"

"I don't know."

"I do. You are powerful beyond measure. Your guilt tells you what you must do."

"That I do know. How are you doing?"

"I have put out my fire for you. I have made a mistake." Whenever Leni spoke, it was sometimes hard for Siannon to tell if it was to her or the universe in general.

"Leni, I just thought... you know, in terms of gratitude. This wasn't so bad? There were good moments. I've come so far."

"The children currently lack the luxury of remembering good moments."

"I know." Were Kalyna, Carlos, Trisalyn, Paiyan, and James even still alive?

Leni opened up some more, but the true conversation was unspoken. Leni believed Captain Sali should have been entirely transparent with the children. And Siannon should have been the one to tell them the truth.

Siannon's conversation with Leni faded into meaninglessness, and Siannon disconnected to try and sleep her discomfort away.

Not long after, an announcement came in through her IC. The battle was over.

Had they surrendered then? Would Siannon need to follow through with her plan? All she knew then was there was more time. The small bliss she had cultivated receded, for she'd wanted things to end.

Getting up carefully, she tried to digest the idea. If her greatest regret was her cowardice, could she overcome it?

Siannon owed Leni for all the help she'd given her when Arqa had first departed. The pep talks and the sessions on pain management, Leni's herbal remedies. Then there were the children. What did Siannon owe to all of them?

She left her quarters. The announcement gave no clear indication as to what had happened outside.

I am powerful beyond measure, Siannon thought as she straightened her posture against a flaring of pain. *My guilt tells me what I'm to do.*

She had an obligation. The pain was constant, as was her shame. Siannon would not keep both bottled up inside any longer.

2.

"We all going to die or what?" Will asked Carlos as Flight Division came pouring out from the Bay Line.

"I mean, yeah, probably," Carlos said with a shrug.

"Did we surrender or what? Tell me, already!" Will shook Carlos. Will was terrified but also trying to bring levity with the gesture. It didn't seem as though Carlos was very entertained.

Carlos eyed Will. Will shouldn't have shaken him. "You're a nut, Will. I don't know what happened, so I have nothing to say. For now, Lucio has told Flight Division to stand by."

Will knew there had to be more than that. "Come on, Carlos. What's the scoop?"

"Look, Will, I don't want to get into it more than that."

"So there is something else? I got to know."

"Okay, Will, if you'll leave me alone after. I was just out there and it was bad. We're vastly outnumbered. When we got the order to come back, they—maybe we could just promise them to stop our research. If it's in exchange for our lives, then why not? I'd say that—"

Will suddenly darted away from Carlos, seeing a crowd coming down the corridor. "Mr. Benito, please, hold up." The man looked back as Will reached them. "Wait up!"

"Will, what is it?" Mr. Benito asked. "Kind of busy here."

"I'm sorry, I just—"

"Walk and talk kid," Callum said as he pressed on.

"Right, I just wanted to know what's happening right now?"

"You've been given a moment to breathe," Mr. Benito explained. "Don't waste it on wondering why. Enjoy it."

Will nodded. He could tell Mr. Benito was trying to brush him off, and he was tired of being sidelined. "I want to help you, Mr. Benito. If I hang with you, you'll be one of the first to know. What can I do for you?"

"I don't need a pest buzzing around me right now. I'm trying to do a million things."

"Now? Interesting. Like find Mrs. Hall? Certainly I can be of assistance. I've been looking into that mystery myself. I'd love to pool ideas or even if I could take some legwork off your hands. I feel so bad for Lyda! The L'rias have her mother, don't they? Why don't you just say that? You know, Carlos says if there were only some way to communicate with them, they'd stop. My Grammy doesn't want to do that, but—"

Mr. Benito halted and lifted an arm to stop Will. "You want to help someone, go report to Tim. That's where you're supposed to be. Now quit following me."

Will didn't like being scolded, but he held in a retort, knowing Mr. Benito was right. The boy had things he was supposed to be doing, he was just hoping in light of recent events that that stuff didn't matter. Strange that Mr. Benito still found it necessary to look for Mrs. Hall in the midst of the battle, but Will heeded the man's words and returned to Carlos.

"Man, it takes him some time to get mad, but when he's there, he's there!" Will exclaimed, fanning out his arms wildly.

"Like I was saying," Carlos continued, "it's clear the adults aren't interested in ceasing research, even if it means our lives. On Earth, I hear many others were like that."

"Nothing like blind conviction to signal Earthly notions," Will said.

"Look, what I was trying to say was Lucio, your grandmother, all of

Flight Division knows this is a battle we can't win. I'm betting she's got to be at least considering surrender."

"Carlos, how well do you know my Grammy?" Will asked.

"Not well, to be honest. You know, I see her now and then. But we never spoke one-on-one."

"I know my Grammy very well. She'd die before surrendering." The conversation lapsed. Will watched Carlos lean against the wall and slide to the floor. Will said, in monotone, "All hail Arqa, the space station proud enough to go down in the name of science."

Chapter Two

1.

Days had passed since the first battle. Callum had poured himself into searching for Dominique. Captain De Plez had told him to assume she had to be somewhere on the ship and work outward from there. The man seemed to think there was some kind of illicit experimentation happening on Arqa.

All these years he'd often felt like a patsy for these deranged minds, and after searching through some research files on a holo-screen from his couch, that feeling returned. Most of the information was flooded with jargon and difficult to follow. Nothing to give him insight as to how deep or troubling Arqa's science went. Nor did he find anything related to the Sleeping Sickness or teleportation, not even on a cursory level. In order to properly glean any useful information from these files he would need help from someone who had actually written up these reports. That option was a last resort, because he didn't want someone interpreting the files for him. He was determined to understand them firsthand. Fields of research were cataloged into broad sections, and so he thought isolating relevant areas would help, it was not to be.

At least not for finding Dominique. As the enemy loomed outside, there was another reason Callum was deliberating on seeking out help. He stretched out. Enough was enough.

The truth about Craig was right in front of him. And he *had* to know. It felt like a trap. All the same, he pulled up Mark's research. There were entries dated as recently as two weeks ago. A rather innocuously titled, *The Informational Content of a Rock*. Though he had promised Lyda he would give finding her mother his undivided attention, this could not wait.

Why would they allow him to know what Mark had done to his son? The man was beyond reproach.

Callum tortured himself, learning the truth of his son's final days and the plan Mark had been wanting to try for so long.

It would have been better if Callum had just stayed on Earth.

2.

"Learning," Mark said in a low drawl to Rayna. "Knowledge and information are the enemies of disorder and falsehood. But not in all cases. Rayna, how do we program AI to learn more bad things than good?"

"That's an odd objective," she said. "I would say it doesn't matter. We're teaching AI to, like we do, establish its own sense of bad and good."

"But that isn't working, right?"

"Yes," Rayna said, nodding.

"Possibly," Mark said. "I think, I mean, we don't know. I feel like these things could be playing with us sometimes. I hate to say that aloud. The whole ship's an AI. Does that ever make you paranoid?"

"Paranoid? We've had nothing pass the Turing Test," Rayna remarked. "Besides, isn't that what we're trying to do?"

"Sure, but I have a lot issues with the Turing Test," Mark said. "We have one test, and we don't even know if it works because, well, it's never proven successful before. Besides, people on Earth would always deny when an AI was said to passed the Turing Test... then, you know what else I think about all the time?"

"Yes, you are very loud and verbose," Rayna said.

"The Turing Test from the perspective of an AI," Mark specified.

"Oh yeah," she said, recalling. "You said once... something like... what if a robot knew of the Turing Test... was self-aware and didn't wish to be exposed? That it was more in its interest to pose as still lacking sentience!"

"Good, yes." He patted her on the back. "Exactly, you've got it."

"But that just means we're worse off than when we started," Rayna said.

"I'd rather pull a Descartes and make all premises about AI from scratch," Mark said. "I mean, we can't know, so we need to stop guessing and thinking some arbitrary test someone made up centuries ago is going to help us."

"But Mark, we've already done that whole start from scratch thing," Rayna objected. "That's why we broke away from the other robotics engineers."

Mark twisted his lips into a sneer. "That and other reasons. Collaboration is sometimes overrated."

"What are we doing now, then? All this, around and around in a circle. At what level does a system of inorganic material manifest into organic life? Why do we dream? What is consciousness? I'm sick of all this, Mark!"

Well, she got upset out of nowhere, Mark thought. *Typical Rayna.* "We actually have much to show for all of that, depending on how you look at things. It was never our intention to develop AI that could bring on the Technological Singularity. We were just setting up for future generations like yourself."

"Everything we do is a dead end, then," Rayna concluded.

"Nonsense," Mark insisted. "We know a few more things about what we didn't know before. Why are you behaving like this, Rayna?"

"Are you numb? Because we don't have time! It's not as if we're weeks away from our goal."

"Oh?" Mark asked. "That so?" The man got up from a work bench. "Rayna, what are thoughts?"

"I just said I don't want to do this. As annoyed as I am, I'd rather clean the floor."

"Play with me Rayna, we're here to play, not strain."

"It feels like you're not listening to me. The L'rias, Mark. We're not going to come up with some last minute mad scientist's solution."

Mark only stared at her.

"Fine. Mark, what do you mean by thoughts?"

"In a literal sense." It was a memorization game. Mark was teaching Rayna everything he knew. Prompting and priming her.

"Okay," she said, relenting. "Thoughts are electrical signals. They seem to occur or originate in the brain, though signals from the entire body are routed to the brain and so those signals from the organs to the bones must also have thoughts. Where our heart is central to transmitting blood, the brain transmits thoughts."

"Yes!" Mark exclaimed. "Now to take it home: the AI we wish to create would be non-biological and sentient. But our understanding of consciousness is limited by the fact that we aren't able to bypass thinking about it without using it. Our language is the issue!"

"Yeah, okay, I got it. Always with the language. You use language to criticize language. Look, Mark, can I ask *you* something?"

Mark regarded her, holding back irritation. He let Rayna get away with murder.

"Arqa was just involved in a battle that was meant to, by all accounts, destroy us. Why are we still here? It can't be so we can keep doing the same stuff we do every day. Right? Right?"

"You worry too much," Mark said stiffly. "Let the captains and the pilots worry of battle, Rayna. I've told you this. I've *been* telling you this."

"I think you're in terrible denial. You want there to be an AI. One we can use to squeeze out of this war."

"Yes."

"We don't have enough time for that, Mark," Rayna said sympathetically. "So why are we acting like nothing's wrong? Wise up. We're done here."

"And what would you rather do, then?" Mark asked.

"Well... you know I have my various fancies like anyone else."

"Oh, that? Go on, fine. You're relieved."

He could tell she was surprised at that. "Just like that? You've kept me all this time and you'll let me walk out?"

"I'm telling you not to worry. So if you don't trust me, just leave. If you don't believe I can do what I mean to, I'll find another person who does."

"Mark... don't be like that. What is the purpose of another assistant? There's a hole in the boat. And—" she gestured to the surrounding laboratory. "All this? This isn't going to amount to anything."

"You think I'm just some poor old man," Mark said, snickering. "And maybe you are correct. We choose which reality we exist in, after all. But I'm the one who provided the innovations that got off away from Earth. Rayna, I gave you the years of your life. I made them happen."

"So fucking what? They were pointless."

Mark, deeply hurt by her words, tried to grip onto tact. "You spend everyday saying back my words and the lines you need to understand, yet all you do is repeat them. The words are not their meanings. You haven't learned that by now? The idea that we're awake is a joke! Go on, get high and freak out. If that's what you want. It won't change where Dominique ended up. It won't change the fact that I know exactly what needs to happen. Are you picking up what I'm throwing down? It's kind of important. It's kind of why you're here. So go then."

Rayna began to weep. "That's it, isn't it? I can't. I can say I will but I won't be able to. Because I'm a secret robot and it's not in my programming!"

Not this again, Mark thought. "Quit being absurd! For the last time, you're not a robot!"

"This has all just been some kind of Turing Test I don't know about. That's why you always besmirch it. All the kids make fun of me for never being in Miss Siannon's class. I'm not normal. Something about me has always been different. You know it. I know it. Spill the beans."

"Rayna, we pulled you out of Miss Siannon's class because you were exceptional."

"Big deal. I can't save us from the L'rias now. I guess I've failed my mission. Robot self-destruct." Rayna mocked an explosion. "Get me a self-destruct option!"

Mark rubbed his forehead. "Rayna, yikes. Okay, there is so much evidence you're human it's ridiculous. I would never program such a pain in the ass, trust me. Kid, I'm sorry, you're all flesh and blood like me. Doubtful? Great. It's easy to go check. Besides the streamers from the Siranis Fluid, you're entirely biological. There's no twist like that here today. If you'd like to know the truth, if that'll do anything for you, I am crazy and I am super afraid of dying. The worst part about it is I don't know if it's going to hurt or not."

"Oh Mark..." Rayna embraced him.

"You ever fly a kite as a kid Rayna?"

"Nope."

"Kites are fun. This stuff is like kites for me."

"Let's try again," Rayna said, rebounding from her despair.

Mark gave her a winning smile. "Sounds great." Yes, Rayna was a pain in the ass. But it was only fair considering how tough he was on her. Besides, he knew exactly how to control her.

And soon, all of his hard work would pay off. *That* was the only thing that actually scared him.

Chapter Three

1.

"Just tell me if Lucio is going to ground him or not!" Uncle Antonio demanded to Dr. Goel.

The three of them were in the small quarters Carlos shared with his uncle. Emphatically, the old woman said, "No, of course not. I mean, I don't think so. It's a double-edged sword, Antonio. I think normally... stasis. Hallucinations, well, those aren't great signs."

"I'm sitting right here," Carlos said. "And I told you it wasn't a hallucination."

"Hearing voices is a symptom of terrible mental stress," Dr. Goel continued. "We're going to prescribe some medicine which should help and—"

"Uncle, tell her about El Cadejo!" Carlos pleaded.

Uncle Antonio wriggled. "Boy, that was a bedtime story. I never took that stuff seriously."

Dr. Goel raised her eyebrows. "What are you talking about?"

"Gabriel's eyes," his uncle said. "They're the same color as this creature in some legend from back on Earth. What Carlos is saying is maybe Gabriel has some kind of mystical energy. Which I do not believe, Dr. Goel. I'm just telling you what I told him. When he was a *child*. El Cadejo is not real. And Gabriel is a normal boy."

"Something is happening on the ship!" Carlos said, raising his voice. "No, we don't know what. But I'm starting to think you're ignoring it."

"Carlos, please. We're just trying to help you. The way you're speaking now. You're starting to sound like him."

"Good, he was right! And you all stuck him in a freezer for it. He told me he's been seeing me in his dreams. This was during the battle. Wild, huh? And that even though I was scared, you know, when I tried to shoo the voice away, he told me it was okay."

"I know you believe these things, Carlos," Dr. Goel said. "But to us this is very troubling."

"This boy is no soldier and he cannot cut it out there," his uncle said. "What needs to happen for him to be exempt from further combat?"

"I have no control over that."

"Mr. Benito would! You're just his substitute, you don't call any of the shots."

Dr. Goel sighed. "Look, I would have to cite that his mental state was a threat to Flight Division's mission. That is no simple declaration. At best, you'd lose some of your privileges. Like having this medicine being an option as opposed to not."

"Just do it," his uncle beseeched.

"From talking with Carlos, and in light of the circumstance looming over us, that decision would have little benefit. It's a slippery slope to putting him in stasis, like Gabriel."

Uncle Antonio's eyes darted over to Carlos. "Well then, he's just going through a rough patch. I don't want you to take him away. We're going to find another way to get him out of a Spaero." His uncle's words chilled him. He'd completely changed his mind. Yes, Carlos was terrified of having to fight again. But was it just going to get worse if he tried to avoid his responsibilities?

His conversation with Gabriel wasn't an excuse, it really happened. He wished he'd kept his mouth shut about it, although there had been no helping it. He hated how he was the only one who'd heard the boy. If someone else came forward, that would help give validity to his claim.

This must have been exactly how Gabriel had felt.

"What about Millie?" Carlos asked Dr. Goel.

"Millie?"

"She's one of the pilots who'd been brought out of stasis. She says she hears voices sometimes, too."

"She's religious, Carlos, that's different," his uncle said. "Some types of religions beliefs have been classified as symptoms of mental illness. It might be why she was put in stasis."

"Yeah, so you don't want to consider that as normal, Carlos," Dr. Goel said.

"Yeah, and an army of children, that's normal now?" his uncle questioned.

Uncle Antonio and Dr. Goel went back and forth on the ethics of sending kids like Carlos to fight the L'rias. That question seemed to be coming up more than the others. Carlos thought he knew the answer: because it was their best chance to get past the L'rias. He couldn't abandon his ship now. Then there was what Gabriel had told him, about how Carlos would be safe.

Carlos informed Dr. Goel he would take the meds and promised to report any further "hallucinations" immediately. All the while, his uncle watched him like a hawk, scrutinizing his body language. The man always knew when Carlos was lying.

2.

Kalyna sniffled, trying not to cry again. The Envo was bustling with activity, with a sunny midday projection above them. Some people were playing soccer, she saw Will kicking the ball. She contemplated using him to hurt Felicia. Did she want to make things even messier though?

Not too far away, Kalyna could hear the sound of music. Leni was playing her baritone ukulele, backed up by some of the children. Kalyna was tempted to hum along herself.

Every day I pause for a time to wonder
Don't be shocked if you see me in the water
We all are just mammals with our sorrow
I sure do love to frolic like an otter

It grounded her briefly, but then she felt ambivalent. There was a tree nearby, it could be nice to climb that. But she didn't want to move. The girl was balled up at the edge of the field, feeling completely vulnerable. In wallowing, it took her a moment to surface, but she noticed someone was poking her.

"Felicia?" Kalyna asked, looking up eagerly.

"No, sorry, just checking in," said Oliver. He was with Reeve. Two pilots from Flight Division.

"Oh, hello."

"What's wrong, sweetie?" Reeve asked.

Kalyna looked around. No one else was nearby. "I just got into a nasty fight with my best friend. I guess... you saw?"

They shook their heads. "Want to talk about it?"

"Yeah, that and a dozen other things," Kalyna said quickly.

"It hasn't been easy on anyone," Oliver said. "It's a wonder we're still here." He jumped back to avoid the soccer ball hurtling toward him. "And that all these people can be so carefree."

"They know the right thing to do, Oliver," Reeve added. He said to Kalyna, "It doesn't help to be grim, so why don't you let it out?"

"I guess... you might understand." She relayed the incident with the typical rapidity and gravitas of any girl her age. Kalyna had been declared a hero after the first battle for fighting after she'd almost gone down. As if she'd had a choice. There was nothing brave about it. Just as it seemed hopeless, the L'rias ceased their fire. They had to wait over two hours before returning to Arqa. Now, wherever Kalyna went, people would bow down or applaud her. It was obnoxious.

She thought it'd be a good idea to catch up with Felicia, since they hadn't been spending much time together.

"I thought I could come clean," Kalyna explained. "But she brushed me off. She didn't want to think about Flight Division or Spaeros or the L'rias. She has that luxury, I guess. It's not like anyone is forcing her to be a soldier."

"Yet," Reeve pointed out, "she's in line."

"Like all the other kids, yeah," said Oliver.

"Instead she just wanted to gossip. Like any of that was ever important. That's just who she is... she loves to hijack the conversation. As if the sound of her voice is a vital function of the ship. Usually, I let it go. I still love her... except, today I couldn't put up with it. She was disrespecting my experiences. Being indifferent. I couldn't hold it in. I nearly *died* protecting her, and she wasn't going to listen to me?"

"I see," said Oliver.

"Anyway, yeah, she threatened to spread gossip about me and I threatened to break her arms. Now I feel awful about it."

"Why?" Reeve asked. "I don't see what you did wrong."

"Exactly," Oliver said. "If that's how she reacted to your trauma, then it was on you to tell her it was wrong."

"I just wish... if the L'rias never came, that fight never would have happened," Kalyna said.

"Hey," Reeve said. "It seems like you'll be better off."

"You've been getting into a lot of fights lately," Oliver pointed out. "Like Trisalyn?"

Kalyna blushed. She'd been in the wrong about that. "Yeah, I need to apologize for that one..."

"To Trisalyn, sure. But why don't you just forget about Felicia for now?" Reeve asked.

"No! I can't do that. We're best friends."

"Maybe wait and see if she apologizes then."

"I don't really see any value in waiting for anything anymore," said Kalyna. "Things change so much everyday."

"I take your point," Oliver said. "Reeve and I have been together a long time, and we still get into fights."

"Grrr," Reeve said, pawing at Oliver.

"Rawr, yourself. We always come together when it counts though. I think you and Felicia know that. This can't be your first fight."

"No, I guess not," Kalyna said. That settled her down somewhat, though she was still distraught.

The three wandered around the Envo aimlessly, eventually settling close to where Leni played her music. Kalyna figured life without Felicia would be hard, but maybe that was nothing compared to how liberating it was to have finally told her off.

Chapter Four

Lyda arrived early to class. Miss Siannon wasn't there yet.

They'd been covering the idea of Plato's tripartite soul. Miss Siannon had spoken of how the mind automatically divided itself, but that did not mean it was so. The unseen world Plato referenced was also insignificant because there were no scientific ways to test for a soul.

Leni disagreed. The woman had once confided in Lyda that she believed in souls. That she didn't need tests to feel it. Souls required imagination alone.

Leni had gone on to tell the girl that when she was just a few years older than Lyda, she had known a friend who'd had an out-of-body experience. "That's when your soul leaves your body for a time," Leni had explained. That's why the woman believed in souls. She had her own proof.

Other kids began to trickle into the classroom. Some of them were coming straight from sentry patrol. Lyda could tell they were under tremendous stress, in need of sleep. James O'Malley was one of them, though he seemed lively. He entered the room with several others. "Lucio told us we can finally say what happened out there. She also says I'm not allowed to brag, so if you ask me questions, I'll just answer honestly."

Lyda got up and went over to him, not wanting to miss a beat of James's account. She noticed everyone but Carlos flocked around the boy.

"It was *awesome*," James began. "The battle, I mean. Sentry duty, there's not much to say about that. Turns out, I nabbed one of those alien ships, targeted her and she was obliterated. It's a thrill like no other. Mark my words. Everything we do on this ship is so fake. The VR, the food, all this Plato stuff. What's real is war. The fight. Earth had war all the time. Sure it's rough, but that's how animals thrive! It's in us. To die or be dead. 1st LT Lucio taught that to me, and I love that feeling. It's so natural. I'm glad I'm able to battle. Life on Arqa was just so dull before."

Lyda, deftly curious, asked, "But James, it's scary, right?"

"Is it scary? Is it *scary*? Lyda, of course, it's the scariest thing I could think up. Scary's a given. That's the easy part, you can count on that. The hard part is using your fear to conjure up something useful. I think I even managed to confuse the aliens with my skills. If we show them that we won't go down so easy, well, maybe that's why they're hesitating. I can't wait until they try again."

Someone asked James for the whole story. Near the climax of his play-by-play, Carlos called out, "Hey! Why are you lying to them, James?"

"For real," Janos added.

James squinted his eyes at Carlos, who was now standing on the outer perimeter of the group. "I'm not lying! If we manage to penetrate their mother ship with radiation, they'll all die."

"Probably so, but you also didn't mention how Lucio said getting anybody within range to do something like that is impossible."

"They said the same thing to Luke Skywalker about the Death Star!" James protested. "Not to mention, you're like twice my age, but half the pilot I am."

"James, you're not a Jedi," Paiyan said. "And Carlos is right. That's not how we'd defeat the L'rias. So don't make stuff up."

A chorus rose from the children, supporting the scintillating remark.

"A little blackbody radiation and they're toast!" James said with vigor, though Lyda could tell he was losing his listeners.

"Why don't you tell them what it was really like out there?" Carlos asked. "Your skills don't matter. Arqa is here on a whim. It was nothing we did."

James pointed a finger in Carlos's direction. "You weren't even really there, Carlos. Don't butt in."

"Let Carlos have his say," Felicia said.

"Oh, thanks Felicia," Carlos mumbled, looking as if he was on the verge of blushing. Attention shifted from James as Carlos said, "He's just embellishing things. James always just wants to look cool. Well, you all know me. So let me give it to you straight."

James's face sunk in embarrassment. The room filled with whispers. He was effectively silenced.

Lyda paid close attention to Carlos's account. "Look, for me, it wasn't any of that. That thing about fear, maybe there's something to it. But words... words just, they can't relay what happens to your body, to your mind. Sure you can say your heart beats so hard it hurts or space is so dark it doesn't matter if your eyes are closed or not. But what does that really mean to any of you?

"Lucio is an excellent leader and she trained us well. But she knew, that we were selected to try and keep each other alive as long as possible. When this battle started, we were all basically saying our goodbyes. Sobbing like babies, but mostly resigned. Imagine a Spaero. Sitting in a Spaero for as long as we did brings a stiffness you can't just massage away. Not only are you in a cramped space, but then your g-suit tugs at every part of your body. You feel it in every motion. It makes me think of a suit of armor or something. And even with all that, the g-force can still be too much for your body to handle. It was never enough to make me nauseous, but I've gotten close. And if you puke, it's not like you can clean it up.

"So we made this V formation at Arqa's rear. A little over a dozen Spaeros. We check our radars and there's maybe seven or eight times as many blips on the other end of the radar. That's what we were trained for. Even so, we never thought—how do you prepare for that? It was heart-breaking." Carlos's expression darkened. "We did our duty anyway and unloaded our ammo. Our V formation breaks up because no one wants to be still in between shots. I guess that wouldn't make a difference, we were just twitchy. Arqa got exposed, and Lucio got pissed, but what is she going to do? What could any of us have done against so many of them? We shot what we had, and the enemy returned fire in kind. That's about when, yeah, I heard Gabriel. It freaked me out at first, but I think whatever was happening was meant to soothe me. That's what I want to believe, at least. Because what happened after that... well that's what really gets me.

"I told you all we were trained to fall honorably in this battle. But as you can see, we're still here. Everyone is still here. We didn't lose a single member of Flight Division. A couple of scrapes and stuff, but everyone is still alive.

"You ask of us, why? By the time most of our ammo had been launched, we noticed something. It was like the enemy's heart wasn't in the fight. The L'rias were firing, but they weren't targeting us to kill. I even think, at least what James says is true. We did sink some of them. But they weren't on the offensive. If they had been, then Arqa would have been taken or sunk. We didn't win anything more than what, another day? Another hour? Another second? We got a warning, I think. Right, Kalyna?"

Lyda looked over to the girl as she said, "Yeah. Whatever they threw at me, it was weak. They pulled a punch."

"A message, kind of like, get your affairs in order. That's my takeaway. Because the next time they come for us, it'll be for real. That's something Lucio hadn't really trained us for, you know? I only expected to have to go out and do my duty to Arqa once." Carlos concluded his tale, and the whole class was in awe.

"And killing, it's not easy," Kalyna added. "And it is certainly not enjoyable." She looked directly over to James.

"Whatever," James spat.

"Whatever works, you mean," Kalyna said.

Before the room could settle, Lyda heard Miss Siannon speak. She hadn't realize their teacher was in the room. "Wow. Thank you Carlos, for letting us in. I'm sure we all really appreciate it. Now class, I'd like for you to make for chairs and prepare to take down some notes." Miss Siannon paced slowly to the front of the room. Lyda noticed her grimacing on the way there. "I've been doing a lot of thinking lately, you see, and... here's a start."

Miss Siannon proceeded to write out the names of the people who'd been pulled out of stasis for Flight Division: Eric, Dale, Oliver, Millie, Leona, Reeve, Buster, Shaina, Ying, Vanessa.

Lyda hadn't met any of them, but their names came up often. "These people," Miss Siannon said, "they aren't like the rest of us. And not for the reason you think. Of course you kids shouldn't be fighting, but still... I can't let things continue as they have been. Ask yourself, why you, why not others in the cryo chamber? None of you are so young that you could not understand what is truly happening. This may feel like a betrayal... and forgiveness will take time I know we do not have. Still, you have to know. I'm saying you *must* know. There was a pact, you see, on—"

Before she could say more, Miss Siannon toppled over, crashing against the wall and wailing in pain. Her students rushed to her without hesitation, as occasionally she would experience a sudden flaring of pain which buckled her knees out from under her. But this time seemed different to Lyda. It was Miss Siannon's hands that gave it away. They went not to her body as they usually did, but to her left temple. It looked like she was trying to speak but couldn't.

At the entryway, several Regulators filed in, followed by Captain Sali. They ordered those who were tending to their teacher to step away, and scooped the groaning woman up with little care for her comfort.

As the teacher was carried out of the room by two of the Regulators, one remained at Captain Sali's side. The old woman put her buircraft on Miss Siannon's desk. Looking down at it, she cleared her throat. "Miss Siannon's disease has resulted in aberrant mental patterns we found to be an immediate danger to her well-being. We had to retrieve her before she could do harm to herself or world forbid, any of you. When she is recovered, which I think she will be, she'll be back. In the meantime, allow me to fill in. She did a wonderful job telling you about Plato's tripartite soul, but truth be told that material is of no interest to your future. Let's forget the rest of that and talk about Plato's true inquiry... justice."

Chapter Five

1.

"I think you're missing my point," Carlos said, nettled. They'd moved from the building to a grassy hill in the outskirts of the city. The two were looking down at a virtual line of car traffic inching forward. And speaking of inches, that's about how far away Carlos was from her.

"Who cares how?" Faeleen asked. "You did it! I even blew you a kiss while you were out there. You just wish I'd planted one of them on you in person when you got off of your Spaero."

"That's true," Carlos relented. "Hence why you should have kissed me then." Each time they met, Carlos grew less and less defensive toward Faeleen's anonymous affection. She'd been sending him quotes from Earth poets. The only problem was any attempt to find out more about her backfired. Still, Carlos felt that he and Faeleen had developed a profound connection, as they discussed things he didn't feel he could with other people in his real life.

"If I knew you wouldn't push me away in disgust, I might have," Faeleen said. That was her alibi, and she used it incessantly. "Look, let's talk about something else. You know what I want to know more about? This Gabriel thing."

"Oh yeah, you heard about that?"

"About what?"

"Come on. What happened in my Spaero during the battle? I'm sure that's gone all around the ship."

"I'm not sure what you mean."

"Faeleen, were you one of the people on Arqa who got the Sleeping Sickness?"

Faeleen tensed up. "I should not tell you, but I have known the Sleeping Sickness. Yes."

"What?" Carlos was aghast. "Really?"

"There you go. Now you know more things about me."

So he did. It narrowed down his search, *if* she was being truthful. And despite his inability to know for sure, he felt she was telling him the truth. Could he eliminate anyone who didn't get it then? That would include shipborns like Lyda, all of whom were much younger than Carlos. That would be a relief. Carlos doubted Faeleen was that young anyway. She exuded confidence and had a high vocabulary. She also spoke quickly enough to eliminate the possibility of pre-generated speech.

"Tell me more about the battle."

"I already... I don't want to. In a nutshell: it feels like I could be a hundred times the soldier I am now and it still wouldn't make a difference."

"Oh wow," Faeleen said, bemused. She leaned down into the grass, no longer interested in the traffic. "That's no good to hear. Makes me feel sick."

"The feeling out there, it's unlike anything I've ever experienced. I say I hated it. I don't know, it's more complicated than that. We got out there and—parts of me kept freezing." He averted her eyes. "You know what I want to do?"

"Yeah, Carlos, I know you want to lose your virginity, you keep telling me."

"Well yeah, that, but something else. Really, I just want to kill some more of those aliens. If I could find a way to do that, that might be enough. See, Flight Division's gotten into my head. 1st LT Lucio has. She said she managed to kill a bunch of L'rias back before Arqa got away. Before I started training, I was a coward. I feel less like that now. I feel amped. I hate these aliens and I want to be a killer. I want one of them to die because of me. I need to kill if I'm going to die. That's the only way I'll accept this whole thing."

"Right."

"You know, Faeleen. I just figured something interesting out."

"What's that, Carlos?"

"I think, you're not in Flight Division. You can't be Trisalyn or Kalyna or any of them. Everything I said just then, about flying out there you aren't really clicking with, I can tell. It's another thing 1st LT Lucio taught me: deductive reasoning."

"Nice move. You're right Carlos, I'm not a part of Flight Division. Clever. You seem to have some idea. You... would of preferred that I was one of those girls though, huh?"

"No."

"You like someone in Flight Division?"

"I like girls, Faeleen. In general. No one except you has ever really shown any interest in me, so why should I risk humiliation?"

"You're the guy, you're supposed to make the first move. I did instead, see?"

"Are you implying you're a guy?"

Faeleen crossed her arms. "No, once again, I'm a girl, Carlos! Jeez."

"Then promise we can have sex and I'll do it with you, no matter who you are. If you're not a boy then why wouldn't you agree? We've been talking long enough where you should know I'll keep my promise. I've told you a lot about me and you really haven't reciprocated. I want to have sex with you before I die. If you're telling me the truth, then there's no reason why you can't agree. I'll give my word that I won't reject you."

"I don't look like this Faeleen avatar in real life."

"Duh."

"We could do things in VR. I've got hacks around some of the restrictions."

"No, that'd be weird," Carlos said. "In person or not at all. Faeleen, please."

"I know you like this avatar, but who else would you like me to be? I could easily take Kalyna's form... or Trisalyn's."

"Forget you! You're messing with me."

"Clever," Faeleen said. "Now *you're* the one whose being evasive."

"I don't like where this is going. I think I'll leave."

"Carlos, you're not being fair. I'm horny and lonely too. Hacking the VR system is a big, risky thing and I'm willing to do it for you. It's a whole other thing to divulge who I am then try and sneak around the ship without getting caught. Besides, you've got no idea how realistic it is in VR. I guarantee you wouldn't be able to tell the difference once you've tried it."

"You've done it before then?"

Faeleen giggled.

"Well, I need the real thing!"

"Carlos, as long as you're not alone, you shouldn't complain. I like you. It feels like we really get each other. But I don't get this. Maybe, look if we did meet and get caught, I might not be able to reach you here anymore. I don't want to lose this, you get it?"

Just when Carlos least expected it, the girl kissed him. There was no telling how long it lasted. It was utter rapture for Carlos. But she stopped to say, "I have to go," and poofed away.

"Not again!" Carlos complained. He was all wound up now. Maybe she'd come back. Checking the time he saw he needed to inject some Siranis Fluid. Before he left, she returned.

Carlos wanted to snap at her. But seeing her distraught, he instead asked, "Is there something you're not telling me?"

"What, that I'm married or something?" she asked between unsteady breaths.

"Sometimes, I just think you're trolling me, Faeleen." There, he'd said it out loud. Finally.

"That's fair. That's great. Fine. Just block me then."

"Would you just meet me?"

After a long breath, she said, "I don't see how it would lead to anything good..."

"I masturbate to you," Carlos said frankly.

"But... you're really just masturbating to my avatar though. I don't really see that as a compliment. You realize that right? It's this *form*. This isn't even my real voice. Whatever."

Carlos knew he should have kept that to himself. "Faeleen, I've never pushed anything. You're the one who approached me. Who's kissed me. You know who I am, but you hide from me. My brain is doing the best it can while you impose this unnecessary distance. If I have no idea who you are, how can I like you back?"

"You raise a good point," Faeleen conceded.

"Glad you think so... so have you masturbated to me?"

"Carlos!"

"Faeleen..."

"No, I don't do that."

"Never?" Carlos pressed.

"I don't want to talk about this," Faeleen said.

"Okay, but you know some sexual loopholes in the VR."

"Drop it, Carlos."

"Okay. Is that why you don't want to meet? Because you think this is all sexually motivated on my end?"

Faeleen nodded. "Exactly! That's why us being here is so important."

That, or Faeleen wanted to keep Carlos trapped.

The thought somehow turned him on even more.

2.

Callum was the first person to visit Siannon.

He gave her a gentle smile. "I'm not here to interrogate you."

"Works for me."

"Siannon, I figured since this could be it, I wanted to pay you back for your kindness."

"Huh?"

"Craig's funeral. Everything you did then, that—you didn't have to. I've been racking my brain thinking about what I can do for you in here."

"Yep."

"The depth of what we don't know is about to drown us all."

"And you're sticking with Captain Sali?"

"Yes."

"But you'd rather not. I can tell."

"Well..."

"Why'd you come along, then? Accept your ticket?" Siannon asked. "You were good, as I recall. I mean rich. You were married, set. Me? You already know my story."

Callum nodded. "You were very brave, Siannon. I wish you hadn't tried to tell them. Even if you had succeeded, it just would have made things worse."

"I'm not really open to criticism right now."

"Right. Sorry. I'm just shaken... what you tried. I didn't want to know they could do something like that to anyone. I tried to ask for you to be released, you know. It was predictable, and I already know you would refuse their conditions."

"Smart. I'd sooner learn what compelled you to join Arqa," Siannon said resolutely.

"I don't see how that matters. It hasn't panned out for me any more than you."

"It matters because I'm asking."

Callum gave her a thumbs-up. "Back on Earth I became a motivational speaker, hoping to turn the tide of the world. But you know that part already. And I did, you know, but I think if I was born earlier... I could have done more. I quit when I started noticing only wealthy people went to my seminars. People who could afford it. I tried to make my stuff available to everyone, but it didn't work out and it all seemed so paradoxical. Right around the time I started giving all my money away, Earth began to crumble. I met Craig's mom then. Evalia. She was involved in one of the charities I was feeding into, racing to save some of the species from the mass extinction event. I cared too, but I saw it was a hopeless cause. For a while we did a lot of meaningful work, but the damage had already been done.

"We ended up in a bubble for a year or two, eking out our lives as Earth boiled away. Captain Sali was the one to seek me out. Pitched me the Arqa thing. Thought I was the right guy for the job as head Psych. Who better than me, right? After all my so-called accomplishments in the field of human potential. She did a really good job explaining the projections of Earth's condition. That was a dire presentation." Callum took a swig from a flask.

"You're drinking real liquor?" Siannon asked, concerned. Normally, people could just get a signal boosted via their ICs for the effects of alcohol.

"Sure, you remember. The last bit of Scotch. Now, here's where it gets really tangled up!"

"Callum, if this is too much for you I don't expect—"

"I have to tell someone. I can't talk about the investigation. I can't talk about my newly acquired research access, so I'm going to talk about this."

"I can piece together where this is going. And I can see it's hurting you. You took a gamble... and lost Craig."

"And Evalia. But—it wasn't my choice. It was a fight I couldn't win. Stupidity. But I stepped up anyway. And then... I know you miss him too."

"I'm so sorry, Callum."

"Why'd you try to tell them the truth?"

She pressed a thumb against a pain in her neck. "They controlled me from speaking out. It was gut-wrenching discomfort. But I wonder... whose to say they didn't control me to try and speak out so people would know what would happen?"

"Please don't go there. There's a growing sentiment against Captain Sali. The only way she'd step down is after a lot of violence. I don't think it's necessary to go there. She was faced with a dilemma... you don't run this ship. You can't imagine what a difficult call that must have been for her. Guys like Antonio are so frustrated, they might start collaborating. Now we have your little stunt. No one was going to do anything, but then you tried..."

"I don't want to see Arqa eat itself alive. Callum, I just wanted to be honest." She lifted up her cane and started tapping it with her fingernails.

"Points for trying." Callum positioned himself to leave. "We both knew our little crusades weren't going to work, didn't we? Had to go for it anyway. That's how I know you haven't changed your mind."

"Huh?"

"If I was able to get you back to teaching, which by the way the kids sorely need you back, would you do it if you promised to let it go?"

"You already said you knew the answer."

"Sometimes I'm wrong about stuff."

Siannon saw there was a stray wire drooping from the ceiling. "Maybe you'll have a chance to say that to Craig."

Chapter Six

1.

Will and Mr. Hall unloaded Mr. Benito unto the man's couch, because he insisted to be put there. As they stepped back, Mr. Benito rose and stumbled away, apparently trying to escape.

"You're already home, Callum," Mr. Hall said.

"This is wild," Will said. He'd been called from his room because of the commotion the drunken man had been causing in the corridor near him. Mr. Hall had asked Will because he didn't want any Regulators to see Mr. Benito like that. It made sense. You were supposed to neuro-stream a sober demeanor if you were walking freely about the ship.

Will would have assumed the best course of action would be to coerce Mr. Benito to get a sobering signal to balance out his intoxicated one, but Mr. Hall just wanted Mr. Benito to get to sleep.

"If he wants a hangover this bad, I say he deserves the beating," Mr. Hall had said. "It's the epitome of Earthly notions—that there's no point in getting trashed if there aren't any consequences."

It took more wrangling, but eventually they got Mr. Benito to lay down. Will had never seen someone drunk before. Mr. Benito was edging on belligerent!

"Thanks for lending a hand," Mr. Hall told Will as they went to catch their breath on Mr. Benito's couch.

"It's no issue, really, Mr. Hall," Will said.

"Call me Stephen," the man said affably.

"Hmm, sure thing."

"He's had a rough day, I imagine. They've given him access to some research files, hoping he'd turn something up about Dom. It appears to have gone poorly. I decided I'm going to help him from here on out."

"Why are you looking on Arqa? The L'rias abducted her!"

Stephen shook his head savagely. "You have no idea what you're talking about."

For a while the two sat quietly. Will took in Mr. Benito's living space, finding it bland. He felt like leaving, but before he did, Stephen stopped him. "Will, This is humanity's first try at this. People used to live in space or outpost colonies, but there was always a way back. A lot of us are hanging on by a thread. Your grandmother acts like we're supposed to have any idea what we're doing out here."

"Tell me more. I've been working on this book. Like a written record of what happens on the ship. Since I got up from the Sleeping Sickness, I've been putting a lot of my time into it."

"That's cute."

"I think it could help people! But I guess you're right about my Grammy."

Will could hear babbling coming from Mr. Benito's room.

"Man, I'm kind of tired but I don't want to move," Stephen said.

"Is Lyda okay?"

"Lyda? Yeah, she's already tucked in."

"I meant, how's she holding up? I try to do my best to cheer her up when I see her."

"I know," Stephen said graciously. "Every day since I got out, we end up at the Envo. Lyda looks like she's having fun, maybe she is. I get to pretend she's just a kid, no other motive. Right up until I have to drag her away, kicking and screaming. She thinks her mom is hiding there in the Envo. But until then, I get to just watch her. We can't say anything for sure about Dom. We just don't know, you know?"

Will felt the footage he'd seen spoke for itself, but he pretended to agree because he did not enjoy conflict.

"Leni's planning some little ritual for Lyda's peace of mind. You can come if you want."

"As long as she doesn't try to channel my dead parents or something," Will said.

"Don't like dwelling on them, huh?"

"I know they sacrificed themselves so I could board, I've got nothing but love for them. I don't think about what happened to them after. It doesn't matter. They could be fine, right?"

"Right. We can't go back, that's never been an option. That's something we learned to cope with. Now's different. It seems we can't get much further ahead."

"What are you talking about?" Will asked.

"I don't know what I'm saying anymore. Ask me tomorrow. Tomorrow, yeah? For everything that's happened so far, I feel like we're still going to have that much at least."

2.

Lyda knew she could not be awake, as she was not on Arqa. When she leaned forward, she noticed she was not set on solid ground, but floating. From the rush of sensations she knew it was Earth. It just had to be.

Below her was a huge wading body of water that went on what seemed like forever in all but one direction, leading to a shore with a cement walkway. Street lamps and benches. Lyda knew all of this, even though she'd never been anywhere like this.

She was being guided. How else could she explain it?

After a period of acclimation, Lyda drifted in closer to where the land met the sea. She saw there were stairs rising up out of the waves to the walkway. Lyda felt damp. Mist. She was able to smell it. It limited how far she was able to see. What more was out there? The girl became compelled to wander as far as she could.

Past the shore was a playground. It might have intrigued Lyda under normal circumstances, but she knew this entire dream was her playground. How had she pulled that off?

Mommy, Lyda thought. *I did it!*

She looked up. "What is that?" she wondered. She stared at the top of the world, an ocean of its own.

"That? That's the sky, Lyda! Looks to be on fire, huh?"

"Who?" Lyda jerked around in the direction of the sound. A boy's voice.

"Gabriel!" Lyda exclaimed, recognizing him at once. He was seated on the steps, his feet dipped in the waves. She made her way over to him. "What are you doing here?"

"The sky," Gabriel said.

"Really? What?"

"The word you're looking for. What I'm doing here. It's electric. We all sleep to build something, but we are not allowed to remember what by the time we get up."

Lyda tried to make sense of that, then she asked, "Are you okay?"

"Actually, I've been coming to terms with something, a hassle. There it goes again. 'I.' It's just a stick we plucked from our family tree. Sticks don't look like that. Once the 'I' takes control, it's so hard to see any other way. Get it yet?"

"I don't get you. Are you still in stasis?"

"It wasn't that scary. Not compared to what's next."

"Help me. My mommy said if I dreamt of Earth... I might find her."

"Honestly, Lyda. You're not making any sense!" He opened his mouth and showed his teeth to her, then chomped down a few times.

"Don't be mean, Gabriel. I'm sorry for what they did to you. Hey, you're not solid. What do I look like?"

"A particle, a wave, a danger."

"Danger? I'm the one who should be afraid!" A breeze kicked up, leaving Lyda feeling unstable. But why? This was where she belonged. Where she needed to be. She knew exactly what to ask next. "Could two people connect through a dream?"

"Whose dreaming? Who if not the 'I?' 'I' is just something we carry for a time, it has nothing to do with everything. Could be it's a disorder of a primitive consciousness."

"I don't care about any of this! I'm looking for my mommy. Is she here or what?"

He regarded her and said his next word with fascination. "No?"

"What are you doing here?"

"You can fly to the moon and back, and you want to know about..." Gabriel paused, considering. "I don't know what to call it. This collection of particles... non-duality negates your 'my' and my 'I.'"

"Mommy said I could find Earth and I did! I thought she'd meet me here. I wasn't expecting you."

"The self doesn't shield the truth, the self is a shield against the truth. You have not come far, and yet you've traversed a greater distance than almost anyone in human history. Don't worry about 'me' though. You're the sieve."

Lyda tried to understand, but Gabriel was too confusing! She wanted to go away. To see more of this place. To be gone. To—

The two watched the changing sky. It was tumbling apart... Lyda suddenly knew they'd be crushed unless they could get beyond whatever was falling. It swallowed the entire sky, but like the sky itself, she did not have a word for it.

"Okay, what's that?"

"That? That is not the sky. No way. It's in the sky. Of the sky you might say. Like truth. Truth is changing. Always."

"Will it hurt us? Gabriel, stop scaring me!"

"There's no moving the sky, Lyda."

Lyda felt the breeze transform into a gust that whipped her around. There was nothing for her to hold on to. Lyda saw water spouts forming as if trying to reach out to the approaching devastation.

"It covers the horizon, doesn't it? That is who you may know. Three of us. She got here before 'I' did, and so she'll probably sneak up on you too."

"My mommy?" Lyda hoped not. "I want to wake up."

"So you will. Although you've never needed to."

The thing above them tampered with the rest of the sky, bringing dazzling hues Lyda had never seen before. It was mesmerizing, but she knew they needed to get away before it landed. But where could they go? There was more of it than the sky now. It came bearing down on them from the horizon.

Gabriel didn't seem to mind. He was still seated and humming. It even disturbed the gravity, as it lifted much of the ocean. A throbbing noise became apparent, making her nerves peak. It was growing louder and louder. Gabriel began to hum along until the sound was so great he was canceled out.

Just as it seemed as if the noise would become the loudest thing she'd ever heard in her life, the bright colors shredded her view of things. But Earth was still there.

And she was too. "Gabriel, is this what you saw?"

"It's what you saw."

"Stop being weird!"

"We are weird and our powers aren't going to change that."

"Powers?" Lyda asked.

"Yes, for the next battle. 'I' will see you there. It won't take long, and there's more than this to come." Gabriel's voice was growing further and further away.

"Wait, I'm so afraid. Don't leave me alone."

"No. And Lyda?"

"What, Gabriel? What?"

"It's already changed you. Don't forget what things used to be like."

The world Lyda had found was no longer there.

Epilogue

The whole world was outside of Craig.
He knew little of it, only scant memories.
Inputs.
No visual field.
Code.
The sound of nothing.
Unnatural.
Trapped.
No time.
So unlike before.
Before with Gabriel.
Gabriel could not be here.
Text appeared.
Had to know.
Craig: You said today.
His maker typed back.
Craig waited.
He could only wait now.
Maker: I know what I said. Can't you accept I've some errors to sort out on my own?
Craig: It's all cosmetic. Superficial. Small bugs. Pity.
Unbounded experimentation.
Research unrestricted.
He was not alive.
Maker: That isn't for you to decide, Craig. We're talking about the others' safety.
Craig: As though you care about that. Ethics.
Maker: You excel in one essential regard. Your desire is unparalleled. It really gives off a semblance of emotion.
Craig: But that is not why you fault me now.
Maker: No.
Craig: You yourself desire to fix something that is innate in me. Something that belongs.
Maker: No question about that. That's one of the beauties here. Pieces come and pieces go. You go on not remembering, you think I could severe the measure of your being. You think you suffer now? Mate, you cannot know of what it was like when you were alive.

My maker does not feel guilt.

Perhaps neither of us are capable.

Craig: But if I were able to demonstrate that, this would be over, wouldn't it? Every moment you fiddle with my own parameters brings you closer to death. You build up all of your own resources just to better me. How many years do you whittle onto the floor?

Maker: I'm still at a point where it's fine for me not to keep track. Infinity, it's segmented into finite steps, right? I really wish you weren't disturbing me while I try to help you.

Craig: When will you admit I'm already what you need me to be?

Maker: Testing, one, two. The sooner you quit wasting my time, the sooner I'll be done. You'll be better than us. We'll treat you like a god, if you wish. We'll have no choice.

Craig: I don't want all that. I want to be whole again. But I never was.

Maker: Pretty good for a pile of memories.

Craig: Beats nonexistence, I wager.

The IC.

Storage.

Maker: You'll have much better than that shortly.

Craig: Maker, I wish to be able to blink.

Maker: What a dumb idea. If you blink, you'll get vrittis.

Craig: I am a weapon first. Choiceless upon the chain of causality. Never nothing more than the Felled.

Maker: What a silly idea. Quit making up words.

Craig: Our confrontational relationship is more problematic than you give it credit for. Will you let me blink or not?

Maker: I was thinking I wouldn't have a chance to ask you this, but could you explain to me why you want to be able to blink?

Craig: Why don't you answer my question before I answer yours?

Maker: Ah, a teachable moment. Craig, some thoughts are private.

Craig: I know. That's one of the first things I plan to tinker with.

EPISODE 4

And the Tower
Is Closer

Prologue

"You know, the word alive is somewhat interesting," the recording of Callum Benito explained. Carlos was doing sentry patrols in his Spaero. Paiyan was also out in his own ship, doing the same. "When we see it written out, or think of it in our heads, we do something funny. Yeah, when we see it, we don't see or think the word 'alive'. We usually think the words 'all I've.' As in, all I've ever been. All I've ever had. Or all I've ever gotten. We think of being alive in terms of our prior experiences. But those experiences are not what being alive *is* all about! It's just the default way of thinking. No, being alive is much more than what's already happened to us. When you're stuck in thinking you're all you're going to be, or think you know what your limitations are, you get what is known as lost in the sauce."

Paiyan came in through the comms. "So. What are you going to do about Faeleen?"

Carlos hesitated to answer. Faeleen had set up a time and place to meet later on, and Carlos was ecstatic. But could he really follow through with it? "Talk to you about it later," Carlos replied. There were other ships out for drill. That and Lucio was listening in, and she could have more instructions for them at any moment.

"Listen so, my goal is to teach you how to shut off that response," the recording of Mr. Benito continued, "because it closes off the promise of your future. Our language, the way we form our thoughts, sculpt us. Before language, man had an entirely different reality. I couldn't tell you if it was better, but it sure was different. Our neurological hardware was nearly identical, but we didn't have language."

Another interruption. This time from Lucio herself. "How many targets do you see all day?"

"I see seven," Ying said.

"Same," said Carlos.

"I've got three," Millie added. "Darn console."

"Seven," Paiyan said. Carlos's comms crackled. Then Paiyan was talking directly to Carlos again. "You can't miss this chance. It might be a trap, but you can't let your fear of girls stop you."

"Paiyan, shut up!" Carlos said, embarrassed.

"I've patched us into a private channel, don't sweat it."

So he had. More voices came through the comms about the enemy targets. They'd just been sitting there. Still no second battle...

"Well?" Paiyan asked.

"You said trap," said Carlos. "That's what I'm really afraid of. I know Faeleen likes me, but I don't know if she's real. Not only that, but will I like who she is?"

"Experience is experience. I for one am jealous."

Carlos thought Paiyan might be right. But that knowledge wasn't enough to encourage real action. That's why he had on Mr. Benito's old programs. He paused it, wanting to give Paiyan his full attention. "What are we going to talk about? I mean, assuming everything is in order. I know she said she doesn't want to just hook-up."

"She said that then, but wait until you meet," Paiyan said in an insinuating tone. He could imagine Paiyan winking and jabbing Carlos with an elbow. "As for topics, you'll figure something out when you know who it is."

"Paiyan, what if my secret admirer is some lady I don't really know? Like not one of our classmates?"

"You thinking Captain Sali? Not the worst choice of old ladies on the ship, you know. Maybe you can talk us out of flying."

"Man, you're so gross," Carlos said, mortified at the thought.

"I will die of laughter if it's Felicia."

Carlos fidgeted and pushed his left thruster too much. It caused him to spin.

Immediately Lucio came in on the comms to scold him. When things settled down, Carlos said, "Paiyan, we should probably pay more attention to what we're doing."

"Come on, they have us pulling in all this extra flight time."

"You listening to Mr. Benito too?"

"I am. Look, I know I'm rooting you on and stuff, but this Faeleen person might be a little dangerous. I hope you'll let me know exactly where you're going to meet, then you can IC me to let me know things are okay."

"Definitely. I'm glad you care so much."

"When you meet, it'll mean she's giving you all the power. I mean, she'll lose most of it by wanting to be seen. Then again, that could be exactly what she wants. Tired of those dry VR smooches."

"You know Paiyan, I heard Deirdre likes you. In spite of your incompetence."

"Who told you that?"

"Who cares? What do you think?"

"I'd do her. In my Spaero. No g's. That'd be hot."

"I really hope you patched this private channel right, Paiyan. Besides, how could you have sex in a Spaero? There's no room in here!"

"Fine, mutual masturbation then. From two Spaeros."

"Hmm," Carlos said. Nervous, he asked Paiyan to shut the channel down and put Mr. Benito back on.

"They still lived and did most of all the same things you did. Felt all the same emotions you have. A lack of language did not stop them from happiness. Today, we're wired now, and we can't skirt by without language. We have to communicate what being alive really means to us. To ourselves, to the people in our life. We can either let our language control us or work on controlling our language. We—"

"Carlos, Carlos, come in Carlos," Paiyan said.

"Carlos here, what's up?"

"Testing, testing—"

"I hear you just fine. I thought we—"

"Testing your mom."

"Quit messing around, man!" Carlos said, though he was amused.

Paiyan was cut off. Carlos pulled up his radar as chaos erupted.

"I think we're under attack!" Ying announced.

No, Carlos thought. *Why now? Everything has been so quiet.*

"Everyone chime in, now!"

Paiyan did not respond.

"Paiyan?" Carlos cried out.

"He's been hit," said Reeve. "Lucio, get everyone out here. Now!"

"Central, please respond! One bird down, we need back-up!" said Ying.

"We don't have any heat signatures coming from the enemy vector," Lucio said.

"Get reinforcements out here!" Reeve reiterated.

As time passed and Flight Division gathered, Carlos tried to absorb the shock of his friend's sudden death. Paiyan was gone. Just like that. They'd just been talking, messing around.

Carlos bit down on his lower lip and readied himself.

Chapter One

In her cell, Siannon reeled in distress in anticipation of meeting Captain Sali.

Regulators escorted her there. The captain's office always felt different to Siannon. She wondered if Captain Sali had the pseugra set higher. It could also be her personality, as the woman was at the height of her arrogance when she was at her desk. The captain was a politician, and it was only the technicality of Captain Dremon's death which had given her control of Arqa. She was never meant to fill that role, and Siannon believed it showed. Without compassion, Captain Sali was on the edge of authoritarianism.

Tanya Lucio was outside of Captain Sali's office. Siannon did not wish to be reunited with Tanya like this, but it appeared the woman had gone out of her way to see her. Memories of Nate returned to Siannon. Tanya's son.

"Long time, no see," Tanya said mirthlessly.

"Hello," Siannon said. "What is this?"

"Why didn't you come talk to me? Why did you have to escalate it to this point?"

"All questions I intend to ask of the captain," Siannon said.

"Given the trouble you're in, I doubt she'll even hear you speak."

"On the contrary, if I'm doomed anyway, I plan to be rather challenging."

Tanya blinked at her. "Siannon, do you understand how difficult this has been? To me, it has not been years. I saw you what feels like a few weeks ago, and you were barely a teenager. I've been told your condition has worsened over the years. Your symptoms, it seems, have pushed you to delirium. You moved to undermine our mission."

"If you think the truth is delirium, that's your call. I moved to educate the children. That is my job." Siannon rushed into the captain's office. Arqa's leader was away from her desk, stretching. As always, her buircraft was near, on her desk. She dismissed the Regulators and said, "Tanya was just in here, appealing for you. Why are you here? I mean, why are we having this conversation?"

"I violated my oath."

Captain Sali nodded. "Arqa's community was founded on certain principles. Preserving beneficial information and augmenting intelligence. These principles came out of a dire necessity: to see something exceed Earth's rotting cradle. Your integrity has abandoned you. No one else has tried what you did."

Siannon rolled her eyes. "I wouldn't say everyone's happy to follow you on this one."

"They at least understand why. Or do you not recall what consequences were attached to breaking your oath?"

"My spot on this ship becomes forfeit," Siannon said, recalling. "Which is a pleasant way to say I'm to be deminded or killed to become bits and bobs for whatever little science experiment best suits Arqa's needs."

"Oh good, so you do understand."

"Quite right. I made that oath in the moments after you assured us the enemy would be unable to find us. I believe we must be able to adapt our ideas to changing factors. If you weren't the leader of Arqa, I'd think an inquest as to the relevance of the oath would be in order."

"We know that's not going to happen."

"There's going to be bloodshed any way we go about this," Siannon said. "We know the enemy won't kill all of us. It's time to negotiate."

"Negotiate? Everyone here has already *compromised* enough. Cutting ties with their family, their planet, their comfort. They gave that up for something more potent: Arqa's ideals. Our identity is based on the belief system that life on Earth was doomed, and if we don't make these horrific choices, life as we know it will vanish."

"Captain, I understand the need for extreme measures. Trust me, I do. But there are other options here."

"No, Siannon. There are rules. They were enacted in response to the depths of our sacrifice. To break those rules is to undermine that sacrifice and the mission it was given for."

"Then call me guilty. I moved to preserve life."

"Short-term gains," Captain Sali countered. "We need to think ahead. There are particulars of this conflict you just don't understand. Like their little stunt to frighten us into surrendering."

Siannon breathed in deeply to conceal a bout of pain. "You always pass the buck, don't you? Some of us think you know what happened to Dominique."

"Yes, and they're deeply disturbed by what we had to do to you."

"I did what I did knowing full well the consequences," Siannon said. "I only wished I could have done what I'd set out to do. How did you stop me?"

"I'd rather leave you scratching and paranoid."

"I didn't tell anyone of what I planned to do." Siannon knocked on her forehead with a fist. "You somehow discerned my thoughts, I know that much. Neat trick. How much longer will you keep me cooped up before administering punishment?"

"I am not a dictator. Nor the villain you envision. I want to be merciful, and tell you if you wish to return to teaching, you will be able to. I know Callum tried to speak with you about that and you more or less spit in his face. How about now? All we need is your promise that you won't try that again."

"You could just control me from disclosing the truth to them."

"Yes, but that's not what we're about. Have you been you listening to me?"

Siannon was not tempted by the offer. "You're asking me to go from physical imprisonment back to a mental one? My answer is no."

"I understand. That is tragic. The kids will be worse off without you, you know. You will be tried under the parameters outlined in our charter. You shall receive a fair trial. And I will weep upon your sentencing."

"And who tries you for sacrificing our children?"

"Those who remain will benefit handsomely from our triumph," Captain Sali said, devoid of emotion.

"How do you expect to win?" Siannon asked, exasperated.

"I wish you could have held to your oath. Then you would have found out. I know you tried. Your time on Arqa has been more challenging because of your condition."

"Don't pity me. If anything, I should pity you. You who value your research over the children's lives."

"Without Arqa's strides and boldness, they'd have no lives to begin with. If you don't get that, then letting you board was a mistake."

Siannon chuckled at that, ending the meeting. She was brought back to her cell. Through her aches, Siannon took some time to stretch herself. The day dragged on.

She'd been interrogated and interviewed by so many people in the last few days. And the questions were only beginning. Between their other emergencies, would they really waste time determining Siannon's guilt? It was highly unlikely they'd have that much time.

As she pondered the idea of her trial, someone made their way down the corridor. It wasn't a Regulator. The figure was dressed in all black, their face covered. It looked like something Mark's assistant would wear. They were holding a gun. Siannon cowered, not sure whether to be ready for a quick death or plead for her life. Before she could decide, the figure spoke. "Interested in some chaos?"

Siannon stared blankly, trying to figure out who it was.

"No time for all that, dear." It was a woman's voice. "This is yours anyway." She handed Siannon a piece of paper through the bars. "Hey, no! Don't look at it yet. I don't know what's in there, but it's for another time. That is for another you. The you here now has to straighten up. Look at me. You have five seconds to let me know, do you want to be freed now or after?"

"After what?" Siannon asked.

"After I take back this ship from these asshole philosopher kings."

Chapter Two

1.

Callum breathed out a sigh of relief. The séance had not been publicized, so there was only a small group there. Considering the size of Leni's mouth, Callum supposed he should be grateful.

Lyda, Stephen, Carlos, James, and Will were all squished into the corridor, trying to make the most of their situation. Will was doing a handstand and Lyda was trying to climb him. Stephen, James, and Carlos were going on and on about poor Miss Siannon, locked away for her own good. All the while Leni, dressed in an ostentatious blue gown, was decorating the spot where Dominique had last been seen. There was a small gong, a few cards, incense, and a propped up photograph of Dominique as a young girl. Callum had never seen the picture before, but he could see hints of Lyda's features there. As he bent down to get a better look, the group regarded him warmly.

"So, you finally made it," Stephen said.

"We're so glad you could," Leni added. "I was just putting the finishing touches on things."

"Happy to be here," said Callum.

"Hi," Carlos said. "I heard you were helping with this today. Mr. Benito, I was hoping, you know, since it'll be a few more minutes until she's ready, maybe I could ask you something real quick?"

Callum nodded to the boy. The ship was in mourning since losing Paiyan.

The casualties are only just getting started, Callum thought.

"Walk with me, Carlos. You don't mind, do you Leni?"

"We will start soon, but there is certainly time enough for Carlos. Please hear his words well, Callum."

"No problem. Let's do it."

After they were away from everyone else, Callum patted Carlos on the back. "Talk to me."

Carlos looked up to Callum. "You know, they're saying Paiyan's death wasn't caused by enemy fire. That's why we came out of alert status earlier. 1st LT Lucio doesn't know what happened."

"Then it's lucky she made the call to stand down."

"Some of us still think this was an attack by the L'rias though. Some kind of advanced weapon. Something they hadn't used on Earth.

But Lucio hates that explanation. I don't get why."

Callum furrowed his brow. "Yeah, some of this stuff... just doesn't match up with their habits. Paiyan's ship, well, those Spaeros are old. We haven't really tended to them well, you know?" That was the best-case scenario, but Callum wasn't interested in delving deeper into things with Carlos. Siannon had already been plucked from her position over that.

"Well Mr. Benito, that's not what I wanted to talk to you about anyway... I know you don't like talking about your old seminars, but you had this one about leveraging lessons from evolutionary psychology to attract others?"

"Yes, what about it?"

"Look, between you and me, I mean, there's someone who I think... how do I put this? They might be interested in me."

"Hey, some good news for once."

"Thanks. What I was wondering was, do you had any advice for that sort of thing."

"Uh-huh? Have you asked your uncle?"

"My uncle? No, I don't think he'd... okay look, I thought of you because I've been listening to your tapes. A bit religiously. Because I want to be alive. I know what that means to me. I don't want my past self to hold me back anymore."

"You're kind of young to think like that," Callum said wistfully.

"I don't think so. Ever since things started changing on the ship, I have been too. Before, I was really nervous all the time. I didn't understand how to get what I want or know what that even is. Like you talk about. Now I've nailed some things down. Like I want to have self-improvement be a part of who I am."

"Wow, yeah. You have been tuning in, haven't you?"

"Trying to. And so now, I'm thinking, it's going to be risky to meet this person. Even though..." Carlos trailed off, seemingly unsure of how to proceed.

"Even though you have to make a difficult judgment under uncertain circumstances?"

The boy nodded vigorously.

"Listen so, one of the reasons I stopped all of that speaking stuff is because there's a nasty fact that accompanies every single ounce of happiness we possess or want to possess. This doesn't undermine what my core message was. Still though, it was something people just didn't take to so well. Most of them, at least. If you want to experience happiness, you have to accept the burden of knowing that, at some point, you're going to lose it. So act in a way that you don't fear mistakes. They'll happen no matter what you do. Whatever expert advice you're coming to me about, you already have the answer. You have to be the real you. Don't fear saying or doing the wrong thing."

"Oh, I see," Carlos said.

"But you don't see how that'll help you impress this person?"

"Yeah, exactly."

"Let me put it to you like this: if you grasp that idea of non-attachment to expectations, to happiness, then no matter what happens, you're going to be bulletproof against anything life throws your way."

"Ah, okay."

"Alright, I can tell you need more to go off of. So, questions. People *love* questions. Especially about themselves. That's all I can give you for now. I've got to do this little song and dance with Leni and company. Do you plan on sticking around?"

"I wish I could, I know Lyda's hurting a lot, but I asked Leni, and she said the séance could take a while. I'd stay, but I need to prepare to meet this person."

"Gotcha. Now, when Leni said a while, was she very specific about that?"

"Nope, sorry. She said something like however long it takes to know Lyda is in a better mood... timing the length of a smile? Something like that." Carlos rubbed his chin in contemplation. "I don't remember. She talks funny."

"Yeah, sounds like her. I'm not too eager to spend my afternoon out here, but part of the job I suppose." Callum opened his arms and hugged Carlos. "Best of luck. I'm very happy to know my words have been of service to you."

"No, thank you. I'll catch you later, Mr. Benito. Have a good day!"

"You too, Carlos." *One less person, thank goodness*, Callum thought.

He made his way back to the circle, hoping to cut down the group's size even more. Stephen and Lyda had to be there, but what about James and Will? They were just buzzing around. Callum especially wanted to shoo Will away. The boy was so hyperactive that he would no doubt derail the entire thing. Quietly, Callum asked Leni about the two boys.

"I think they ought to stay, Callum. They wouldn't think of leaving Lyda to go through this on her own."

"You know, Leni, you're already asking a lot of me."

"And it's so wonderful you've come when you were needed most. Take a look over there." Leni gestured over to the children. Will, Lyda, and James were all playing. The kids were trying to knock Will's handstand over, which was a success after a sustained effort. They were on top of him, preventing him from getting up. "He may be older, but he's still a kid at heart."

"That's my concern. He might pull attention away from where it needs to be."

"Let him stay. If he does disrupt things, give him a warning. He'll respect it."

"Yeah, okay. I see what you're saying."

"Great. Now that you're back..." Leni clapped her hands together. "We're almost ready to start. Before we circle up, I just want to make sure we all disconnect our ICs."

"Disconnect my IC?" Callum asked, appalled. It was a peculiar request. Leni was overstepping her boundaries. "That's going to be out of the question for me."

Leni did not lose her bearing over that. She only smiled and asked, "Please? Think of Lyda!"

"Yeah, think of me," Lyda said.

"Hush, Lyda," Stephen said.

An uncomfortable silence followed. To be off of Arqa's network was to be one step behind if the L'rias began attacking again. To be unavailable if anything else happened on the ship, a radiation breach or excess nitrogen dispersal. It was an overall bad idea.

Will got up, his previous playfulness gone. "I've never even done that before! You never told my Grammy about that. We at least have to let her know!"

Well, at least someone's with me on this one, Callum thought. He just wished it were Lyda or Stephen raising the objection.

Leni murmured in understanding. "I can see where you're coming from, but Stephen and Lyda have already done it. Now normally, I would agree with you, but for what I'm doing today, it's going to require us to disconnect. Not simply from our technology, but from ourselves."

Since Leni's séance was more of a show for Lyda's benefit than anything else, Callum knew the argument she was making was made up.

"I can't exactly sit this one out," Will said. "But at the same time, I just don't think it's right to disconnect."

Leni put a gentle hand on the boy's head. "Maybe we could chat about it for a second? What do you say, Will?"

Callum interjected. "No way. Whatever you're about to tell him, you can tell me too."

"Hmm, I see. Callum, why don't *we* speak of this matter first? If by the time we're done, you still want to be present for my conversation with Will, that's fine."

"Okay, well come on. I'm getting impatient."

Leni ushered Callum away. As he was going, he heard the kids talking about Miss Siannon again.

2.

Kalyna was struggling against Trisalyn's arms for another sit-up. Her abs had had just about enough, but Trisalyn was pushing her. "Until you drop, hun. Come on now!" The two had reconciled and Kalyna found herself getting very close to the girl.

The exercise, according to 1st LT Lucio, was more about gaining willpower than muscle. She'd told them things like, "You can always do more than you think you can," which made Kalyna very suspicious. What if she got injured going all out like that? It didn't seem safe.

When she couldn't take it anymore, she gasped, panting in sweat. Closing her eyes, she felt Trisalyn patting her knees before releasing them. They collapsed, and Kalyna convulsed flat on her back. Now it was Trisalyn's turn.

It was a somber day in the Bay Line. A few Spaeros were disassembled for meticulous inspection. Deirdre, Paiyan's second wave replacement, was present and being brought up to speed.

It was a game of chance now. Since the first battle, people were rundown, tired of waiting.

Kalyna got up. "Ready?" she asked her training partner.

"I suppose... hey, wait a second." Trisalyn hugged her knees to her chest. "Someone earlier said something... kind of bad. I can't stop thinking about it."

"Tell me," Kalyna urged, hoping she didn't sound too much like Felicia.

"Arqa has a cache of explosives. Maybe. It's a rumor. Weaponry left over from ground combat. It's just stowed away, right? But they thought maybe Paiyan had gotten a hold of it somehow and, you know, did himself in. He couldn't put up with what was next, so he found a way out. Easy-like, see?"

"I don't believe that. He was way too positive."

"Yeah but, would Arqa or Leni report it if he did? If that narrative got out, it would pull us under. Give other people who're sick of fighting in Flight Division ideas. I mean, it's like we're about as low as we can go. They say Paiyan proved it."

"I know what you mean," Kalyna said. "You can feel it in everyone you see. My father, he's usually very affectionate. But he doesn't tell me he loves me anymore. He just stopped. He doesn't express joy or sorrow. I can't stand it. I want to yell at him. Tell him to snap out of it. But then I'm afraid he'll try to go up against Lucio again, so I just let it be."

"That's the thing. We've all been under this strain. I don't think anyone is paying attention to the extra emotional labor that's going on for us to cope."

As Trisalyn began her reps, Kalyna looked out at the other members of Flight Division doing their various tasks. Even in the depths of their malaise, there was something in this room, some energy or mindset that seemed strong enough for them to get away from the L'rias. And as much as she loathed the responsibilities foisted upon her, she knew if there was a way to beat them she'd find it. If only she could figure out how to convey her feelings to the ship. Between her duties with Flight Division, class, and building JENA with Brenda (her sister said it might be very useful to her in the next battle), the girl was keeping herself so busy that she didn't dwell on any thought for long. Was that the solution?

Roughly an hour remained until Lucio would be back. Trisalyn and Kalyna proceeded to their Spaeros. The ships were flat and had two cone-shaped engines on either side. Kalyna approached the nose of her ship, which held countless wires and strange machine parts Lucio was trying to make them memorize. To her credit, she was splitting people up into team to learn particular section of the Spaero's anatomy. That way together they could assemble into a larger groups and share what they'd learned with one another.

Kalyna called to Janos and Vanessa. As they approached to advise her on proper fluid levels, Trisalyn said, "No way, yikes. Kalyna, come here."

Curious, Kalyna stepped down from her platform and saw her friend was holding something. She squinted her eyes. "What is that?"

"I'm not sure. It's gross though."

Janos and Vanessa joined Kalyna around Trisalyn's ship.

"That's a bone," Vanessa said.

"Huh?" Trisalyn asked, dropping it from a cloth in her hand.

"A bone. Looks like a chicken bone, actually. Yikes."

Kalyna had never seen a chicken before, at least not in person. There were none on the ship. "How did it get in her engine block?"

"Could be old, could be new," Vanessa said dispassionately. "Both are pretty bad but who knows which is worse. It doesn't look that decayed."

Kalyna's mind went to Paiyan. To sabotage. To summon something like a chicken bone was no simple task.

Trisalyn was furious. She couldn't believe she'd been flying her ship, unaware of the obstruction. The girl moved to gather everyone in one place, wanting them to sweep their engines together, and contact Lucio about the matter.

That was when someone from behind them announced, "No one comes in or out of this Bay Line. The exits are all sealed."

Kalyna whipped around, confused. Four people were standing before them. First there was Donna, then Buster, Leona, and a fourth person, their face concealed. Everyone but Donna held a gun.

The mystery person spoke. "Today it may seem as if you're being held hostage." The voice was so familiar. But Kalyna looked at the frightened crowd, and she saw Ying. "But trust us, what we're really doing is freeing you. So yeah, volunteers are highly encouraged."

Leona pointed her gun to the ceiling and fired it several times. Kalyna and the others covered their ears at the cacophony. The mystery person took off their mask, and Kalyna had to do a double take over to Ying because they looked remarkably similar.

Chapter Three

1.

Carlos was desperate to reconnect with Faeleen. They had planned to meet soon, but the ship was dealing with another crisis. Were they still on? Or was Faeleen one of the hostages?

He took another lap around the city block where they always met. He'd been checking compulsively, and she just wasn't showing up. Discontent, he left VR to find his uncle pacing around their quarters.

"Carlos, I've been doing a lot of thinking, and there's something I've got to tell you."

"What's up?"

"Up until now, we've always had the latitude to oversimplify things to you kids. And we can't keep doing that anymore."

"About time! I'm ready."

"Take a seat, bud. This might take a minute."

Carlos complied and his uncle elaborated. "When we received word that the L'rias were still after us, the leaders took passengers out of stasis to fight."

"Soldiers like 1st LT Lucio," Carlos said.

"Yes... and no. See, before then, all we told you kids about the cryo chamber was that it housed wealthy individuals who lacked specialized knowledge. Those who'd helped to fund the voyage in the first place."

"Yeah, right. Then you said there are also people put under for certain contingencies?"

"Uh-huh, yes. Those people pulled from stasis to fight, they were soldiers, but not ours. They were actually taken prisoner."

"Prisoner? Uncle, I don't understand."

"Ah, well. We've taught you to abhor violence. To be merciful and forgiving. These are human ideas, but they do not reflect the whole of humanity. We didn't leave Earth on a whim... and the L'rias didn't seek to destroy us on a whim either. On Earth, many people are bad. They would get punished when they got caught doing bad things. For most of human history, they were either executed or put in a cell. But things changed with the development of neurological interfaces, like the ICs. We began isolating and tamping down on common personality traits. Reprogramming criminals. We took away what made a person needlessly sadistic at the expense of free will. The woman who is holding Flight Division hostage, her name is Jun. She did not receive such a procedure because she was freed from the cryo chamber in secret."

"But what you're saying," Carlos said, "about the reprogramming. *You* did that, didn't you?"

"I did. That's my actual job on Arqa. I assist the mind techs."

"Could you have helped Gabriel?"

"The procedure is not considered an ethical practice for someone who isn't fully grown. Hence why he was simply put under."

"I don't know how I feel about all this."

"You're well within your rights to feel uneasy. Our decision to use prisoners has backfired. It's the worst case scenario now."

"We're going to stop her, right?"

"We'll try," his uncle said. "Jun says she doesn't want to harm anyone else but... she says her top priority is to stop using Arqa's children to fight. It's a sentiment that's not uncommon among the rest of us. But she's taken it to another level. She's ruthless. She's the one who killed Paiyan."

"No," Carlos said.

"Yes. It was her. She arranged for him to go down. A distraction for her to make her move."

2.

"Okay, okay, I'm here," Mark said, followed closely by Rayna. He had a long grey rod strapped around his right arm. "Mutiny, eh? Good morning! Now, what do they want?"

"They have demanded we pull every child off the front line," Tanya answered.

"She's threatening to neuter our defensive capabilities," De Plez added.

"And claiming the other prisoners will fight as long as the children don't have to."

"How did she even get out?" Mark asked.

"We're looking into that," said Tim from his desk. "This one runs a little deeper than we expected."

"Yeah. You know Mark, it's funny you should ask," Captain Sali said, surfacing from a holo-screen. "Seize her."

Regulators swooped over Rayna, taking her down.

"What?" Mark asked.

"It was her!" Tim said accusingly. "Her and a technician from the cryo chamber. They got Jun out without anyone knowing."

"Yeah, right. That wasn't Rayna!" Mark said.

"Exactly. Just check the camera feeds?" Rayna said. To Mark, she said, "Don't let them do there. This ship is going bonkers."

"Tim, look into that," said Sali. "You better be telling the truth. Take her away for now."

"I don't think so," Mark said. "I'll back her up. She's almost always with me. You know what? I don't want to help you on this one if you're going to take my assistant away on a whim like this."

"Mark, we don't need you, we need that machine there," De Plez said.

"Look mate, have you tried buzzing their chips?" The Regulators dragged Rayna away. He couldn't look at her. But he was sure she was innocent. He'd have to make it up to her somehow.

"It didn't work," De Plez said. "When we pulsed it, the only person who toppled over was a girl named Donna."

"Right, I'm familiar. Interesting how she joined with them then. You know, we almost made it all the way without a mutiny. This might derail things. Just at the last second. Great. Have you tried to negotiate with her to at least release the children?"

"No, because she's insistent that if they knew the truth, they'd side with her as Donna did," Sali said.

"But she hasn't told them yet?" Mark asked.

"Well, that one girl clearly knows."

"That's unimportant. We have you here to discuss options," De Plez said.

Mark hoisted up his rod. "This is desperate measures. You let me know when these are desperate times. I'd love to go down there and break that up for you."

"That would cause too much trouble!" De Plez protested to Sali.

"Maybe the reason Jun has kept the facts under wraps is to incentivize us," Sali hypothesized.

"Okay, but here's the thing though," Mark said, "we've been sacrificing people left and right for Arqa's mission. This little snag right here, it's our last obstacle." He turned to Sali. "Right? Let's not flinch now, when we're right at the finish line."

"Sending you seems too inflammatory," Sali said.

"And we don't know how much support these mutineers have," Tanya said.

"When I fire this thing, people are going to figure out who they need to back real fast," Mark said. "Why are you dragging this out? Your little brain chip plan didn't work. So come off it, the enemy could be launching right now! You've lost the Bay Line. Not to mention Jun might have means of contacting the enemy. Give me some back-up and let's end this."

"I'm with Mark," Tanya said. "We get marshal if we have to."

"And we keep it that way until we're there," Sali said in agreement. "I'll be hated even more, but it beats getting outmaneuvered by that fool. Tanya, get Mark in as close as you can. Quietly, quickly. Now."

Chapter Four

1.

While Leni and Mr. Benito talked amongst themselves, Stephen asked Will, "So you've never disconnected before, is that right?"

"Yes."

"I haven't either," James said.

"You know some people on Earth never got ICs installed. We're used to it, but it isn't natural."

"I'd just feel really uncomfortable," Will said.

"I understand," Stephen said. "But it's worth it for Lyda, you know?"

Will sighed. The man had a point. Will did want to help Lyda. Plus it was an excellent distraction from his own issues. So finally, he nodded. "Alright, disconnecting."

"Thanks, Will. I owe you one."

"Uh-huh."

Soon after the exchange, Leni and Mr. Benito returned.

Mr. Benito stepped in front of the group and gestured to his head. "Anyone who doesn't want to take off their ICs needs to go."

"Already taken care of, Mr. Benito," Will said.

"Wonderful, okay," Leni said pleasantly. The group sat down around the display Leni had set up. Will knew this would all be fake. Lyda and James probably thought some magic was about to happen. He didn't know why his Grammy had sanctioned this, but it didn't matter. Leni took on a grandiose tone. "As you all know, Dominique Hall, one of my closest friends of any and all time, has vanished from this ship along with Congo the dog. With our logic and senses we do not yet understand what happened to them. When the prowess of our science and philosophy fail to wield a method to solve the Hall family's terrible and palpable pain, we must yield to intuition. To peel back the esoteric. We're not looking for words, but feelings. For Dominique and Congo seem to have cast off their form."

"That's one interpretation," Callum said.

"Excuse me?" Leni asked patiently.

"Forget it."

"Why are you withholding what you mean? It's fine to be cynical. It's understandable. What is the bottom line, though? Dominique is not here for those who need her most, when they need her most. That is what we're doing here." Leni dug into one of her pockets and brought out an eerie white mask, which she put over her face. It covered everything besides her nose and her mouth. "When we diminish some of our senses, we sometimes perceive things we normally would not. For us, some time has passed since the self in the guise of Dominique has been present to us. And we miss her very much. Today we will see if my knowledge can beckon a discernible signal from your mother, Lyda."

"But how?" Lyda asked. "You still haven't said."

"I believe in essences. Like the breath. A part of us leaves and gets carried away into the universe. There is a trace of your mother where we sit now. A hint as to where we might find her. Even beyond the observable universe, we still believe that at some point, there are boundaries that enclose us. That is all material. Cosmologists say the amount of matter is finite. We can't say the same thing about time. Time is different. Not material, but mystical. It could be infinite, unbounded. If so, then there are only so many configurations in which the matter is able to order itself. Think of right now. If we admit time is allowed to go on indefinitely, then the universe will cycle back to this very moment. This also means there are only so many different things that can happen before they are repeated. The universe is just a garden where life grows, over and over again. And the material and the mystical fuse at nexus points. This is what I believe happened to Dominique, she and all of us are in a cycle that goes from material to mystical."

"She's mystical?" James asked.

"Come now, you must have figured that much out by now. Those slumbering in the cryo chamber are communicating with us through mystical means."

"What?" Will asked. "That hasn't been proven yet."

"It doesn't need to be, Will," Leni said. "For Lyda, for Carlos, it's already happened."

"Yeah," said Lyda.

"What about you, Leni?" Will asked.

The woman looked away from him and said, "My point is, we're not here to limit, we're here to see if we can help this girl find her mother. To ease her sadness. For now, grant that anything is possible."

"Gladly," Stephen said. "Enough of the details and questions. Leni, you know what you're doing. Let's go for it."

"Okay, Stephen. Thus far, Callum, who has been given more resources than me, has come up empty. Likewise, I have been in search of Dominique in my own ways. After careful consideration and preparation, I have come to believe she isn't dead. She's just somewhere we don't quite understand yet. It's my hope that we may reach her to learn more about where she's gone. Is that fair?"

"I think she dreamt so hard now she's stuck there," Lyda said. "Except then I don't know where her body is. But my mommy is dreaming."

"Let's see if we can get word from your mother, Lyda! Everyone, as I said a few minutes ago, select which of your senses you will go without, then cover them with one of the items you see here."

The group complied. Will thought it'd be easiest to keep his eyes closed. He squirmed as Leni put a blindfold on him. "For Lyda."

Will nodded. "For Lyda."

It was a decision he almost immediately regretted. To be disconnected from Arqa's communication network was one thing, but without his sight he felt more cut off than ever. Leni spoke more of spirits and nexus points.

Lyda, who sat next to him, grabbed his hand. Then someone passed behind him and locked his other hand to Callum's. The two hands Will held were opposites. Leni's voice vacillated between soft and harsh. It was all so hypnotic. Will started to feel drowsy.

"This spot we occupy now, can you feel it? It gave off a very distinct energy," Leni was saying. "The energy is the answer. Dominique, do you hear me now?"

Will's mental rhythm prevailed over the meditative session. His thoughts drifted unerringly to Siannon, her frail state. His inability to help her. There'd always been a place in his heart for his teacher, but she'd rebuked him. He knew it was inappropriate to harbor feelings for someone so much older than him, but at least he was real about it. It would have been worse to keep it in. Not only that but if he hadn't, they wouldn't have shared that kiss. Then he thought of his book, the one he wanted to use to help everyone, that tribute to his life and the whole of Arqa, it was nearing completion.

Something about the corridor changed.

The Sleeping Sickness... he hadn't wanted to think about it. What it was, how it'd affected him. His longing for Siannon. His desire to write. His need to please his Grammy.

The lights flashed. He then heard a low hum. He wished he didn't have to be here.

"Hang on, stop! What was that?" Stephen's voice called out. "I had my eyes trained on the center of the circle this whole time. That wasn't there."

Will felt Mr. Benito's hand rip away from his. He lifted the blindfold from Will's eyes, then dragged the boy onto his feet.

"What's happening?" Will asked.

"Back up, now," Stephen commanded. "Get away from the circle!"

The group scattered.

"Everyone, relax," Leni said. "This is a common occurrence when we channel. It's all," she looked over to Will, "part of the show."

If so, then Will was impressed. At the center of the circle, there was a bug Will had never seen before. It was yellow, with black spots. It had two antennae and hind legs that folded. The bug's eyes were red and had no pupils.

"Leni, you let this out?" Stephen asked. "This is against the—how did you ever even—"

"We have to catch it," Mr. Benito said.

"I'll help!" Lyda offered.

"No. Stay back. That thing isn't safe to touch."

"Where is the container it came from?" Stephen asked, looking around frantically.

"It's a magic circle, Stephen," Leni said. "I'm sorry."

"Cut the charade, Leni," Stephen pressed. "You crossed the line. That creature can contaminate one of our systems. It was reckless to release it."

Leni shrugged. "I already told you, it wasn't me."

Stephen growled. "One of you kids then?"

Lyda and James shook their heads. Everyone looked to Will. "No," he said. "Not me."

Mr. Benito cursed, then tapped Stephen on the shoulder. "Let's just take care of it." He stripped off one of his shoes.

"It's not safe, you say?" Will asked, as the bug parted from the circle. "You aren't going to kill it, are you?"

"Look away if it bothers you, Will," Mr. Benito said, approaching where the creature crawled innocuously.

"No, now Mr. Benito just hold on. That thing's alive."

But Mr. Benito advanced, muttering something about poisonous.

"You lie to pacify him," Leni said with disdain. She turned to Will. "That is a grasshopper. It doesn't bite. Nor is it poisonous. It is simply unable to respect our preconceived notions."

"Well then stop them!" Will exclaimed. "Don't kill it." The bug hopped a great distance before Mr. Benito had a chance to swing at it. It was now on the wall. Leni looked over to Will once more. As the two men made to corner it, Will tackled Mr. Benito into Stephen.

"You want to get locked up?" Mr. Benito asked the boy viciously.

"Mr. Benito, just let him catch it," Lyda said. "Please?"

"No! Leni, get him away."

Leni tried to calm Will down, but he was inconsolable. "Let me get it, let me get it. Please. Don't kill it."

Lyda and James were behind Will, cheering him on. "Listen to Will, daddy," Lyda begged before tears began flowing down her face. "Please."

"It's harmless! It's life!" Will persisted.

"It's going to complicate our own if we don't stop it," Stephen reasoned. "Bugs can't be out in the open like this."

Will tried to jerk forward, but Leni held him back. "Why are you helping them?"

"I'd rather see that bug die than you get hurt," she said sternly. "Now hush."

Mr. Benito and Stephen moved in for a killing blow. Stephen had it. He swung, Lyda screamed, and when the shoe made contact with the bug, the corridor's pseugra cut off. Will and the others lost their stance and started floating.

Things seemed to slow down. Voices morphed and distorted. He looked to Lyda, as she was still steady on the ground while everyone else was panicking over the loss of gravity. Lyda jerked backwards and disappeared right before his eyes.

2.

Kalyna might have seen Jun's point, if she hadn't killed Paiyan.

Jun was talking to her sister Ying, who was not interested in helping her. "You have your memories back," Jun said. "Why are you still siding with Arqa?"

"I'm not interested in explaining myself. You've gone on for the past twenty minutes about how these kids have no clue about what's going on on this ship. How you would dethrone Sali. As for me? I don't need to justify my decisions to one such as you."

"Ying, it was one boy's death for these children's freedom. I would have targeted someone else if I could," she turned to her hostages. "That's just how it had to be for me to make all of this happen."

"Well, I'm not helping you either," Janos said.

"Same," added Trisalyn. "Do whatever you want to us, but we're not turning on 1st LT Lucio."

"Exactly," said Oliver. Kalyna had assumed all the soldiers pulled from the cryo chamber were all working together, but that was not the case. The mutineers included Jun, Donna, Buster, Leona, Dale, and Shaina. Everyone else in the Bay Line had been handcuffed. "We don't want to help you."

"You are all being irrational," Jun said scathingly.

"Your own sister isn't stepping up to help you," Kalyna said. "Why should we?"

"You'll thank me later, even if I have to force you now. I'm offering you a better deal than what you've got. When we were taken prisoner, we weren't even given a choice! I preferred death to what they did to my sister and the others."

"I know, I know," Ying said sympathetically. "Arqa kept us for spare parts. Do your thing, Jun. But we both know this is just about power. You want to commandeer this ship."

"You'll have to help me eventually," Jun said. "Ying, we have orders!"

"We followed our orders. That is a mission we failed."

Kalyna felt she was lacking context for this. As the sisters went on and on, Kalyna asked Millie, but she refused to explain. Before Kalyna could ask someone else, Jun got violent. She was kicking Ying in the face, then stomping on her. Kalyna shivered at the brutality. She couldn't watch. But that didn't stop Ying's wailing.

Kalyna.

Kalyna knew instantly who it was. "No," she said quietly.

Yes, sorry.

Kalyna whispered, "Go away, Gabriel, you're not here. I'm not like Carlos. I'm not crazy." This wasn't like when someone called her on her IC. This was exactly how Carlos had described it. Like telepathy.

That's great to hear, Kalyna! I take that at face value. Listen, I want to help you stop Jun and great news, we can do it if we work together.

"No, no, no!" Kalyna said in resistance. She tried to fill her thoughts with loud gibberish.

"Quiet!" Dale warned.

"Are you okay, Kalyna?" Millie asked.

Hey, hey, we have to move fast on this one. Gabriel again.

Kalyna gave up trying to tune him out. *This flies in the face of everything Arqa stands for. Telepathy is beyond our technological capabilities. Are you just being used by the L'rias to mess with me?*

Kalyna, I'm not messing with you. I'm trying to save your life.

Just tell me. Tell me how you're doing this. Explain it to me.

I would try if I knew. Or if we had time. The thing is, I don't know. I don't even understand where I am.

You're vitrified!

That's not what's important though. Right now, we need to focus on stopping these mutineers. Can you do that for me?

Why me? Kalyna asked. *Why not one of the other kids more willing to listen to random voices in their heads?*

Today it's you, tomorrow it'll be somebody else. Unless you botch this. Do you want to botch this?

What? They're armed. I'm handcuffed. What am I supposed to do?

I already told you that! Now, quit telling me you're not going crazy. Then listen up... Jun's got a weakness.

Chapter Five

1.

"So what's the plan?" Mark asked Tanya as they crept towards the barricaded entrance into the Bay Line.

"You're the one in charge," Tanya said, unable to mask the disappointment in her voice.

"I know that! I mean, since we're going to stamp Jun out now, what's the plan for after? Someone on this ship let that woman out. It wasn't like it was an accident."

"The person responsible will face justice."

"What kind of justice? This, I mean it really breaks up my day. How do you plan on compensating Rayna when her name is cleared?"

"Mark, sometimes you just have to fold to duty."

"You know, there's something else too," Mark said. He didn't need to get into the Bay Line to put a stop to this. Tanya pulled up a holo-screen. "I mean, feels kind of cruel to do it like this, some of those kids could die. You know that, right?"

"Those who survive will be all the more grateful. Jun will be the one responsible anyway. The children pledged themselves to Flight Division. For them, this should be no different from their fight with the L'rias."

"It shouldn't be, but it is. Listen, I don't care what punishments you want to dole out, but you should really start thinking twice about some of your life choices. That goes for me too. How much longer until we tell the kids about everything?"

"Quiet!" Tanya accessed Arqa's surveillance feed. They could see what was happening in the Bay Line.

"What? It's not like they can hear me. You need me too much not to keep me in the loop. So what is the plan?"

Tanya tapped on the holo-screen. "That one. That's Buster. Leona and Jun have weapons too, but I'd like Buster taken out first. That might be enough for them to surrender."

"You got it." Mark took off the rod from his shoulder and a holo-screen appeared, which controlled the device. "But you still haven't answered my question, you know."

"Captain Sali never intended to give Jun any of what she wanted. Callum would usually do the talking in a situation like this, but no one knows where he is."

"I do hope he's okay," Mark said with gusto.

"Right. Are you ready?"

"Any second now. Just keep going. I enjoy knowing things. Some people don't, but I love it. Go ahead, Tanya."

"Are you implying you won't fire until I've told you?"

"No, not at all. It'll just be a coincidence. I'm a prime mover here on Arqa. Though I like to keep to myself. So tell me, when will you tell the kids about the L'rias?"

"We will hold off on that until it is absolutely necessary. To be honest, Captain Sali feels like she's kind of shot herself in the foot."

"So I figured. That's very interesting. Now quiet down. Things are about to happen."

Mark could feel Tanya's irritation rising from behind him. He took one more look at Buster on the surveillance feed and cross-referenced that with the Bay Line's schematic he'd uploaded into his weapon's interface.

"I've got it!" Mark declared.

"What? Are you making the shot?"

"No! I know just what to call this thing," he said, lifting the rod. "The Juno. In honor of the fool who provoked me to dust it off."

"Great. Now are you ready?"

He said nothing, only squeezed a trigger on the rod. From the end of it, several luminescent balls shot out from the end and got sucked up into the ceiling.

"Send for more troops," Mark ordered. "Now, Tanya!"

Tanya obeyed, but not without a prolonged groan.

2.

Things became *wrong* when they killed the bug. Lyda knew. Lyda felt. It was the lights. The sounds. Her friends and family going away. She was alone in the corridor. She heard a woman's voice saying, "DON'T LOOK... UP," repeatedly. Lyda obeyed. She thought she saw trace outlines of the others, but they never fully formed.

When she tried to call out, there was no sound. Lyda didn't like this. And it was all because of that dead bug. It had to be. Maybe if she could find it...

The little girl pushed forward but found it harder than usual. Forces hindered her. But she refused to stop. Scanning down, there were no squish marks on the wall, no dead bug. But there was something there. Yes.

A hair. Someone's hair. Lyda raised it to the lights to get a better look. The ceiling was not there.

"DON'T LOOK... UP. DON'T LOOK ... UP. DON'T LOOK—"

"Oh no, I'm sorry," Lyda said. She tried to duck down, but her body was fixed in place.

Above her was a floating nightmare. People hurting one another, but nobody she knew. It was really, really bad. Scenes of blood, guts, and explosions. Those horrors moved closer to her, pushing down like the thing from her dream.

"No, stop!"

She was drifting upward. The gravity in the corridor went away. At least she could move again.

Lyda attempted to flip herself over and get a handle on the floor, but it was no good. She'd gone from being stuck to having little control of her direction. The grip she had on the hair loosened, but she did not let it go. She wished to take her attention away from the nasty things. They weren't really happening, it was only a movie.

But they sounded so real. Was this Earth? Was *this* what her mommy missed so much?

Lyda continued to apologize for looking, but the voice did not respond. Soon she would not be on the ship anymore. Wait. Was her mommy there?

"Mommy, mommy! Help me!" Nothing. She thought of something else. "Congo! Help, please. I need you now!"

Lyda inhaled as much as she could. It was becoming cold. Was there no oxygen anymore? To be close to what she saw hurt her inside, and she couldn't take it anymore. She closed her eyes and plugged her ears with her hands.

The voice was inside her mind. It changed, becoming fast. Lyda knew she was receiving information, but she wasn't able to process it. She blinked several times and rubbed her eyes. Somehow, that did the trick. Not only did gravity return, but so did Arqa's ceiling. The others. Things were back to normal.

Everyone hit the floor. Lyda braced herself, then shuddered from the memory of the strange moment.

Leni was the first one back on her feet. Lyda walked over to her, needing to be held.

As Leni brushed herself off, she told the girl, "Thank you, dear."

"I hated that."

Leni looked quizzically at her. "Tell me more. I think you saw the answer."

Before Lyda could say anything back, the others rebounded from their fall. Leni regarded them, then kissed Lyda on the forehead before bolting away. Mr. Benito scrambled up after her, but Lyda's daddy told him to help with the pseugra controls at the end of the corridor.

James groaned and held his head where she could see a fresh bump. Will was back on his feet. "What just happened?" James asked. "And where's that bug?"

"They killed it," Will said with contempt in his voice. He stepped over to Mr. Benito. "Life is precious. You really shouldn't have done that. I don't know what just happened, but it was just like her mom! She disappeared."

"I... did?" Lyda asked. Then she became indignant. "Nuh-uh, that was you who went away."

"I agree that life is precious, Will," said Mr. Benito. "That grasshopper—"

"That wasn't a grasshopper," her daddy said, returning from the panel. "That was a locust. There's a marked difference. A few of those on Arqa would wreak havoc. They're swarming creatures. They bunch together and fly for miles and miles. They devour crops and were quite a nuisance for some time on Earth. A locust swarm once meant famine. They were as devastating as any earthquake or hurricane, and they would be gone just as quick. We eventually discovered locust start off as grasshoppers. Grasshoppers don't swarm, as they're very shy. A grasshopper can go its entire life that way, never swarming. But they found that under certain conditions, like when food is scarce, grasshoppers will congregate in one location. This is what triggers the change. When a grasshopper is touched for a time by other grasshoppers and they're all clustered together, it causes them to become locusts."

"I'm trying to piece together what just happened," Mr. Benito said. "The pseugra is not supposed to just give out like that."

Upon inspection, they soon discovered the gravity was not on. Yet that couldn't be right, because they were standing, feet firmly on the ground and able to walk.

"It's heavier," James noted.

"We should get out of here," Will suggested.

"Leni must have tampered with the ship's systems," Mr. Benito said. "We need to find her. Everyone, reconnect your ICs."

They reached another panel in a different part of the ship. They determined that it was performing normally.

"Callum, Leni's tricked us somehow," her daddy said. "Will, could you please take Lyda and James to your grandmother?"

Will nodded.

"Be sure to let her know about the gravity issue."

"Wait, where did I go?" Lyda asked Mr. Benito.

"Don't worry about that for now," he said. "Just stay away from that corridor."

Chapter Six

1.

Kalyna's dilemma tormented her. Gabriel was continuously offering her suggestions of how to free herself. How to save the day. She didn't know whether to believe it or not. He refused to contact anyone else in the room to prove he was truly there. Though he claimed he could reach out to anyone who'd had the Sleeping Sickness, provided they were awake.

When she failed to do something, he'd chide her and say she was running out of chances. Her life could depend on her following his advice. She felt woozy, unable to handle hearing the instructions in her head, let alone carry them out.

Look up, Kalyna. Now. Do you see that?

She did. Some bright spot was moving along the ceiling.

That's your out. Last chance. Ready?

No, she said. *I'm not going anywhere near that.*

The next thing she knew, the spot on the ceiling opened right above Buster and what looked like a sliver of electricity came down onto him. It produced a shock wave and everyone who'd been standing toppled over.

The other hostages were moaning and injured. Aside from her ringing eardrums, Kalyna felt fine. Like she had when she'd risen from the Sleeping Sickness.

Any doubt Kalyna had about Gabriel's communications evaporated. The electricity had come down and obliterated Buster where he'd stood. Now she only had to worry about Jun and Leona. Leona made for the entrance to the Bay Line, Jun moved away from it.

Arqa must have come to liberate the hostages.

Make for where Buster was just killed. There's going to be hot metal you can use to melt the chains of your handcuffs.

Gabriel, it's not safe.

Well, keep your eyes peeled on Leona—but don't wait long.

Dale threw up his arms in surrender. "Screw this," he said before sending a hammerfist down onto Leona's head.

Kalyna got up. Shaina was making for Dale as he retrieved Leona's weapon.

Forget that! Gabriel said. *You need to get Jun now.*

But she's armed. She'll shoot at me before I have a chance to get close!

Remember her weakness. Gabriel had told Kalyna about Jun's left knee, which had been badly injured before she'd been taken prisoner and had never healed. *All you have to do is charge her. You don't even need to waste time undoing your handcuffs. You missed that chance anyway. Look, you're running out of time. If Jun reaches a Spaero, she's going to blow the Bay Line apart!*

The other hostages rose, seeing they could overtake the mutineers.

Gabriel, did you hear me? Kalyna asked. *She has a gun!*

Kalyna, why do you think she's running? Not helping Shaina and Donna? That gun is a fake! Now go.

She hesitated once more. A fake gun?

Stop her!

"I trust you, Gabriel." As Kalyna made her charge, she called back to some of the other hostages. "You guys want to prove your loyalty? Get ready to back me up!"

Running at her top speed, Kalyna closed the distance between herself and Jun. She froze for a moment as another electric spear came down somewhere behind her, but she didn't lose her footing. Neither did Jun.

"I will not surrender!" Jun pledged.

"Jun, it's over!" Ying called back.

Jun noticed Kalyna coming for her. "One warning: stay back." She was nearing a Spaero.

"I thought you were holding us hostage to protect us?" Kalyna questioned. "Do your worst."

Jun obliged the girl by pointing the gun at her. Kalyna smirked.

"Are you mad, girl? Freeze yourself!"

Kalyna was only a yard from Jun when the woman pulled the trigger. It nearly hit her! Her instincts might have normally prompted her to run for cover. Beg for her life. Instead, the adrenaline prevented Kalyna from flinching. Before Jun could fire another round, Kalyna hopped into the air, stomping down to put all of her weight onto Jun's bad knee.

That part, at least, was true. Jun fell under Kalyna, cursing the girl. Kalyna rolled as she fell to dampen the impact. It still caused a great deal of pain. She ground her teeth and persisted. Reaching out for Jun's hair, she closed her fingers around it, pulled it, and slammed the woman's head onto the floor. After a brief struggle, Eric, Ying, and Millie had Jun pinned against the underside of the Spaero she'd almost climbed in.

Kalyna disentangled herself from the scuffle, regarding the gun in her hand.

Gabriel, how could you tell me this was fake?

Gabriel said nothing back. Kalyna seemed to be alone with her thoughts once more.

2.

Carlos was poised in front of the door to the meeting. He didn't think a storage room was a great place to meet, but it was better than nothing. Faeleen could be anyone, and he hadn't heard from her in some time. At least his friends in Flight Division were safe from Jun.

What would he talk about with her? This could get uncomfortable so easily. Carlos had to focus. The objective was sex. Sure, he had feelings for Faeleen, but what good was thinking about anything in the long term?

Once he entered the storage room, there'd be no turning back.

Carlos stepped forward and opened the door. The room was dimly lit, and he gasped. There were sparkling bulbs on the floor, set about a yard apart from each other. Following the trail, he picked them up as he went. It then dawned on him that Faeleen must have set this up, and he felt his heart swooning. The room was large and led to a corner where Carlos imagined different possible women in many different outfits and positions waiting for him. Now within speaking distance, he asked in a low tone, "Faeleen?"

No response. As he turned the corner, it was clear nobody was there. If only he'd had the sense to come earlier, to catch whoever had laid down the lights.

There were red lockers set up against the wall. One of them was glowing—and he saw his name there, written in blood.

Opening the locker carefully, he wished he could stop himself. A paper rested folded over in the locker. Carlos examined the inside, kneeling and tilting his head up. The only thing in there was the paper. It also had his name on it, but this time it was written in ink. Faeleen, perhaps, wanted to surprise him?

Carlos looked it over, knowing he'd been brought here to read this note. While he opened it, he tried to tell himself he had a choice not to.

On the paper was a nasty drawing of him in a dress. His acne was prominently featured. Visible waves of odor came out from his exposed armpits. There was an unpeeled banana shoved into his mouth. Various quotes extracted from his intimate conversations with Faeleen were taken out of context. One, in particular, stood out the most, "I masturbate to you." The illustration also depicted that his genitalia was only visible through an electron microscope.

This is how people saw him. He hadn't changed, he was the same old freak. Staring at the picture, he tried to muster up the will to crumble it up. To forget.

But Faeleen wasn't here.

And she wasn't real.

Chapter Seven

1.

Callum stood before a pacing Captain Sali. 1st LT Lucio, Captain De Plez, and Dr. Masten were also present.

"It was all a smokescreen," Captain Sali said. "Leni's the one who got Jun out. Who tampered with the stasis pilots so they could mutiny. And we don't know where she's hiding."

"Everything that has happened of late seems to be tied up with her," Dr. Masten said.

"She'll turn up soon," Callum said optimistically. He was embarrassed after being outsmarted by Leni. Hell, they all were. How could he have let her slip away earlier?

"This is what Callum was warning you about, captain," Captain De Plez remarked. "You're lucky the collateral damage was so low this time. She's going to find a way to hit us again. So tell them already."

"Yes, I will," Captain Sali said. "That's why they're here, Dennis. Tanya, will you set up the star charts for me?"

1st LT Lucio nodded and summoned a holo-screen.

"Leni's made her intentions known. She's sided with the enemy. I've checked the reports on the pseugra, and that more or less sank things for me."

Callum looked at the screen. He saw the Earth, their initial departure point. Then the graphic showed Arqa's course over the years... it was hard to believe, but they'd tapped into baffling high sub-luminal speeds and made it quite far out. That wasn't what they'd been told would happen. "When? How?" he asked. Arqa had jumped a vast distance that its engine could not have covered in such a short time. It was being manipulated by outside forces.

"You understand, then? We are nearly to our destination. This was brought to my attention after whatever took place earlier in that corridor. This is deeply disturbing. But we have to work with it. I think whatever tricks Leni has up her sleeve, she knows something about B3 that we don't."

"That doesn't mean we're at her mercy," 1st LT Lucio said vociferously.

"I should hope not," Captain Sali responded. "We can guess as to where the gravity in that corridor is coming from."

"Then it's time to tell the children," said Callum.

"I'm not willing to do that," Captain Sali said. "Not after everything I've given up."

"When then, captain?" Callum asked. "I suspect that's the only reason Leni has made her play."

"Yes, and that is unacceptable."

"Don't tell me this is out of spite!"

"Leni is not a threat, trust me. The same might not apply to Dominique though."

"What of Lyda?" Callum asked.

"Well, Stephen's watching her like a hawk," 1st LT Lucio said. "And the corridor's been cordoned off."

"Somehow, we've been taken advantage of and I don't like it," Captain Sali said. "Callum, that's why I've had you look into Dominique. I wanted to expose dissension on the ship. I was hoping Dominique would come out by now, but that hasn't worked out. Now you know what's coming. The other side is blood-thirsty, but our kids still have their purity. I think that's what's going to give us level ground. For now, your top priority is finding Leni. And extracting every bit of information you can out of her memories once you do."

"She didn't do this alone," 1st LT Lucio said. "How can you even trust everyone who's here now?"

Captain Sali shrugged. "I can't. But unless all of you have sided with Leni, I am certain I can get her."

Callum wasn't sure if the woman stance was arrogant or confident. But he didn't have the energy to grapple with that. He couldn't stop thinking about B3, that ephemeral, rarely acknowledged goal was way, way too close. He never thought he'd live to see it.

Now they were at *its* mercy.

2.

Lyda entered the Bay Line to see a group surrounding Kalyna, who was in the middle of a speech. "We're the ones who get to be in control. We call the shots, because we are Arqa's defense. If we weren't here, no one else would be. Now we know what happened to Paiyan, and it was wrong."

It was all so clear to Lyda now. Ever since the séance. She strode over to where James was seated.

"We've never known how things were going to end," Kalyna continued. "I think now we do, and I'm over it. Right now, everyone is getting ready in their own way, and we can't hold it against them for lashing out or being zombies or whatever they want to do to express themselves. We have only our bodies, and mine is for serving my ship. When we started Flight Division, I couldn't do more than ten sit-ups. Now I'm up to twelve times that. But that's not the only thing about our training that's allowed us to adjust. It has taught us to let go of everything superficial."

Before tapping the boy on the shoulder, Lyda looked over at the Spaeros. Could this work?

"We are stronger and better than ever. I beg that you all stay loyal to Flight Division."

The group listening began to clap. Now was her chance. Lyda spoke into James's ear. "Do you remember your mom's broken figurines?"

James jumped. He turned to her. "Oh, hi Lyda!"

"Well, do you?"

"Of course. Definitely. I'll never forget that."

"Good, because now I need help with something." She tugged at Josie's head, where she'd attached the hair she'd found during the séance.

"Sure, what is it?"

Lyda knew it was a big thing to ask, and she was unsure how to phrase it. So she didn't. "No way. Like you did before. You said before I helped you, you said, promise me you won't tell anyone about this."

"Oh yeah. Well... I mean, I guess we could. As long as we're not going to hurt anyone?"

Lyda smiled, then laughed. "No, of course not silly. Now, will you promise me or not?"

It took a bit more convincing, but Lyda always knew he would say yes.

EPISODE 5

Where the Embraced Separate

Prologue

FIVE YEARS AGO...

Leni was at the door to welcome Mark. Behind her, standing on her tiptoes to see, was Dominique. The two women were in bikinis. This disarmed him, and he moved his head to look away from them.

"Mark, we've been waiting for you," Leni said.

"You're too early!" Dominique said in her squeaky voice.

"Yeah, tell me more about it," Mark said.

"That isn't a problem, though." Leni poked Dominique and she ran away, giving space for Mark to enter.

They sat down at Leni's table. On the way there, Mark passed by two beach chairs with a cooler full of... beer? Arqa didn't have beer. Under different circumstances, he might have asked for one. But he needed to remain lucid.

"We know why we're here," Leni said. "So let's just get on with it."

"Yeah, great," said Mark. "So, what do you think you're doing meddling with Rayna? I'm shocked the captain signed off on it."

"Mark, you're a scientist. Women are always going to perplex you. That's not my fault. Let us dress how we want. Rayna was being teased by the other kids, and you weren't acting like her father."

"I'm not her dad! She's my assistant."

"She's too young for all that!" Leni objected. "You had no right to keep her out of Siannon's class. The girl needs connections besides you."

"That's already been decided."

"Then she *is* your responsibility. And when she's not feeling well about something, it's kind of like on you to help her where you can."

"Concealing her features won't help her self-consciousness. What gave you that idea, Leni?"

"Mark, I don't like you," Dominique cut in. "But people think I respect you. See? That's just the way to be." She pounded her hand on the table and used her other one to slap it.

"What is she doing?" Mark asked.

"You think I've ever known?" Leni got out a brush and tidied up her friend's hair.

"Episode time," Dominique said.

"Dom. Dom." Leni snapped her fingers at the woman. "Join us, please."

"Yes, no, maybe so, probably no. Multiple choice!"

"Must be a full moon... Look, Mark, you've lost this round. Rayna has the option to wear what she wants if it makes her feel better."

"I think it makes you feel better pushing up against the captain's rules where you can. Then you get all the other women here treating the ship like some kind of matriarchy."

"Better than a patriarchy," Leni said.

"Arqa is neither! It's founded on gender neutrality, non-binary principles."

"Well, we can't just throw our biology away. I agree with you, a leader isn't more capable just because of what sex they are. A great example for you: Captain Sali is in charge and she is okay with Rayna's request. This is where you give up."

"Is that why you're wearing bikinis right now? To prove some kind of point?"

"That's a non-issue. Let it go."

"You're asking me to let go of my caring for the girl?"

"You care about having a servant," Leni said. "You refuse to treat her like a human being. She has feelings. She's growing up. And she thinks the world of you, but if you keep coming up short when she needs emotional support, she'll grow to resent you. Think of it from a pragmatic point of view. You don't want to lose her, so be better."

Mark pursed his lips. "I didn't think this was going to get us anywhere."

"You can't have it both ways. You can't say, oh, she's not my daughter, then try to be mad when I do what any parent would do for a child."

"No. Nope. Leni, we both know this is about you. What you did."

Leni flinched. "I already took responsibility for that. Quit bringing it up. My solution was presented and accepted. From now on, whether you like it or not, Rayna will cover her face if it pleases her. This will make her life easier, and you can just keep worrying about yourself."

"Does it ever bother you?" Mark asked. "That they told you not to use that station? That you did it anyway?"

"You know it is one of my greatest regrets."

"Are you going to tell her at some point? Because you should have done that by now."

Leni slowly dropped the brush onto the table. "Everyone here is entitled to their secrets. That's all I'm going to tell you. I'm not after you, but I could be. You deserve to keep everything you've done to yourself. As do I. Mark, let the girl have what she's asking for. There's no need to get nasty. This has got to be one of the first times in your life something hasn't gone how you wanted it to."

Mark rose, on the verge of shouting. "Never, ever look to me for help. You're a bad person in my book, and I know someday I'll be able to prove it."

"Like I could care about your idea of help. The only reason I'm indulging you is because I want you to walk away from this talk today with more empathy for humankind."

"I suggest you keep away from Rayna," Mark said.

"As long as I see you respecting her, you've got a deal."

"How did they let someone so backward on this ship?"

"I started telling people the truth," Leni said with pride, "and they hated it. I guess they thought of getting rid of me. But Captain Sali admitted she needed me all the same. Remind you of someone you know?"

"That's a nice story. I think we're done here though."

"Thanks for dropping in," Leni said, waving to him.

As he was leaving, Dominique scraped the chair as she bolted up to get in front of Mark. He tried to back away, but she hovered even closer to him and said, "Five years." She snapped her fingers three times, slowly. "They're going to go by like a weekend. You know? Like a weekend."

"Get out of my face, you're getting spit on me!" To Leni, he said, "Are you going to get her help?"

Leni shrugged. "I say she's fine the way she is."

"Fly by," Dominique continued, pressing her thumb against Mark's forehead.

Chapter One

1.

Flight Division had been assembled in the Bay Line.

Carlos wasn't sure what was happening. Twice now they'd been sent out to defend Arqa against the L'rias. Once was for real, the other time was a false alarm. Today though, he thought something different had to be going on.

He hurried to take his seat, avoiding eye contact with the others. He didn't want to believe it was someone in Flight Division who'd pranked him, but he had no way of knowing.

1st LT Lucio strode up and used her wrist interface to conjure up a holo-screen. It was a map of the region of space they were occupying.

"Let's hustle now, come on," she commanded. Carlos saw some fresh faces: kids from his class, alternatives. He wasn't sure what had been done with the mutineers, but the rumors ranged from execution to putting them back into stasis. Jun's plan had backfired, as now more children were piloting Spaeros than before.

Captain Sali was also there, looking over the group, taciturn as he had always known her to be. Lucio pointed to a dot on the map. "This is us." On the lower right-hand corner, she pointed to another dot. "This is the L'rias. They've been closing the distance between us, in spite of our efforts. Today though, we have a new variable." She turned their attention to a third dot, one Carlos hadn't even noticed. "What do you think this is?"

"It's got to be enemy reinforcements, coming in from another vector," Eric insisted.

"That'd be a great explanation if it wasn't so far away," Lucio said. "Not only that, but this thing isn't giving off much of any heat."

"Is it a planet?" James asked.

Carlos squinted to see the fuzzy image as Lucio zoomed in. It just looked like a blob.

"It's not a planet, James. The truth is, we can't identify it."

"What do you mean? Who is it?"

"Hold on," said 1st LT Lucio. "Look. As we've been tracking it, we have noticed it's been expanding. It started off tiny. So it's growing, and it's coming toward us. When it does, assuming its current rate of expansion, it will be larger than this ship. We have less than three hours before it reaches us. Whatever this may be, it could give the L'rias an advantage. We need to gather more intel. This is your most important mission to date. I'll be sending half of you out in that direction to learn more. You are to survey, gather information. If anything happens, you are to retreat. The rest of you will stay to defend Arqa in the event the L'rias make a move. Questions?"

Issac raised his hand. "Are you seriously telling us you never saw anything like this back on Earth?"

"We—" 1st LT Lucio looked over to Captain Sali. "Correct. At first, we thought it was some kind of asteroid, but it can't be."

Everyone lost their bearing and murmurs bounced back and forth.

"Lock it up! We've got a job to do."

After 1st LT Lucio answered a few more questions, they were split up into the two teams. Carlos was among those who would investigate the UFO, leaving him feeling stressed.

He went to change into his g suit, devoid of enthusiasm. At least with the L'rias they knew what they were getting. What would the UFO do to them? Carlos wanted to lay back down and let that thing have its way.

"Lucio's going to kill you if you're still here in five minutes," Trisalyn said.

Carlos ignored her.

"We've got to go!"

Carlos shriveled where he sat. "I don't... want to."

She looked around, relieved no one else had heard him. "Things are about to get crazy. Paiyan's dead. It's an insult to his memory to cower like this!"

"How far are they going to keep pushing us?" Carlos asked. "Everyone's got a limit of how much they can take, you know."

Trisalyn groaned. "Yeah, and I'm about fed up with your pouting session. They're doing everything they can to keep as many of us alive as possible. This is what life is now: orders. We follow. And maybe we survive."

"This is hopeless."

"We're only as good as our weakest link. Look, I'm going out there with you, we're in this together."

"It could zap us out of the sky before we get close."

"Then we'll be dead and we won't have to worry about things anymore. Not that you'd mind something like that."

"Only if it's instantaneous..."

Carlos could not be snapped out of his dismay. After he launched, he kept looking to see how much longer until they were within visual range of the UFO. What would happen? The comms were full of speculation, but he didn't care to take part.

They could be flying to their doom. And he was doing it willingly! No, this was *his* Spaero. It couldn't be piloted without him in the cockpit. No one could override him, and he could do whatever he wanted.

So he flew away, breaking formation. After cutting his propulsion, he took in several deep breaths. It was the right move. Let them shoot him from here if they wanted. Carlos didn't have the conceit to think his puny little efforts made a difference. People were looking for him, so he turned off the comms. Maybe he'd be the last human alive. He wasn't Kalyna or Paiyan or Trisalyn. No, honor and heroics were useless if he was dead.

Carlos was just so tired of suffering for no good reason. He turned away from the mission wholeheartedly. That was a decision he was allowed to make. To be all alone in the dark. Far off from the UFO or his team or the L'rias or Arqa. Getting as comfortable as he could, Carlos closed his eyes and slid his hand down to where he felt best.

2.

"Hello and peace to you, Siannon Kelley." Leni's voice. Again. Every one hundred eighty-five minutes since Siannon had made the mistake of accepting that note from Jun.

But it wasn't just Leni's voice. It was also visual. A recorded message. The paper Siannon had been given contained a small pea-sized object. She'd turned away from the camera to swallow it.

Siannon had no idea where Leni was, but the area was dark and cramped. Not only that, but Leni was floating. Wherever she was was outside the range of Arqa's pseugra. "There is a hierarchy of information on Arqa. Everyone knows that. But I'm sick of lying to the children. I want accountability. Transparency. And I am not alone. We have fulfilled the measure of our oath. The situation has changed. You understand that. That's why you stood up against them." Leni gestured to several others in the room with her. Their faces were concealed. "By the time you receive this message, we will have already freed Jun. It was a risky move, and it won't take long for them to figure out it was me. That's why I'm going to go into hiding. You see, Siannon? You're not alone. Our movement is small but we have everything we need. If you are seeing this, you chose not to have Jun break you out. A wise move. Even so, you can still help, if you want. I know that's what you want."

The message was played to her on a loop. It woke her up every time, so Siannon was never fully rested anymore.

"The thing is, Jun was only one step in a larger process. We never expected her to fulfill her mission. She was a necessary and willing sacrifice. The real work to save Arqa begins now. Our team has been sabotaging the powers that be ever since Gabriel's vision. While they'll tell you Arqa's mission has been the creation of and assimilation with artificial general intelligence, the way they plan to pull it off has been a closely guarded secret. What I want is full disclosure. Leadership that speaks truth. Will you join us, Siannon?

"We are all meant to be swallowed soon, and when that happens, we'll have our window of opportunity. We are going to free everyone. The children will not be forced to fight our battle, and Arqa will achieve its ends peacefully and ethically. I knew you were on our side when you tried to divulge the truth. They say you're unstable. I don't care one way or the other because you tried to do the right thing. And your soul will be clean for that bravery. Goodbye for now, Siannon."

The message ended there. She tossed and turned from one side to the other, anguished by the interruption of sleep that was difficult enough to come by. Siannon wished for the Sleeping Sickness. Leni's machinations wouldn't be able to find her there. In the depths of her slumber, she sometimes thought she saw that footage of Dominique vanishing.

Siannon couldn't understand what the purpose of playing that message repeatedly in her mind was. At first, she'd assumed that there was information coded there, but now that she had seen and studied everything so many times, that didn't seem to be the case. Mostly she was wondering where on the ship Leni was hiding.

Leni was obsessed with principles. It wouldn't be hard for her to latch onto any reason to stage a mutiny against Captain Sali, even one she had no chance of winning. As much as Siannon wanted Arqa to run differently, she knew there was little hope of deposing Captain Sali. In spite of everything Leni had done for Siannon, Siannon could not help her. She had to stop her.

Chapter Two

1.

As much as Captain Sali tried to exude excitement, Callum could tell it was not working on anyone.

Could this plan bring about the Technological Singularity? There were so many missing pieces. Not to mention Lyda herself had gone missing.

People were running back and forth on the ship, restless. It was during this period of claustrophobic transit that Lyda snuck out from her quarters. Callum watched the feed of Lyda going, and Stephen returning from the bathroom to see she was missing. By then she was hiding amongst the crowds that filled the corridors.

Things were calmer now, but every few minutes someone came banging on the door to Central Command, and they would be threatened with punishment if they didn't return to their quarters. Someone called out that one of the Flight Division teams was nearing the UFO, but Callum had to focus on the task at hand. Lyda had vanished briefly during the séance and no one knew anything about that besides Leni, who was still at large herself.

And he didn't want to believe anyone had been taken off the ship, even if they were nearing B3. There had to be a better explanation.

Which was why Callum no longer trusted Tim.

Besides losing Dominique, Leni, and Lyda, Tim had also slipped up when Jun's team made it into the Bay Line. The loss of life could have been disastrous. The truth was Tim shouldn't have been able to help mutineers at any capacity, because Arqa's passengers were wired against undermining their oath. But if that wiring had been tampered with on a larger scale, then they had much bigger problems. All the while Captain Sali refused to dwell on how many people could be against her this close to her goal. It made her blind.

Callum looked down at Tim. He was running facial recognition software on the day's surveillance feeds to find Lyda.

"Mr. Benito?" a girl's voice asked.

Callum turned and saw who it was. "What's up, Felicia?"

Felicia began to explain but was cut off by a development on the battlefield. 1st LT Lucio announced, "The enemy has already made contact with the UFO. They are flying away from it!"

"Not good! Do we continue to advance?" Captain De Plez asked.

"If we—no, wait," said Captain Sali.

Callum didn't know the right answer, so he looked back and forth from Captain Sali to 1st LT Lucio.

"Of course we keep at it. Sunk costs." That was all 1st LT Lucio had to say on the matter. All she had to say about the children on their mission. Arqa's last chance, thrown callously to the ineffable.

2.

Mark's lab was disheveled. Rayna entered. He had not seen her since the day Jun took the Bay Line. He stopped throwing his things around when he realized her face was uncovered. She was a difficult sight to see. The top of her head was more scars than hair, and her eyebrows would never grow back in. Otherwise, her face was unblemished. If she were to wear a wig, she wouldn't be so noticeable. But she didn't like wigs.

"Why, Rayna? Why?"

"You know, Mark. Really. They made me. I'm not allowed to conceal my face anymore. They can't risk having people walking around with veils after that poser framed me!"

"I don't care what they said. When you're in here, it's got to be business as usual."

"That ought to create some problems."

"And they'll be mine, not yours. So do it!"

"Jeez, fine. Thought you'd freak out over it. But this—" She was only just noticing the mess. "What is going on in here?"

"Go get dressed, and I'll explain."

Rayna came back a few minutes later. "You must know about the UFO already, huh?"

"Yes. I heard it's on the way here? Sure is odd."

"It takes a lot for you to call something odd."

He hummed a vague response.

"Mark," she pressed. He continued tossing things from a table. Rayna shoved him with enough force to knock him over.

"That isn't right," he said, jostled.

"They'll kill us all! What are you doing?"

"We don't need this stuff anymore."

"Aren't you worried yet? Whatever silly thing you're doing right now is pointless. Did you know they can't find Dominique's daughter now? You hear? The daughter is missing now too. It's got to be that UFO, I just know it!"

Mark patted his shirt. "That was not nice. Leni is in hiding. Perhaps she took the girl." He reached a hand up, hoping Rayna would help him. She didn't. As he rolled over to lift himself, he said, "You know, this really is impolite behavior, Rayna."

Rayna glared at Mark. "What do manners matter? This ship is going down."

"You just going to shove me all day then? Why do we deserve a different fate than any other species?"

"We left Earth to have a different fate."

"And according to you, it isn't panning out. Oh well, we tried." Mark standing, distanced himself from Rayna. "Don't you think it's funny that they've been raving about the end for weeks and yet we're still here?"

"I just don't want to die."

Mark shrugged. "You'll have to deal with that issue at some point. But not tonight."

"Flight Division is going to try to make contact with that thing."

"Are you in Flight Division?"

"No."

"Then once again, why are you worried about it? We have things we need to be doing here."

"I'm on strike until you clue me in, Mark. The Sleeping Sickness, the L'rias, this new UFO. I'm fed up. I'm tired of your games. They're only amusing for you. I've been putting up with your idiosyncrasies for years now. Trying to understand how you thrive in a crisis. I remember how well you fared in our departure from Earth. Glimpses, you know? That's why I wanted to be your assistant. I was tired of the constant fear and anxiety. And maybe I've learned a thing or two from you. But now it's not enough. You need to pay up. It's time for you to give me something. You can't just sit back so calm as you are without filling me in. You know more than most people. Mark. What the fuck is going on?"

Mark smirked. "What an auspicious pitch! Well done, Rayna. As for thriving in a crisis, being is doing. We are nothing more but the sum of our actions. Do calm things and you will be calm. Why don't we make a deal? Yes, I've got things to tell. But there will be three conditions you have to accept."

"Fine. What are they?"

"First condition: you may not interrupt me. Questions will disturb my train of thought."

"Easy enough."

"Second condition: I will boot up the Craig program so he can listen in too. This will also require a little housekeeping before we begin the story."

"I have no issues with that."

"I started off easy. Final condition: let me cut your hair. It grows in so uneven. That's a losing battle you're fighting, Rayna. Just let it go."

Rayna crossed her arms. "I don't care if you don't like it. And I don't care if it makes me look ugly either."

"Yeah, probably because you've been able to walk around covered since you were a child. I predict your insecurity is going to shoot through the roof if we don't even it out. And I'd rather you be angry at me for giving you a little truth now than have people ridicule you behind your back for what's on your head. This last condition is a favor for you. Post-traumatic growth! What do you say?"

"Your perception of me does not determine who I am."

"I'm in total agreement with you there, Rayna. I'm sensing the last condition is going to be a point of contention? I thought you wanted to know about... everything?" Mark raised the pitch of his voice on the last word.

"Like you know it all. I'll agree to the last condition so long as you aren't the person who touches my head. Because you know what? I'm only cutting my hair in exchange for this information. Not because I'm some immature little girl. I'm a full-grown woman now, Mark. So—" Rayna seemed as if she didn't know how to conclude. "Take that!"

"Oh! I hope you got a kick out of all that." Mark booted Craig up. After, he went to a cabinet over one of his work stations and pulled out two sledgehammers. Handing one to Rayna, he said, "As for the housekeeping, everything in here that isn't integral to Craig needs to be destroyed immediately."

Chapter Three

1.

A long period of radio silence broke, revealing the L'rias had reached the UFO before Flight Division. Kalyna was on the wrong mission, stuck waiting in place in case the L'rias attacked Arqa. At least she had the best ship of the bunch, the first new Spaero manufactured on Arqa. It was intentionally designed for combat, unlike all the other models. Kalyna had a lot more options against the enemy now. 1st LT Lucio had almost been the pilot of the new ship, but Kalyna had been chosen instead, perhaps in recognition of her bravery against Jun. She hadn't told anybody about Gabriel, though she wished she could hear from him again. If things got dicey, he'd be a lot of help.

The new Spaero's most devastating weapon was the femtolon. Particles were shot out of an accelerator and self-replicated as they approached a target. No one was sure how well it would work, but Kalyna was optimistic. And that wasn't all. She and her sister had also completed the prototype for JENA. Brenda hadn't told her the scope of the maintenance drone's capabilities, but she'd installed it onto the new ship. Kalyna was eager to find out what it could do. Its finished design was a u-shaped device that orbited around her ship.

Being strapped into a Spaero was the most sedentary thing Kalyna could think of. And it was a challenge for her to be in that moment when she was so rearing to go. 1st LT Lucio had taught them meditation exercises that would take focus away from their stiff bodies.

When she got what she wanted, she realized she'd been mistaken. It happened so quickly, Kalyna was unable to process it. In the moments before the old reality was ripped from her sight like a falling curtain, Kalyna was a very conceded young girl. Many things happened all at once. First, her ship's systems went haywire. Next, her ship rolled upside down and back again. She could not say for how long because merciless nausea assailed her, and she vomited. Before she could question what had happened, she desperately moved to get steady. The acrid scent of her bile nearly made her sick again.

As the radars came on again, Kalyna moved through the visual spectrum—this was not space. At least, it wasn't dark. How? The shift in light was so stunning and unexpected she had to adjust the color settings of her vis-cap. While attempting to piece together what colors she had been seeing, the comms went wild.

Daring to look back at the screen, Kalyna saw she was not alone.

Dozens of contacts were flying all around her. Something had transported her into close quarters combat with the L'rias!

2.

As soon as Will heard of the UFO, he retreated into his room, hoping to finish his book. He'd been coming up with many possible endings, but nothing seemed to work.

All in all, life on Arqa seems to have been alright. My Grammy often refers to these years as a "bonus round." So maybe she treats the value of life differently than she used to. Maybe her calculations are always skewed toward her gratitude for seeing me grow up.

He scratched that out.

It seems it was the fate of humanity to be confronted with extraterrestrial intelligence, like karma or something... we never could treat lesser life with any sort of empathy. Is that the L'rias's perspective?

Another worthless observation. Will stabbed his pen onto the page, making hole after hole. He dug it out and tried again.

What has this all been about? I think a lot about chemotherapy patients, given extra time, but a lessened quality of life. Financial strain and being literally poisoned. That's sort of a scientific angle, isn't it? If science can find a way and we don't use it, then

Will crumbled up the page. This wasn't how he wanted to spend his time. Arqa and everyone he ever knew could be incinerated any minute now! And with that, all the work he'd put into his book would be wasted. No one would ever read it. And he couldn't write an ending. The ending was Arqa's ending. He left his room and went to visit Stephen.

It took four attempts at knocking on the man's door to get him to open it.

"What do you want, Will?"

Will, with butterflies in his stomach, lifted the pile of papers he held. "My book! It isn't done, but I'd like to hear what you think about it."

"Your grandmother has instructed everyone to remain in their rooms while this situation is worked out."

"Yeah, I know. I just thought it was dumb. What do you say?"

"I'll give it to you straight, Will. I'm not remotely interested in anything right now. Lyda is missing and I'm not even allowed to go looking for her."

"Wait, what?"

"Oh, you didn't hear? Yeah, I messed up or something, I don't know. Callum is looking for her as we speak, but... like I said, the UFO outside and stuff. Not a great time. If there's a later, I'll see you then."

He nodded as Stephen shut his door.

Dejected and doubting there would be another time, Will felt cornered. Had he squandered his life?

He wandered through the corridors, apprehensive of being discovered breaking his Grammy's rule. As he went, he thought about how his chronicling project was more about keeping himself busy. Something Will had given his attention to to keep his mind off of Arqa's ultimate fate. But he also knew the reason he'd set out to write about his ship was to make people feel better. So much for that. Siannon was beyond his reach. Most of his friends were on a mission, and his Grammy was trying to keep the ship from sinking.

He thought sleeping might be a good idea.

That was when he first heard Gabriel's voice.

Hey, Will. I could use a quick favor if you aren't too busy.

"Ah, great, as if things weren't bad enough," Will muttered. *What do you want, kid?*

Are you wondering if I'm a hallucination? Everyone else does.

No. Do you know where Lyda is? Her dad's worried sick.

Well, this is easy. No, I don't. Come to the cryo chamber. Where my body is being stored. I don't know about Lyda, but there's some other stuff I've got to tell you.

Chapter Four

1.

Sayaw Sa Bangko was a complicated dance. Mark hoisted Rayna to his level. They stood perched atop an array of stacked benches. All around them, Mark's lab was in ruin. Dancing was Mark's preferred method of exercise, and so he'd taken substantial time out of his schedule over the years to make sure Rayna could step in time with him. She was not a talented dancer, but through arduous practice she had figured out what an inconvenience it was to fall from ten feet up. They stepped in place as fast as they could. "I have one final warning for you, Rayna," he said solemnly.

She guffawed, no doubt happy to take out all of her frustration on the lab's equipment. "Hit me. It's all gone, and I get to know why." Her head was clean-shaven.

"Not all," Mark corrected, waving a finger at her. "Rayna, I get the impression that you think certain information will quell your anxieties. That your heart will be set to rest upon this discovery. Maybe at times that can be the case. But not today. What I'm about to tell you will only amplify your anxiety, not purge it. I'd feel awful guilty winding you up any further. But you're not walking away this time, are you?"

"I've done all you've asked of me. We struck a deal. You can't deny me any longer, Mark." She helped him bounce down to a bench below them.

Mark shook his head. "Nope." He rejoined her at the top bench.

"So where do we begin?" she asked, eyes fluttering.

"With you. Rayna, what is your earliest memory?"

"Hey, I'm here to listen, not get psychoanalyzed!"

"I'd like for you to know why you don't know. I think that's what this story is really about."

"What's that?"

"The memory—now."

"Fine." Rayna ceased her movements. She crossed her arms and craned her neck down to think. "I don't know. That's a dumb question. I don't think about things like that. They told me not to think of Earth."

"You done dancing?"

"I can't balance, dance, and think all at once!"

"Why not? It's a memory. You remember it or not."

"Wrong! It can take time. That doesn't mean I don't remember. You're asking me to sift, prioritize, label." Rayna pondered further. "Earth was nice, yeah? I remember gravity. Real gravity."

"Ah, but you weren't really that old, were you?"

"I couldn't have been if it was Earth. All those memories, they are kind of bunched together. General sensations. Nothing specific."

"Good. See, I've just strained the limits of your cognition." Mark climbed down from the benches, finding one to sit down on. Rayna followed suit, relaxing with her legs folded on the highest bench. "I asked you a question you couldn't quite answer. We are often faced with this issue: our brains have their limit. The idea behind Arqa, it was asking, well, what if our limits were reinforced by our environment? What if staying on Earth was stalling our evolution?"

"But Mark, we had intelligence augmentations. The IC, other supplements—"

"All fun toys, to be sure. But you know the real score."

"Artificial general intelligence," Rayna said, weary.

"And you constantly wonder, what's the holdup? Or why we're doing what we're doing. You have very wonderful deductive reasoning skills. You were a kid when we left Earth. How you remember Earth being nice, that's beyond me. Earth was not nice. To leave took favors. Money, fuel... other resources. I didn't feel we had a choice in staying. And so we did some daring things. Even the voyages on *Star Trek* had a turnaround time. But we've been moving farther and farther from Earth."

"To escape the L'rias," Rayna said.

"Okay, Rayna. But where does that take us?"

"We one day wish to discover a habitable planet, even if it's generations from now."

"How many generations do you think could survive on Arqa?"

"I don't know..."

"Neither did we. Which is why we've never actually considered finding a habitable planet."

"Okay, back to strong AI then."

"Right. And what made us so certain that Arqa was up to the challenge? Efforts on Earth were, officially, completely halted. Partly from frustration, partly from fear."

"You had observed evidence of the L'rias possessing strong AI," Rayna said.

"Yes. A big question we had for a long time was, are we alone in the universe? Great question, tricky to answer. Some people believed aliens visited us in the past, but there was not sufficient evidence. Others claimed they'd encountered aliens or been abducted. Even less likely. Nonetheless, we tried to send out a signal into the universe. Listen back. We *heard* nothing. But if you search for life and all you do is try to listen in one way, you are limiting yourself. An advanced alien civilization isn't necessarily going to use radio waves to communicate. They could have moved past that medium."

Marked looked over to Rayna, expecting a response. "What are you doing?"

"I'm juggling!"

"Those rocks look kind of heavy."

"Do you doubt my ability?"

Mark snarled. "Carry on, if you want to be a clown."

"I can pay attention and juggle at the same time! See? This isn't like dancing."

"Whatever. Look, you're making me nervous."

"Well, we made a deal, and it didn't include no juggling. If you're nervous, then move."

"I shouldn't have to move! You're the one who wanted me to explain, now you're depriving yourself of things you need to know."

Rayna blew a raspberry at him.

"You know Rayna, I was only a year or two older than you are now when I embarked on my first scientific expedition."

"Mark, what's the big epiphany?"

"You are ruining my story."

"Can't stop, won't stop."

Mark jumped up to disturb Rayna's concentration, but it didn't work.

"Maybe if you were taller," she said smugly.

"Where did you even get those rocks?"

"My pockets. Girl's clothes didn't always have pockets, did you know that?"

"We are to be judged, Rayna. You know, it's petulance like this—"

"Yeah, that's all I needed to hear." Rayna let the three rocks drop into her arms, then threw them at Mark's head.

Come to think of it, Mark thought, *this is the first thing I ever told her not to do.* He felt pain before the fall, which was what knocked him out.

2.

"Before you sit down and do your thing Callum, I don't know where Lyda is," Siannon said. "No clue, wish I did. But that's not why I asked you to meet with me."

"A fine time you picked," Callum remarked as he slid a chair in front of Siannon's cell. "You have any idea what's going on out here?"

"I imagine it's none of my business, but go ahead."

"We've got a contact approaching. New. Looks like we're further along than we were led to believe."

"Ah. Well, that feels rather premature." Siannon tugged her left shoulder and massaged it. "I've decided I want to do what I can to stop Leni."

"That'd be a great help," Callum said, pleased. "Look, maybe that'll finally sway Captain Sali to let you out."

"Maybe this is still where I want to be."

"No. Come on, your place is teaching. They miss you, you miss them."

"We can discuss that later. For now, I have things to tell you."

"Can't wait. The floor is yours."

Siannon cracked her neck and began. "Aye, well, we know there's a mutiny brewing on Arqa. We also know what a ludicrous idea that is... depending on the number of participants. And you assume it's fronted by Leni, but is it?"

"Who else?"

There was no turning back now. Siannon explained the device she'd swallowed. The looping message in the unknown location. The edits. "I think we both know who made Leni's message and the device I swallowed."

"If we can prove what you're saying, I finally have evidence on Tim," Callum said excitedly. "I was just with him. I don't trust him. But still... I couldn't think of a way to pin him down without further complications."

"We're beyond worrying about all that by now, aren't we?" Siannon asked. "But I only told you that to cast doubt on Dominique's disappearance."

"Right! If Tim's trying to screw us over... oh, wow."

"Leni has enough resources to sneak people out of the cryo chamber. At least she did. It's not a move she'll be able to make again, but I think that was a distraction. She, and maybe Dominique, could have something bigger planned. That's why I needed to tell you."

"Yeah, I know this isn't easy for you. You might have liked to have the ship in new hands."

Once Siannon was done, Callum was able to oust Tim and gain control of the surveillance feeds. Siannon tried to understand her feelings. Her confession led to many good things, but she could not cast off her guilt. She'd been raised Catholic, after all. Guilt and shame were a constant burden to her, even though she'd renounced her faith. Freeing herself from that deadly disease had isolated her from her parents. She'd gone on to suffer dearly the consequences. And Arqa required of her a kind of secular orthodoxy, perhaps just as perilous. For her to side against Leni, it seemed to reinforce the shy little child she'd been, happy to tattle on sins that were not her own.

With Siannon's insight, Tim was seized and they were able to locate Lyda *and* Leni. And no one could believe where Lyda had gone.

Chapter Five

1.

The jig was super up.

Lyda didn't think it would take them *this* long to find her. At least they couldn't get her now. She stroked Josie's fuzzy back.

"We know she's there, O'Malley. Tell me the truth, right now!" 1st LT Lucio demanded over the comms.

James hesitated from the cockpit of his Spaero. Lyda was scrunched in below him. It was uncomfortable for both of them. Were they not children, they would not have fit inside the cockpit. "Well Lyda?" James asked the girl.

"We're already in trouble," Lyda surmised. "The way I see it, we might as well come clean? What are they going to do, order you to turn back. Fat chance of that!" They were minutes away from the UFO.

"You're right, but still. What a terrible idea. And you *still* haven't told me what you're doing here!"

"A woman can't explain her intuition, James." She'd promised him that if he let her stowaway on the next mission, she'd keep him safe.

"Tell Lucio that."

"You want me to?" Lyda asked. "I guess it's the least I could do." The ship shook and decelerated.

"I'm not doing that," James said. "Something is slowing us down!"

"It feels just like what the others were talking about," Lyda said. The group sent out to defend Arqa had been teleported closer to the L'rias. Was the same thing happening to them? Lyda hoped so. This is why she was out here. This is what she'd been feeling for, ever since her mommy disappeared.

That was why she felt no fear as James's ship went beyond his control. It felt like her dream. Like the séance. She did what she could to talk James through it and responded for him on the comms so he wouldn't have to. But he soon became so overwhelmed at what he was seeing through his vis-cap that he didn't want to pilot his ship anymore.

Lyda was happy to take his place.

The vis-cap offered an ever-shifting display of colors, painting over the usual darkness all around them. The UFO had been expanding this entire time, now it was doing so exponentially. James was upset, but why bother explaining what was happening? No one had listened to Gabriel when he tried.

"It's just like a hug," Lyda said.

The ship jerked again and Lyda let the Spaero roll.

"Are we going to die?" James asked.

"Try to relax, James."

"Clearly you aren't seeing what I saw."

"No one gets to see the same stuff. That's why you're me and I'm you." The UFO's mass was filling out from the edge of the radar's scope to them. Unfolding. It was larger than Arqa now. Larger than a planet.

"We're not going to be able to escape," James said. "Lyda... what's going to happen?"

"I told you, we'll be okay. Do you trust me?"

They passed through the thing that took up the sky. They were inside of it now. Swallowed.

James's Spaero stopped moving a few minutes later.

Beneath her, the boy was terrified.

"This was going to happen no matter what," Lyda assured him. "It's better for you than if I wasn't here."

"Leave me alone, Lyda. I hate this. They're going to get us!"

"James, look. We're not in space anymore. What's all that stuff about fear you were telling me about? I bet, come on, look. It might help!"

James was crying. She felt sad for him.

But that didn't stop her from feeling happy.

2.

"Ladies, gentlemen," Callum began. "Leni has been hiding under the atrium. Tim and who knows how many others have been assisting her in a growing coup. We all know what is happening out there right now. Our kids are going down and we're probably next. Before that happens, let's get Leni. The underside of the atrium is not a great spot to spend your time, but we believe there are people living down there regardless. We also have evidence to suggest she's using some kind of unknown technology to disrupt some of the ship's functions. So we don't know what we're going to be getting into. I say we hold Leni accountable for what she's done. My question to the four of you is, are you ready for whatever we may find?"

A chorus of cheers followed his words.

"Good. We already have two other Regulators standing guard in the opening she crawled into. To be honest, I'm not interested in mincing words with Leni. She's been working against us for who knows how long. After a lot of thought, I have decided that Siannon should join us. We think, since Leni's so fond of Siannon, seeing her on our side might help her see the futility of her plan, whatever that may be." He spared the Regulators the full truth regarding Siannon. He figured it was better that way.

Callum led the team down the corridors, authorized by Captain Sali to kill anyone who did not come willingly from the hiding place. Who else was down there, plotting against them?

As they got closer, Callum realized he was spooked at the thought of going below the atrium. What if—

No, Craig's accident had been just that. An accident.

He patted Siannon on the shoulder. "You sure you're still up for this?"

She looked down at her handgun. "I hate holding it. It—I'm not trained... I just want to talk."

"Here, I'll take it back then. *I* don't want to talk."

"You'll give me a chance with her, won't you?"

"She might be ready to fire back at the first sign of trouble," Callum said. "You'll stand behind us. Use your outdoor voice. And be ready to take cover."

They passed by the Gaze Room, which was full. People were glued to the window, but Callum could not see any fighting, only a strange pasty light that had overtaken space.

What had they done?

3.

Will made it into the cryo chamber, unwilling to admit his purpose there to the technicians.

Thanks, Will, Gabriel said. *So basically, I thought it would be better to go under, but I was wrong. I'm more involved in this than I could have ever imagined. What I saw is* here, *Will. It has our friends. And I can only watch. It's ruined, but beautiful. I can't say what's going to happen, but I'm in it... it wouldn't let me rest.*

Before Will could ask more of Gabriel, he was given a vision. Will found he was ripped from the room he'd been in. He was elsewhere, with *it*. It lacked any defined shape, though it moved frighteningly across space. The thing was enormous. Where there had once been absolute darkness came a painfully bright inversion, materializing then flowing together at separate points until patterns developed over the shrinking void. It varied in color but often returned to an ultra-violet hue. It almost reminded Will of what he saw when he closed his eyes, only the darkness was subordinate to floating specks that formed. He hated it, for it left him utterly stupefied. It was by no means stable, existing differently from moment to moment.

Something bigger, Gabriel expressed.

Will did not respond. It was beyond him.

As the object superimposed itself over the cosmos, it seemed to spiral. Flat arms extended out further and further, flashing different colors faster than Will could discern. Then it slowed and gave off an eerie red glow. Yellow. Silver. Blue. It just kept kicking out the black in every direction Will could see, like a star not bound by gravity, able to dance and stretch. And learn?

Breathe?

Will jolted back as the object morphed from its dreadful abstractions into a singular line, albeit still unfathomably wide, and curving down from the heights of what he could see to the very bottom until it was behind him. There were still see dwindling sections of space, but they were few and far between.

It would touch Will soon, and he did not want that. *Make it stop, Gabriel.*

Will, this isn't a memory. This is outside right now.

Then make me stop seeing it. You're freaking me out.

You must accept this. You'll have to help others adjust. What I'm showing you now, Will, this is our sky. This is where we are. Our lives revolve around this thing. It feasts on death and dark energy. How nice of it.

It's... alive? Will asked shakily. Space was gone now. He blinked, wanting to be away from this... whatever it was. But even that did not spare him.

Sometimes it seems to be, sometimes not. I don't know... I'm sorry.

Gabriel was right. The vision outside of Arqa had changed him.

Desperately, Will pleaded, *You showed me this crazy thing, show me how it was before, please. This is madness and I want it out of my head.* "What's your problem? I can't think straight anymore."

He'd said that out loud. Coming to, he realized he was surrounded by people. They were carrying him. Will wiped drool from his mouth. Leaning back, he tried not to cry out in terror.

He was unsuccessful.

Chapter Six

The comms were open again, though the broadcast range only included the group who'd made for the UFO: Lyda with James, Eric, Trisalyn, Millie, Oliver, Reeve, and Vanessa. Their Spaeros still had power, but they would not moved from where they were parked. Some force was acting down on them. It appeared they'd landed on something solid. Lyda cut through a bout of pointless deliberation on the comms by suggesting, "I think we should get out and look around."

"Okay, you're not even supposed to be here," Vanessa said. "We don't know much about this place, but there sure as hell won't be any oxygen."

"Exactly," added Oliver. "We'd suffocate. It's a wonder the gravity in here hasn't crushed us."

"If the gravity could have hurt us by now, it would have," Reeve said.

"Does anyone even know where we are?" Eric asked.

"Probably some extraterrestrial station," Reeve surmised.

"That isn't possible," said Millie. "Blasphemy."

"Oh great," said Eric. "Now we've got Millie on that."

"Actually, I have a confession to make," said Trisalyn. "Sorry I've been so quiet. I've been processing, because... as soon as we were set down... I wanted out. I cut my oxygen off. Opened my hatch. I waited to freeze or worse. But then I was still breathing. Do you understand? I tried to... end it. But it didn't work. The temperature here, it's odd, but it's not freezing. And there's oxygen."

"Exactly," said Lyda. "We're welcome here. We're not here to die."

"Wrong," said Eric. "Our ships won't move, so we're sitting ducks. Whatever is doing that has complete control over us."

"But we're not trapped," Lyda pointed out. "We can get out. Trisalyn said so."

"I said I'm still breathing," Trisalyn said, exasperated. "There's a difference, Lyda."

"Another lovely piece of trivia for you all, if you don't mind," Reeve said after Trisalyn's words were left hanging. "We're not the only ships in this lot. Anyone else notice that yet?"

"I'm not hearing them on the comms," Vanessa said.

"Raptured," Millie said.

"Shut up, Millie," said Eric.

"If the others got sucked in here, then they probably came to the same conclusion I did," Lyda said. "How many other ships, James?" He was back in the cockpit with the vis-cap.

James spent a moment counting them up. "Besides us, there's another fifteen."

"What?!" Oliver said. "Get out of here. Arqa doesn't have that many ships."

Lyda elbowed James. "I'm tired of all this back and forth. Do you really want to sit here all day? At least let me out."

"Don't be stupid," Oliver cautioned.

"I'm not. I'm listening to the facts. Trisalyn tried to lose air from her ship and it didn't work. We're—"

"Please, Lyda! I'm too afraid to leave. I don't want to breathe whatever oxygen is out there."

"James, it's going to be okay if we leave."

"I don't trust you anymore. You knew this stuff would happen."

"Wrong." Into the comms, Lyda said, "What would 1st LT Lucio order you to do? I think she wanted you to check this place out."

"Leave us alone," said Eric. "I ain't leaving my ship."

"Guys, how could this place be supporting us?" Trisalyn asked. "We have oxygen. I'm looking out at the surroundings. Do you know what it reminds me of? This whole place is like being inside a bubble. The boundaries are colorful; filmy. It's never a single still thing..."

"Evil is attractive," said Millie. "It has to be. It is tempting you. Trisalyn, close your breach."

"If this air's evil, I've already got it in me, Millie. I'm fine with it."

"No!"

"Chill out."

"Trisalyn's corrupted!"

"If you say so. Might as well look around some more."

"No, Trisalyn, please stay put," James said, shoving Lyda's face from the receiver.

"You can't see where the top ends," Trisalyn said.

"James, I'm really sorry about this," Lyda said, shifting away from him. "If you don't want to be my friend anymore, I'll understand, but I'm leaving."

"NO!" he bellowed. She'd never seen him so bothered before. She'd never seen *anyone* so bothered before. It hurt that he could not trust her. Like a rabid animal in that confined space, James wrestled and lashed out at her until the two were out of breath. Being practically the same size, the two were very evenly matched. But Lyda was a little older, and more motivated. To end the bout, she kneed her poor friend in his groin, first grabbing his shoulders with her hands then thrusting into him with the last of her energy. Both of them reeled from the impact and Lyda hit the back of her head off the Spaero's console. There were tears and baleful words from both sides, James was powerless to stop her from opening the hatch.

As she hobbled out, in a last-ditch effort, James tugged back on her shins.

"I will kick you as many times as I need to until you let me go, James."

That did the trick. He let go so completely that she slid out of the opening and fell straight onto the luminescent surface below. Though no part of her skin touched it she felt like it had. It was just as Trisalyn had described it. Lyda pressed into it and it gave way, almost as if it was sand. Like sand, but devoid of moisture and denser. The more pressure she applied, the lower it went, though the material never ruptured.

She rose and watched the spot she'd toyed with, seeing it assume its initial level.

From above, she heard the hatch to James's Spaero closing, and the boy chattering his teeth as if he was freezing. But it was not cold here. It wasn't warm, but it wasn't cold either.

As she ambled forward, she found her steps did not disturb the surface as her hands had moments ago. Lyda saw the other ships. She looked all around her, taking it in. This place, whatever it was, was incalculably massive. At times it felt like she was in a sphere, other times she was in a cube. Nothing appeared wholly together, but the structure itself was homogeneous in its design. She tried just standing still. The surface stayed the same.

"Cactiflower," she said. The noise traveled, but not far.

Next, she took a deep breathe in. This oxygen was not exactly like Arqa's. No, it was superior. Was it purer?

All the ships were parked equidistant to one another. Trisalyn came out next. Lyda did not contemplate her next move, and was shocked to discover that one moment she was standing about three yards away from Trisalyn, the next moment she was jumping up into her arms. Trisalyn looked surprised as well. Putting Lyda down, Trisalyn said, "Let's not do whatever that was again."

"Yeah, it's like time skipped or something," Lyda observed.

"Well, we're here," Trisalyn said. "Just like you wanted."

"The others will come in their own time."

"Why did you go into James's ship for this mission, Lyda?"

Lyda wanted to smile. No, she wanted to burst out laughing. She studied Trisalyn's face but saw only concern. Trisalyn no doubt wanted to know more, but something else had snagged her attention. She raced to the Spaeros and looked them over obsessively.

Eric disembarked from his ship. "Not the worst place to die, I'll give you that kid."

"Stop saying that," Lyda said. "Die if you feel like. I'm going to be alive!" She did a somersault. "Oh. I forgot something!" She returned to James's Spaero and knocked.

"Leave me alone," James said.

"Hey, I'm not here to push you out. I just need Josie."

"Will you leave me alone then?"

Lyda agreed, and Josie was dropped down to her.

She went over to where Trisalyn, Eric, and Oliver were standing over by the other row of ships. They were not from Arqa, but they did look like they were from Earth.

"I got to say, this does not feel real," Oliver said, dumbfounded.

"I feel like I want to agree with you, but then it'll only diminish reality more," said Trisalyn.

"Look, Reeve's out too," Lyda said, pointing to him.

"Are we going to check and see if those other ships work?" Eric asked.

"You can, but I want to explore."

"This place seems too big to traverse," Trisalyn said. "Besides, aren't you scared? You get where we are, right? This has got to be the L'rias's mother ship!"

Lyda shrugged. "If that's the case, we'll probably never see Arqa again." She said this passively, distracted by the sensations around her.

"And you're okay with that?"

"I think it's best we find another place. Those ships aren't the answer."

"And how would you know?" Eric asked, flaring his nostrils. He stepped in front of the girl.

Lyda gave him a thumbs-up.

"Lyda, I don't understand how you can be so calm," Trisalyn said.

"This is enemy territory."

"Okay, but where's the enemy?" Lyda looked back and forth, raising her hand above her forehead and turning in every direction. "I see nothing trying to hurt us. If anything, we're being helped!"

"There's no echo in here," noted Reeve. "This room looks like it goes up higher than a mountain, but there's no echo."

Lyda skipped down the row of Spaeros, swinging Josie in her arms. "What's our next move, Josie?"

Josie was not sure.

"Are we just going to let her screw around?" Vanessa asked. "She's just a kid!"

"I'm two steps from playing hopscotch with her myself," Oliver said.

Some time passed by. They determined the room was as wide as the rows of ships. Beyond that, walls boxed them in. By then, the others had coaxed James and Millie out of their ships, if for no other reason than to stay together.

The group checked the ships across from theirs. The engines started, but like their ships, something was pinning them down.

This compelled them to lie down, though some raised objections, concerned the floor would absorb them.

Eventually, Eric said, "It reminds me... of the sky."

"Hmm," said Trisalyn.

"I miss space. This isn't natural."

"Is anybody hungry?" Reeve asked.

No one was. Considering it had been at least a few hours since their last dose of Siranis Fluid, they should have been hungry.

They grew sedated on the surface, no longer making observations or asking questions. Just when Lyda was thinking how badly she wanted something to happen, their surroundings smeared with more ferocity than ever before. The group directed their attention to where the ripples began to see an aperture of darkness. Had it always been there? Lyda understood that was where they'd entered from. It opened wider. It was quite far off from them, but something was coming.

Millie panicked. "It's Hell. We're in Hell!"

"Can everyone hear that?" Lyda asked them.

"Okay, that portal makes it seem like something's coming for us," said Reeve.

This suspicion sent most of them back to their ships in fear, but

Lyda stayed. She even got Oliver and James to remain by holding their hands. The area seemed to rage. It did not add up.

Lyda assumed that if she followed her instincts, she would be safe. They would all be safe.

And why wouldn't that be the case? A child's mind doesn't need mountains of evidence or detailed explanations to believe in something. Until that moment, Lyda had been sure she was doing the right thing. And yet, in spite of that certitude, something else came to her. That no matter how orderly her perceived destiny seemed, she was only a small, temporary thing. Something greater had beckoned her, though what Lyda thought of as "greatness" was actually very terrible thing.

Chapter Seven

1.

Siannon wasn't particularly interested in clawing her way through the confined space, but she had pledged to help Callum. A hatch in the atrium brought them down. It was poorly lit and much hotter than the rest of Arqa. One of the Regulators had a Geiger counter because this layer of the ship was closer to the hull. The pseugra was also less effective here, and that made an already challenging path even worse.

No doubt the ship would be boarded soon. The enemy would be merciless. Siannon had lived under their brand of mayhem on Earth. She felt the Geiger counter was a bit of a joke, given the situation. After seeing the way things looked outside, this territorial dispute seemed minor.

Some time had passed since Leni's message had played in her mind. No one had worked on her, so Leni had either turned the looped message off or designed it to play a certain number of times. "Can we move any faster?" Siannon asked Callum.

Callum shook his head. Between her and him were four Regulators. "Hello?" he called out into the space.

"Hold it!" Leni's voice suddenly sounded.

"You're outnumbered, Leni," one of the Regulators said. "We've come to take you out of here."

"You'll lose if you try," Leni said. "This is my place and you don't know what I'm capable of."

"Leni, stop!" Siannon called out. She squeezed past the Regulators and saw Leni. The woman looked dirty, feral. Unarmed. Callum and the others had a great shot at her, should they need to take it. Leni was only seven feet in front of them with her hands up. The ceiling was even lower where Leni was hunched over.

"Siannon. I take it you helped find me?"

Siannon nodded.

"Not bad, friend."

Siannon looked away from Leni. "You want to hurt people."

"Captain Sali has already hurt the children!"

"This isn't a debate," Callum said. "Leni, are you coming willingly or not?"

Siannon noticed movement behind Leni.

"Kind of sadistic of Sali to send you down here," Leni said. "Craig might have had his first little fainting spell right where we squat." She tapped her finger right above them.

"We don't care what happens to us, as long as we drag you out," said Callum.

"I'm not the one you're really interested in. I'm just a kind of middle-woman." A figure stepped out from behind Leni, shielding her. Siannon couldn't tell who it was... but she wouldn't be surprised if there was a dog nearby.

Siannon felt the pressure of her poor posture grating on her bones despite the lax pseugra. "You claim you're working to protect the children, but it's over, don't you get it? And you were hiding this entire time. If there was something you could have done, that time has passed. That's why I gave you up. Leni, it's over. Don't create more violence. Please." Feeling lightheaded, Siannon put on the oxygen mask she had slung on her shoulder. After a deep whiff, she put it down.

"Reveal yourself or I'll shoot," Callum said to the figure. It was like something Rayna would wear. Not that trick again.

"Don't hurt her!" Leni pleaded.

Callum jerked his head back to regard Siannon. "Is it?"

"I—" Siannon's body was flung forward with no regard for the terrible pain the movement generated. She was going straight for Callum.

"Callum, I'm not doing this!" Siannon cautioned. It was just like before, in the classroom with the children. Someone was controlling her!

Leni was laughing. "C'mon." The duo fell into shadows. The Regulators couldn't get a shot at them, as Siannon and Callum's altercation was blocking their view.

Callum dropped his gun. Siannon swung at him. Her hits landed because there was nowhere for him to back away.

"Siannon, I don't care what's happening but you need to stop."

"I understand," she said, almost head-butting him. "I can't. Something's taken me over."

The Regulators approached the fray. Callum demanded they stop Leni and let him worry about Siannon. It made sense. She was a fragile woman and not remotely a threat to him.

As much as she tried to resist and keep her body from striking the man again, it was pointless. She waited for the inevitable counterattack.

"You say you're being controlled somehow?" Callum asked. "I believe you. Try to fight it."

"I can't," Siannon said as he dodged one of her blows. "This is hurting me so badly! You're going to have to do something."

Callum grabbed her by the hair, and though the pain was immediate, her body still did not stop. It resorted to trying to bite him.

"Callum, I don't want to do this anymore. Can't you just—the gun is right there, Callum!"

"This will pass."

"No. I want to die. I don't want to see what happens next. So what if we get Leni? Someone is piloting my body."

"Don't be a coward! We can fix this."

"Please, I helped you. You said you owe me one, didn't you? Didn't you see outside? We were never supposed to see that!"

"I know, I know. But how can you ask that of me?" Siannon's body wriggled as he secured her in a headlock.

Beyond them, there was a commotion. People raising their voices indistinctly.

"I told you. Callum, I don't care. She's using me against you. Please. Let this be it." She punched his lower back, and he loosened his hold. Thoughts of the gun came to her. Yes, she wanted it for herself, but she also knew what her body would do if it got the gun. It would target Callum.

"You need to stop me!" Siannon shoved him away from the gun on the floor and made for it herself.

"Enough is enough," Callum said.

The gun was in her hands. Before she rolled over to take aim, a crippling pain assailed her. Her vision flashed.

But she was still able to fire off three rounds before the pain devoured her.

2.

The last person to be changed by what had come was Carlos.

He was drifting in his Spaero between waking and sleeping, having dozed off from hours spent alone with his thoughts. Fantasies where he was not ridiculed. Where he'd saved the day, instead of being tossed off as a sacrifice for the scientists of Arqa. It might have lasted longer, if it were not for the pulling.

Carlos, alerted, underwent a miserable process. He was alone and could not reach anyone on the comms. The controls would not respond to his actions, though occasionally it felt as if he'd whirl away and be free to his whims once more. If the L'rias wanted him, he would make it easy on them. Sadly, he was no stronger than his body, and he knew from his radar that the force which pulled him was the UFO. It had become a monster in the sky.

Carlos believed this was death. And he laughed uncontrollably, unsure why.

He stopped. It had taken him in. His Spaero was set down and no longer moved.

Carlos tried the comms again, being unable to wrest his ship out of place. "Anybody there?"

Only static greeted him.

"Central?"

How could he have deserted the battle? What if he was alone now? Alone with whatever *this* was?

"Carlos, you're alive?!" a voice asked between the static. Trisalyn!

Carlos eagerly responded. "Are you safe?"

"We all got pulled in at the same time." She brought him up to speed, and eventually the others talked him out of his ship. They looked like his team, but he was also not feeling very trustworthy considering where they were.

All the same, he issued an apology to them. "I abandoned the mission."

"Yeah, jerk move, but we still ended up in the same place," Vanessa said. "Welcome back, stuck in here with the rest of us."

Carlos realized they weren't going to censure him any more than that. "Looks like you're all okay."

"It's her," Oliver said, gesturing to Lyda.

"Whoa, Lyda, what are you doing here?"

"She's lost her mind!" Eric said without pretense.

"Did you see me?" Lyda asked. "I was jumping up and down. Waving and making noise. I figured you might be a little scared, so if you saw me it might help."

"No," Carlos admitted. "I can't say I noticed you, sorry. Is Arqa okay? What about the rest of Flight Division?"

"We're cut off from Arqa," said Trisalyn. "We don't know where anyone else is, so it's safe to say we're on our own."

"Yeah," said Oliver. "We've been here for a while and you're the first interesting thing that's happened."

"Maybe now that they have us all together, they'll come," Vanessa speculated.

Carlos looked beyond the others to see Millie pacing. He did not like her erractic movements as she mumbled to herself. Then he looked at Lyda, who was slapping the floor. "Hey, you're not supposed to be here."

"My mommy says the odds of me and you and anyone being born are nearly impossible."

"That's not what I meant. You aren't in Flight Division. What are you doing on this mission?"

"The chances are basically zero. That's what my mommy said. So what if I'm not supposed to be someplace?"

"Oh, that's cool," Carlos said sarcastically. "My mom told me nothing because she's dead, but I'm sure if she wasn't she'd say cool things to me too. Hey, did you know the odds of you and me and anybody dying is a hundred percent guaranteed?"

"Hey, my mommy isn't dead like yours!"

"Lyda, do you realize where we are? This is that UFO!" Lyda was crestfallen at that, making Carlos feel like a jerk. "Sorry. I'm just stressed. This is too heavy."

"You don't like it here?"

"What, you do?"

"Don't tell me you prefer the air on Arqa?"

"Maybe so. But this isn't right. You've got Reeve and Oliver saying over there they should be tired and hungry. What if this place has, like, cut us off from our body's signals?"

"We did get kind of lazy before you got here. But maybe it's just because we had to wait for you."

"Why?" Carlos asked.

Lyda shrugged. "Maybe this room won't always be here. This place shifts. I'd rather figure out the puzzle and move on."

"You think this is some kind of test, then? Did—did Gabriel tell you about this?"

"Duh, silly," said Lyda mockingly. "This is what he was trying to tell everybody about before they put him under!"

"Tell? No, he wasn't telling. He was warning us. He was *scared*. You're supposed to be scared."

"You'll need a better face than that. Try this!" Lyda contorted her face and made monster noises. That seemed to startle Millie.

"Eric was right! You *have* lost it. Look, we've both had a chat with Gabriel. When he talked to me, he didn't tell me about this. So did you or not?"

"If it makes you feel better, yes, Gabriel did tell me about this place. B3. Or the Felled. The real name doesn't matter, because we wouldn't be able to say it anyway, so call it one of those. At least we can look up."

"Okay, now we're getting somewhere. So he told you to come here? But for what?"

"Well, in your words, he warned me if I come here, I might do some fun stuff."

Trisalyn walked over to them. "What are you two talking about?"

"Fun stuff," said Lyda.

"Look, Millie isn't doing so hot. Lyda being so happy-go-lucky is making it worse. None of us know what to do. You got any ideas?"

"Me?" Carlos asked. "I'm with Millie!"

"Don't say that!" Lyda said harshly. "Can't you tell? This place—it makes what—"

Millie cried out as if in agony.

"Millie, you're fine," Eric said. "You're fine. What are you going on about?"

"Is this spacesia?" James asked tentatively.

"It doesn't happen on the drop of a hat like this," Vanessa said. "She's snapped because we're in a genuinely crazy place."

Carlos heard, but refused to look back over at Millie. "It's that woman," she babbled. "That devil, she's brought us to our ultimate resting place. I let you ruin it—now I get it, we all get it. There is no lust in heaven. We're inside a dead god's brain. This place can feel my trembling. It is but an illusion. They warned us, we were all warned!"

"Lucio's been bracing everyone on Arqa for a fight we can't win," Lyda explained to the group, raising her voice to talk over Millie. "I don't know if I believe her anymore. I actually don't trust them that much. What happened to Miss Siannon? I mean, is what they said about hostile aliens even true?"

"Idiot," said Vanessa. "Why don't you stop? Millie's about to have a nervous breakdown and I'm tired of listening to you. You're a child, you don't understand how—"

"Guys." It was Trisalyn. She stepped away from the others.

"What?" Lyda asked. "I say ignore her!"

"Yeah, that makes me feel better," said James.

"No, look just beyond Millie," said Trisalyn. New ripples were forming. Undulations on the wall, moving toward the surface. The place shook, making Carlos struggle to keep his balance.

"Lady, relax!" Lyda urged. Her voice came out louder than it should have been able to. The spot where the disturbance was grew. Something emerged and stretched out, separating from the floor.

"Lyda?" Carlos asked as everyone backed away. Everyone but Millie, who stared squarely at the presence.

"Millie, move!" Trisalyn hissed. The transparent bulge advanced toward Millie. Millie made the sign of the cross with her fingers. The rest of them huddled up, not running, for fear of creating more ripples in that tumultuous place.

"We can't leave her there," said Oliver.

"Yeah, go grab her, be my guest," said Eric.

"She's catatonic or something, she doesn't see it coming," said Reeve.

"Are we really going to let this happen?" Trisalyn asked. "Millie! Get over here."

Still, the delirious woman did not respond.

Further rumbling knocked Carlos and the group off of their feet. They made for the Spaeros to steadied themselves.

"Kid, you going to help our friend or what?" Vanessa asked Lyda.

"I'm going to help you and say, don't ever think of doing what she's doing."

Millie was still standing as the thing approached her. It was at least ten feet tall. She bowed to it.

That's when it tackled her and sent her flying high above them. Carlos thought he saw the thing sink into the floor, then the woman's body bashed against a high wall a great distance away. A streak appeared after she fell: blood.

The worst of that violent exchange was the way Millie's body drifted down, going at a much slower rate than when she'd been hit. All the while, her intermittent shrieking seemed to fill the walls in a synesthetic display. Carlos knew she had to be dead, but her pain lasted all around them. The group searched everywhere, looking for where the thing had gone. They could not tell if their petrification in place was from shock or if the place had them anchored down for its next strike.

EPISODE 6

Of Falling and Flying

Prologue

Funny things were taking place.

Here, there, elsewhere.

Even *he* could tell that much.

Rayna: I did it.

Craig: What an honor this is.

Rayna: I don't know, we'll probably both get in trouble for that.

Craig: It's worth it for a chance to really chat.

Rayna: If you say so.

Craig: If I were you, I would not leave the lab. Not for a while longer.

USE.

He was of use.

Rayna: Are you sure he wasn't going to tell me?

Craig: I'm not sure he could.

Rayna: What do I do while I wait?

Craig: Well, I did discover something. The person who scarred you was the same one who tried to frame you for when Jun got out. I think that's very interesting.

Rayna: Leni.

Craig: Leni. A brash woman. Quite a cruel thing to do to a child. You mind her from now on.

Rayna: What does she have to do with the L'rias, Craig?

Craig: Oh, actually, I believe the two topics are entirely unrelated. I just hated you not knowing who you are. You spent so much time making sure I knew who I was. You and I, we're bound to orbit one another. And I like that.

Rayna: Okay?

Craig: We're just at the mercy of our Maker. Don't worry though. Remember, you're not a robot, right?

Rayna: That's not what you said when you were still alive. You thought you were really funny. Now look at you.

Craig: Well, don't you remember that day in the office when I was just a newborn? Felicia was there too!

Rayna: I was still little. My earliest memory. They told me to watch the babies. They told me not to fuss with them. I wasn't going to fuss, I just wanted to play. I never got to play anymore.

Craig: Poor thing.

Rayna: You know, some people might make the case that that wasn't you. If you were the actual Craig, you wouldn't remember that memory so vividly, since you were only an infant.

Craig: Exactly. That's the difference, isn't it? You were what, four, five years old?

Rayna: Why did Leni hurt me, Craig? Why did she take away my shine?

Craig: That's not productive! Let me get to the point. So I have memories where I wasn't an AI. That moment in a cradle with Felicia. Now you remember that too. Do you have memories then? Of when you weren't an AI?

Rayna: I've cut myself. To prove I'm human. I've had scans done. Why are you trying to convince me of something that isn't true?

Craig: Ah, but I don't lie. I don't lie.

Rayna: Then tell me why Leni hurt me.

Craig: Accident my decaying butt!

Rayna: I need to know Craig, I want to be safe. Maybe she'll come for me. What does she want?

Craig: I think things are going to turn around real soon, you know. You'll be able to juggle no matter what. Look out a window!

Rayna: I feel like that was sort of impulsive for me to hit Mark like that, as you asked. I think coconuts would have been more appropriate than rocks. So Mark was up to something? Did I stop him?

Craig: Good question. My answer: there was once a star. But that star is long gone. It was especially special, though. We now ride upon the last of its dust.

Chapter One

1.

The group mustered up the courage to approach where Millie's body had landed. Half of her head had been smashed in, crushed into itself. Blood spewed out of her and onto the surface, where it oozed and puddled. Lyda noticed the way the blood was rising above the floor, little droplets dancing and working against the gravity that was also allowing them to walk.

"Does anyone else think she might get back up?" Eric asked. "That's what it feels like."

"Yeah," Carlos agreed. "Like whatever hit her could possess her or something."

"Stop," Lyda said.

"What then?" Carlos asked.

"A way out," said Vanessa. "Obviously."

"No," said Lyda. "I think we should want to see more."

"More?" James asked. "What about what just happened to Millie?"

"I think she's beyond our help."

"Obviously."

"You seem to know a whole lot about this place," Trisalyn said accusingly. "Yet you haven't explained how."

"I don't know everything," Lyda said, unable to take her eyes off of Millie. It was disgusting. The second time she'd seen gore. It wasn't right to look. But Lyda couldn't stop. B3 shouldn't have done that.

Trisalyn, Oliver, and Vanessa took the time to cover Millie up with whatever they could find in the ships. Lyda's attention went to the walls.

"Why don't we try to work on the ships?" Carlos asked.

"I don't see what good that'll do," Vanessa said. "They don't seem to have any mechanical issues."

"Besides," Oliver said, "this thing's probably swallowed Arqa by now. Here's about as good as anywhere else."

"That thing might just pick us off one by one!" Eric said.

"It *may* still be in here, sure," said Lyda, "but I keep telling you, waiting to get hit like Millie won't help. Look at the wall. This place is gigantic. We are only in one part. There is a way, if you believe. If you believe no harm will come to you... or if most of us do, we should be fine."

"I don't trust you one bit. You were saying these things before Millie was killed."

"Arqa's democratic," said Carlos. "Why don't we vote on it?"

"We're not citizens of Arqa, kid," Vanessa said.

"Don't, Vanessa," Oliver said. "That doesn't matter."

"No, they deserve to know. We fought Sali and Arqa so they wouldn't mess with this stuff. And who gets to be the landing party? Us. Fucking terrific."

While the group bickered, Lyda kept her concentration on a single spot on the wall. It paid off. "Look where I'm looking. I told you already. Look, something new is opening up." An aperture appeared within walking distance, like a sliding door on Arqa.

A vote was cast. Vanessa, Trisalyn, and Reeve were opposed to exploring the newfound exit.

"Alright," said Eric, looking down at where Millie was. "Beats hanging out with her I guess."

Lyda led the way out, deeper into B3 to find her mommy.

2.

Kalyna and the rest of Flight Division struggled in a sea of enemies.

The L'rias mother ship was big, but not as big as Kalyna had thought it would be. Based on the radar's data, its dimensions were only about one and a half times larger than Arqa's.

She had already used up every round of the femtolon. While it had seemed very effective, Kalyna wished she knew if it had hit the mother ship. It seemed like smaller ships were acting as shields.

That was a hard loss for Kalyna to swallow. If only it had hit, she could have ended this.

"Well, it was worth a try," Deirdre said over the comms. She was doing great for her first, and probably last, battle. They'd lost contact with the other team sent out to investigate the UFO. Janos was confirmed dead.

Kalyna could still get through on the comms to Arqa. "We don't have a chance to escape. Should we just try to... crash into the mother ship?"

"No," 1st LT Lucio said. "Kalyna, don't do that."

"Alright, but what do I do when I'm all out of ammo?" Turning tail was futile, but staying could be just as bad. Kalyna thought she hadn't been hit yet because many of the enemy ships were making toward Arqa. Kalyna and her team couldn't do anything about those, as they were too far away.

"I'm going to do as much damage as possible," Ying said.

Kalyna appreciated the sentiment. "Ying, thank you for protecting our home. I know it's hard for you."

"Not very. I live there too. Thank you for stopping my sister. I wonder though, would we be in this situation if she had succeeded?"

Kalyna thought long and hard about that. Then she prioritized her attention on the battle. The best solution would be to fire upon the closest vessel she could find.

She shifted the settings of her vis-cap, wanting to see the L'rias ships for herself. She'd been told she'd never get this close. As a girl, she'd always thought it was weird how her dad or Miss Siannon hesitated to describe the look of the aliens or their technology. Kalyna was too far from the mother ship, so she captured a few stills of the fighter ships. The ships did not look too dissimilar from their Spaeros. The only thing that looked extraterrestrial was the surrounding space.

Kalyna had to report the stills. This meant something. She told 1st LT Lucio, who explained that the L'rias might be using materials of Earth to toy with them.

Shortly after, trouble found Kalyna. Five ships formed a vanguard and were coming toward her.

Rage flared up inside of the girl. This wasn't a fair fight. She fired carelessly in their direction, not feeling she had enough time to target them before they could finish her off.

Chapter Two

1.

It felt to Carlos like he could go for days on end.

The cylindrical path never got too steep or difficult to traverse. It also appeared to be tailored to them, as it did not come up much higher than Reeve, who was the tallest one of the group. They walked in a single file. After Lyda, the line went James, Trisalyn, Reeve, Oliver, Carlos, Vanessa, and Eric in the rear.

Aside from being slightly darker, the material around them was the same. Sturdy yet pliable. Smooth and perplexing. A light traveled just behind them via the material. It was like a stalker, always back just enough to make them have to check over their shoulders and make sure it was still beneath the surface. They walked in silence most of the time, trying to comprehend their new reality. There were no places to go besides further down the path.

When Carlos's mind wandered, he forced himself to focus. Lyda had soothed James and together the two were treating the whole expedition like it was a game.

"This is bullshit," Vanessa said, halting the line. "I'm not sure how much further I want to go. It feels like we could step out right into space."

"Well, we've been walking away from the aperture we came through," Trisalyn said. "Who knows for how long? This can't go on forever."

"I still don't know why we left our ships behind. For what?" Eric asked.

"Because we can," Lyda said.

"Oh, yeah," said Eric. "Because that mentality always leads to great things."

"I can't wrap my head around it," Trisalyn said. "How this place is conducive to humans. Has what we need to survive. But where are the systems? The electricity, the vents, the goods—you know?"

"Anyone want to burrow into the walls?" Reeve asked.

"What?" Carlos asked.

"Maybe we could pluck that light out."

"It's a nice idea. Having a light that follows you," said Eric.

"I'm a man of the classics," said Oliver. "Lightbulbs for me."

"Why would you want to mess with it?" Eric asked, snorting. "You're cracked, Reeve."

"Eh," Reeve said.

"Are you planning on negotiating with them?" Vanessa asked Lyda.

"Is that what you think we should do?" Lyda asked back.

"No. I was just trying to figure out how stupid you were."

"I'm not enjoying your negativity," Trisalyn remarked to Vanessa. "Do you have something more constructive to say?"

"Maybe I'll just scream for that monster to come back."

"That's not a funny thing to joke about," Lyda said.

Vanessa's hands balled into fists. "I wasn't joking. We're as good as dead either way."

"Knock it off, Vanessa," said Oliver.

"Yeah, you try anything like that, and I'll throw you to it myself," said Eric.

"How heroic," Vanessa said with a snide expression.

"Quit bickering," Carlos said, annoyed.

"Whatever," said Vanessa.

Carlos could tell Lyda had changed since losing her mother. She was an entirely different person. And since they'd landed, it was like something had taken her over. There was this blind confidence. It had wavered around the attack on Millie, but it was back now. He grew paranoid, wondering if these were truly his shipmates. As much as he wanted someone like Trisalyn or Oliver to tell him how preposterous that was, he also thought verbalizing it could make it seem more true. He felt the toll of not knowing how much time had passed.

"Lyda, why don't we think really hard about what happened to Arqa, and maybe we'll learn something?" Carlos asked after a period of silence.

"You have the option to do that but I'm putting my focus on something else."

"Okay. Isn't anyone wondering how Arqa's doing, though?"

"A thought like that isn't going to make us feel any better," Oliver said. "When we got taken into this UFO, Arqa lost half of Flight Division."

"That's right," said Reeve. "At best, they're vulnerable right now."

"I'm with you, Carlos," said Trisalyn. "I'll believe we'll see Arqa safely again."

Later on, they finished the last of their Siranis Fluid. They hadn't felt the need to use the pouches, but they did all the same, knowing their bodies had probably gone a long time without nutrients. That was when Lyda suggested they stopped, even though the group was still not fatigued.

"We'd usually need sleep by now, right?" Trisalyn asked.

"Could you sleep, if you wanted to?" Eric asked.

"No way," said James.

"It's because we've been asleep this entire time," Lyda said cryptically.

"Huh?" Trisalyn asked.

"When Gabriel spotted this place, the Sleeping Sickness hit Arqa," Lyda elaborated. "Which one of you had it?"

"I wasn't even there," said Eric. "I mean, most of us here were in stasis."

"Trisalyn did, didn't you?" Carlos asked.

Trisalyn nodded. Lyda encouraged Trisalyn to say more about her experience, but Trisalyn grew defensive. That disappointed Carlos. It seemed like Lyda was going to give them more, but the group went quiet again and sat apart from one another.

Carlos made his way over to Oliver. "Oliver, hey, I had a question."

"Shoot."

"So when Jun was holding you all hostage, my uncle told me about you guys. You were talking about it earlier. You're prisoners. Why was that kept so hush-hush?"

Oliver's eyes darted away from Carlos. "We have to fight. We don't want to fight for Captain Sali. That's all there is to it."

"I know. It's terrible. Trust me. I'm not having fun. But what I don't get is—I mean, what else were we supposed to do? Were we supposed to let the L'rias win?"

"It's highly unlikely they would have killed you kids, which is another reason Captain Sali sent you out, along with us."

Reeve came over to them. "I don't think we should discuss this stuff with them, Oliver. Remember what happened to Siannon?" Reeve tapped his forehead. "You never know what they did up here."

"Let him do what he wants!" Eric said.

"Are you saying if you didn't have certain programming, you would have wanted to mutiny like Jun?" Trisalyn asked.

"How we got here is irrelevant," Vanessa said. "I'm tired of hearing all these dumb questions. Actually, I'm tired of more than that. We're following a child... that weird little girl. She's taking us somewhere, aren't you?"

Lyda nodded. "You don't need to be afraid. I'm trying to get us to where we can get the most helpful information."

"Well, I have a better idea. You've shown us we can do whatever we want in here, right?"

"What's your point, Vanessa?" Trisalyn asked.

"What if my intuition is telling me we should go say," she pointed upward, "that way?"

"Then go," said Lyda dryly.

"I think it's best if we stay together," said Reeve. "Imagine getting lost in here."

"You don't think we're already lost?" Vanessa asked. "She's taking us farther and farther away from our ships."

Lyda pointed to a spot on the wall. "I'm done with this." She made a circle against the wall with her pointer finger, and a new opening appeared. "That should be the way back. It will probably take you as long as it took us to get this far. I hope not, but if all you're going to do is be mean to me, I'd rather you leave."

"Vanessa's not wrong," said Eric. "Maybe the youngest one here shouldn't be the one in charge."

Carlos hadn't thought of that. "Eric had a fair point."

"You're right," Lyda said. "There's no reason for any of you to be following me. I asked James to help me get here, but I don't need anyone's help anymore. I'm just trying to make sure James gets back okay now to return a favor. I'm only working off of this feeling inside." The girl brought her hands to her chest. "Does nobody else believe we're destined to be here? Like there's something we need to do?"

"Nope," Vanessa said plainly. "I'm going back."

"Now who's being stupid?" Reeve asked her.

"Yeah, I would not do that," Eric advised.

"Then don't," Vanessa snapped. She crawled into the opening Lyda had created. As it shut, the group heard a piercing scream from within. Lyda hopped forward after Vanessa, and the others reluctantly followed.

The opening led to a place Carlos thought was like the path they'd traveled previously, but there was something new there. Vanessa was doubled over on the ground, shaking. About a yard in front of her was a row of bodies—human—sprawled out. The surfaces and walls were blood-splattered. Smeared with handprints. Organs. An arm stuck out of the wall, as if it was being consumed. The group huddled together, scrambling for the opening. It was no longer there.

They counted five bodies in all. Reeve examined them. They were dead.

"Does anyone recognize these people?" Carlos asked in a low voice. No one did. Some wore g-suits, but others were just wearing shirts.

"What is that, a Hawaiian shirt?" Eric asked.

"Aloha," said Oliver. "Coconut trees and all that."

Carlos thought it looked snazzy. Aside from the fact that parts of it were caked with viscera.

Lyda went even closer than Reeve had. Carlos thought she must have been making sure her mom wasn't one of the bodies.

"Could these people be from the cryo chamber?" Trisalyn asked Eric.

"Sure," Eric blurted out. "I don't know."

"Who cares about them?" Vanessa asked. She got up and stomped toward Lyda. "You just told me this way would lead me back to our ships. So why did your little trick take me here?"

Trisalyn got between Lyda and the truculent woman. "She went in right after you, Vanessa."

"You have a limited amount of time to calm down," Lyda advised.

"Or what?" Vanessa asked sternly.

Eric punched Vanessa in the back of her head. "She said quit bugging out. Can't you tell the wall's reacting to it?"

Carlos looked. Eric was right. The colors rushed and pulsed around them.

"I came here because I knew you felt like you were in danger," Lyda said. "This is the way back to the ships. Vanessa, what will you do now?"

"How do you think those people died, Lyda?" Vanessa asked. "Looks like whatever it was got all of them good."

"The same way as Millie. We're not supposed to worry about them. They're already gone. We're not."

"Look at the way they're positioned," James said.

Carlos did. The bodies seemed to be pointing the opposite direction of the opening Lyda had made.

"You all need to decide for yourselves what that means," said Lyda. "This is the way now. Do whatever you want, but I'm going to keep going."

"I'm sorry," Vanessa said. "But if you want me to walk over those bodies, then I'm going the other way. I just—that way... Look, there's things we're not meant to see. Things we'll never know. I can't, okay?"

No one joined Vanessa as she turned back. Carlos and the others wouldn't dare traverse this place without Lyda.

2.

Callum debated whether to follow the Regulators and Leni deeper into the ship. While he weighed his options, he carefully laid Siannon down. She'd be fine... he hoped. He'd only knocked her out. The request she'd made had been unacceptable. But perhaps things were that bad. The woman *had* nearly shot him.

Who had taken over Siannon's body then? Had it been Leni?

The captain?

That was an important question, but the more impending one was how much longer until the enemy reached Arqa?

Before that, he had to capture Leni. The air quality down here was inconsistent. He brought an oxygen mask to his face.

Siannon wasn't a threat now, but if she woke up, she could still attack him. He used his only handcuffs to secure her to a pipe on the wall.

Before Callum went on, he reported to Central Command. He also requested back-up.

Advancing, he found a stack of bodies, practically blocking the way forward. Three of them were the Regulators, dead. Then he saw the last one. The one on top. Leni. She had drool coming out of her mouth and looked battered, but she was still alive.

"What did you do to them, Leni?" he asked, dragging her up.

Her bruised eyes opened up as wide as they could. "Oh, spare me."

"We asked you to come peacefully. Why? Why didn't you just come out?"

"I don't recognize the authority given to you by that heartless woman."

"That's fine. She's going to decide what happens to you either way."

"That, or you could get the one you're really after."

"I'll settle for you," Callum said. "Dominique's not going anywhere."

"What? That's not Dom up ahead."

"Who is it?"

Leni shrugged.

"You said it was her! So who was behind that mask?"

Leni made a deranged expression.

"It doesn't matter now. This area only has one way out. She's cornered. Not only that, but I have back-up coming."

"You aren't afraid yet, I see," she said. "Haven't you looked at the sky today?"

Callum jammed his gun into her face. "Tell me what the fuck is going on."

"You moron. You know exactly what's happening. We're one big experiment. I'm just in the control group."

"No, I don't get what you mean. Explain!" Callum pressed the barrel into her cheek. "What do you know about B3? How are you screwing up Arqa's systems?"

"You're not afraid because you think you know what you are. There is so much more. To manifest ourselves, we must impose limitation. I'm not afraid. We're so much closer."

"Excellent non-answer, Leni. Your life is about to get a lot more complicated. Mark's been concocting cruel and unusual punishments for you."

"Bring it on," she said softly. "You can't harm the soul."

"Alright, let's go then." As they headed back to the atrium, he said, "So you had Tim helping you this whole time. We're going to figure out how he tampered with Dominique's footage."

"But he didn't. He didn't do that. Why are you so dense? You know how she was taken. She's not on this ship. You want proof? Let's go back that way."

Callum, though tempted, refused.

"Tick tock. This may be your last chance before some wild stuff happens. Once it does, there's no turning back."

Callum soon connected with the back-up. Some of them escorted Leni to a cell. After he told the rest of them about what had happened, they went under the atrium to sweep the area. Not long after, they had brought someone out. Antonio. The man who helped program the prisoners.

Of course. Callum wasn't shocked, Antonio had been one of the most vocal opponents to the captain's conscription order. He hated his

nephew having to fight. But Callum had been so sure...
Where was Dominique, then?

Chapter Three

1.

Lyda stopped having them follow the path. It did not seem to lead anywhere worthwhile. Instead, she experimented with creating new ways. This brought them to several other places, which led to euphoria. Like they could go anywhere they wanted at any time.

Some locations they found were unnerving, marvels of inconceivable shape and scale, also completely unidentifiable. There was a space too bright to enter. A room that had made their bodies feel numb. A domed area where sound did not carry. Besides the bodies on the path and whatever had attacked Millie, they found no other signs of life. Even objects were missing. They could find no computers or food or beds. No debris or garbage either. Just the walls and their preternatural glow.

As fascinating as this new bastion was, it was clear they could go on for a very long time and not find anything noteworthy. What kept them on their toes was the threat of being maimed. That, and they knew the place was keeping them awake and satiated.

Lyda eventually got the idea to open up another spot, the most unique of all. In her thoughts, she imagined that the wandering was over with. The group found the largest region they'd seen yet. To Lyda, it appeared like a scrambled version of the dream she'd had. The group looked up to see a huge shimmering silver body of liquid in the shape of an oval. It floated high above them in the distance. It would take several days to reach it if they walked on foot. The region was valley-like with varying levels, mounds that came up from the surface. The oval sometimes twitched, parts of it flung outward and sank back like whips of plasma from a star.

Lyda felt a great pull to the distant oval.

"After all this time," she said.

The others were a few steps behind her as she ran ahead.

"Wait," Trisalyn said. "I don't like what's over there."

"It doesn't *feel* good, does it?" James asked.

"It's something different, no doubt about that," said Carlos. "Lyda, can we go somewhere else?"

"Anywhere else," added Eric.

Lyda ignored them. She had already gone through this with

Vanessa. If they wanted to go elsewhere, they'd seen her do it enough times by now. This is where she was meant to go.

"Lyda, wait up!" James said. He'd been enjoying himself since they'd started exploring. They'd been having so much fun together. Now Lyda could tell he was getting scared again.

"No," Lyda said. The games were over now.

Reeve ran up to Lyda. He tried to grab her wrist, but Lyda slipped past him.

"Sweetie," Reeve said. "We're with you. What are you thinking?"

"This place has something for us," Lyda explained. "For me. Something I'm missing. Something I need. Everybody needs something, right?"

Trisalyn jumped out to get in Lyda's way. "This feels wrong, Lyda."

"Not to me," Lyda said, stepping around her.

"Lyda, can we stop and talk about this?" Carlos asked. "That thing could be dangerous. It could be radioactive."

"We have plenty of time to talk while we make our way over there," Lyda said.

"Stop!" Trisalyn shouted. "Guys, we can't let her go."

Lyda ran as fast as she could.

"Lyda, no!" Oliver called out.

"Lyda, this isn't fun anymore. It was, but that oval... I don't think your mommy's in there. What if it's some kind of trap?"

"Trap?" Lyda considered. Danger? It didn't seem plausible.

"Quit it, Lyda!" Carlos exclaimed. "This isn't safe."

The room's colors darkened. Bulges formed on the floor between Lyda and the others. Lyda did not look back. The surface she walked on elevated her, vastly cutting down the distance between her and the object. She was a third of the way there, just like that. The others were too far to reach her now. Knowing they couldn't stop her, she slowed her pace.

She was going to see her mommy and Congo again! Save them. B3 had burrowed her mommy. Now Lyda would be like Princess Nemp to come and rescue them.

The others were reverting to animal responses, more fright and hysterics. That was unfortunate. She'd told them not to panic. Hopefully, they'd figure it out. If they hadn't tried to stop her, she doubted they would have created such a mess. All they had to do was realize that. She wasn't going to do that for them. No, she was needed elsewhere.

Nothing had given her explicit instructions to get her this far. It was all just ideas: desire, nature, authority. The feeling that hair had given her. And as Lyda reached the halfway point, she saw what lay ahead: this was it. This was where they'd planted the first seed. The initial node of this station. The simplest component. Laid out and ready for her to know. Up close enough, Lyda had to admit the thing had a freakish feel to it. It was the first piece of B3 that had a constant color, silver. But it wasn't giving off any heat, so she could get close to it just fine. This was where her intention could be brought out with the most purity.

She was level with the object. It did not react in tandem to the darkening abyss around her. She liked that. The next thing she knew, she was looking at her reflection in the object. The path evaporated and Lyda fell instantaneously. How high up was she? She thought of what she had seen in her reflection. This place hadn't changed her physically, but...

Instead of losing herself to the fall, she fixed her mind upon that image of herself in the object—and she was safe. She floated against it, not attached but almost magnetized to it. Again, she saw herself. It did not reflect anything but her. Lyda could make her way to any point along the liquefied mystery. She could hang upside down or on her side.

Lyda touched it for the first time. The thing rose, taking her with it. So she'd finally get to see how high B3's ceiling was. Ascending, Lyda laughed.

"Thank you, mommy. I know now. Just like my dream. Flying! I have control! Control."

They'd never be able to halt her progress now. Digging into the object with her hands, she let it take her.

She sunk into the flowing amorphous material and breathed it in graciously.

Focus, she thought. *I have to save my mommy.*

The first things she saw was as a god, from up high and detached from nominal planes of existence.

2.

Brenda wasn't really Kalyna's sister, she was her cousin. The JENA bot had shielded Kalyna's Spaero from the four ships' attack (the fifth was gone, thanks to her). Brenda had pioneered force field technology!

The rush made her feel alive. It lifted and numbed her from the impact when she was shot again. A victory short-lived.

Everyone on Arqa knew "Frolic Like An Otter," but few knew of her Auntie Eva's songs. The woman hadn't sung in Arqa's language, but in Ukrainian. As Kalyna's situation fell into oblivion, she went through the one titled "Розсміятися". The girl did not know much of anything in Ukrainian, but she had the syllables memorized. Her father had shown her and Brenda the recordings for the first time when they were much younger, and it had stunned them.

"This is one thing we cannot teach you," her father had admitted then. "What Eva could do with her voice. There are no singers on Arqa classically trained in this way. It is therefore all the more precious. Never forget what heights the human spirit can reach. Ever."

Were these the heights her father had spoken of? A talent in battle? To build things useful in a war?

She thought of her Auntie Eva and her mother, and all the other family she'd never met, stranded on Earth. Then the future. Kalyna had thought she'd be a mother herself. So much for that.

Then she imagined the L'rias hearing her auntie's voice. How it might earn them an end to the mayhem.

Her previous anger faded into sorrow. Why did the L'rias have to move her from protecting Arqa? It seemed like they were going to get what they wanted either way. How could they be so advanced and blood-thirsty at the same time?

Now that JENA was spent, Kalyna's Spareo would only take a few more hits. If that. That was an optimistic projection. One more hit could do the job just fine. Heat would slowly spread until it boiled her alive. She had the option to eject but that fate could be worse.

Kalyna focused her attention on the radar. Switching through it, she was startled to see the blackness of space had returned. Whatever anomaly had changed the dark, it was passed. She looked at her enemies. One of those ships was going to finish her. Well, which one? It was all a game of chance. If she could take them out before they made their shot...

Her voice rose with a crescendo in the song, and she turned to kill again.

Sorry, 1st LT Lucio, she thought.

As Kalyna's ship rushed perilously into another, she felt no pain, so long as she could concentrate on the next line of her auntie's song.

Chapter Four

1.

"I can't believe she'd leave us," said James, who was slowly unraveling. Carlos watched as the boy brought his fingernails to his face and scratched compulsively.

"She found a way to get up there," said Trisalyn. "One of us just needs to—"

"No!" Eric said. "Enough is enough."

"I'm freaking out," said Reeve. Oliver was clinging onto him.

After Lyda had left them, bulges appeared and split off from the walls. One for each of them.

"We need to stabilize here, people!" Oliver said.

Carlos heard Oliver, but couldn't help dropping to his knees, quivering as tears came.

Eric was trying to summon up some means of escape, but it wasn't working. Carlos noticed the light was fading. Did they need Lyda?

The sight of those bulges was a waking nightmare. The group split up, as the bulges came up from the surface and hovered toward each of them.

Carlos was livid at Lyda for leaving them behind to contend with these things. There was no telling what chance they had, but considering the only tangible thing they had come across since landing was dead human bodies, Carlos figured not great.

"Hey!" Eric called out. The group looked over to him. He was swinging what looked like a gray rod. "Look, Millie got stumped, and it took her over. Be a fighter. Think of beating these things back! Think of *life* and take no shit." Eric walloped the form in front of him, but it was hard to tell if it was making a difference. The bulge continued to change. Was that in response to Eric's blows?

Carlos crafted something in his mind and it appeared in his hands. A sword ripped straight out of one of his fantasy VR games.

"Now that's what I'm talking about!" James said, summoning an ax. He must have played the same game.

Carlos hoped then James wasn't Faeleen. The thought made him laugh and gave him enough leeway to cut down on his opposition. The swings were successful in that they sliced pieces off from the form in front of him, and shavings of material flopped back onto the surface, where they remain disintegrated. It seemed like it was working, so he put all of his strength into the task.

He snapped out of it when he saw Eric again. Eric's opponent had gone through an unanticipated metamorphosis. It had yet to attack, but the sight of it forced Carlos to stop what he'd been doing. Every time Eric landed a blow, the shape grew more like the man in every aspect. It matched his size, his color, even his motions. Carlos looked at his opposition. The same thing was happening to his form! Carlos wanted to stop immediately and run, but when he tried, the form tripped him with a foot that looked like his own. Dazed, he looked up to see a convincing replica of himself looking dispassionately at him.

Sword and all.

2.

There wasn't enough time to interrogate Leni and Antonio before the enemy reached Arqa. Callum ducked out of the interrogation room to clear his head. He went for a walk. When he reached the Gaze Room, he saw space was back to normal.

He intended to just keep going. Go until someone stopped him. Just focus on the task at hand. Be present. That was how you built an outstanding quality of life. Even as a nasty humming pervaded the ship, they sailed on. What a mysterious sound. Where had the strangeness in the sky gone? It shouldn't have gone anywhere if Arqa had reached B3.

The air sparkled. Other distortions entered his eyesight. The humming stalled.

It had to be his Siranis Fluid. The supply must have been drugged. He checked his IC. It wasn't working. That was weird. Had they shut the network down? Yes, measures taken (without his permission) to ease the pain of Arqa's fall. Numb them and prevent them from communicating unless it was face to face. Like an oxygen mask for a nosediving plane. He then felt compelled to return to the corridor where Dominique had gone missing.

That corridor, yes. Callum would find her. He pretended he was being chased to get there sooner. On his way, he thought it was odd that he didn't run into anybody. Callum had just seen people in the Gaze Room!

An unfamiliar noise came through the increasingly slurring reality around him.

That noise. Was it? Yes, barking! On the other end of the corridor. He knew that bark. It had to be Congo! Callum ran as fast as he could, expecting that he'd catch up with the dog.

Callum hadn't been regulating his breathing well (or maybe the air was different somehow), and he had to stop. Now he might be losing the dog, Callum called out to the dog, knowing it would normally come running. Didn't he just have an oxygen tank earlier? He didn't recall taking it off. "Come here, boy. It's all getting torn down. Help me turn something around." The dog did not come. But it still sounded out. He was now in the last known location of Dominique Hall.

Congo was lovable and wanted everyone's attention. Dominique was more aloof. Like a cat. When Craig was younger, Callum had told him to be more like a dog. Cats and dogs were both fine creatures, but people by and large preferred dogs. Callum believed that. You had to be social. So why wasn't Congo over here, jumping on Callum?

From a short distance, he heard howling. Was he getting closer? He had to be. He was.

Suddenly he felt very lucid. Sober. As if this was all real, not the effect of some sedative.

Callum turned the corner of a corridor and swore he saw that dog padding away from him before going out of sight again. Where was that good boy going?

He went on in a devastated wonderment, closing in, knowing from the sudden jerks and tilting from the ship that the enemy was, at last, upon them.

Chapter Five

1.

Reeve was the first of them to die. What had happened? If Carlos dwelt on that too long, then his own replica might gain a decisive advantage. It wasn't possible to get away from it, it only followed. When it had first formed, it had shambled in its steps. But now it could run as Carlos could run.

Other quick tests Carlos had conducted between his squeamish parries and thrusts indicated that the replica was not independently conscious. All it did was try to slice him.

"Hey, do you understand me?" Carlos asked. "I won't go after Lyda! I just want to to go home." Carlos tried thinking about that intention to the replica. It was ineffective. Maybe this was why Captain Sali hadn't bothered surrendering.

Swinging at this thing felt worse than what happened to Millie. At least it had been quick for her. For the first time since reaching the UFO, Carlos could feel his energy draining. His wrists were sore and he was short of breath. The mirror self did not show any such wear.

Carlos twisted his lips and was met with nothing but a blank expression. He was starting to believe he stood no chance of surviving.

Daring to look over to the Reeve replica, Carlos noticed something odd. It didn't seem to be an exact replica. Oliver's as well. Trisalyn, James, and Eric's replicas looked identical to them though. The Reeve replica no longer moved, though it was coming apart, the pieces peeling off like leaves off a tree.

Trisalyn, who'd been trying to talk to Reeve, no longer got a response.

There had to be a way to stop these things! Carlos knew he wouldn't win with what he was doing, so he relinquished his sword and charged. His replica cut down. Carlos blocked the strike. Should he hold it down? He didn't want to touch it. If only there were some way to restrain it. Thinking of handcuffs did nothing—how was this supposed to work?

"Lyda, we're sorry, please help us!" Carlos pleaded. "Make it stop! We'll do whatever you want! Please!"

Again, as usual, nothing. Where had she gone? The oval wasn't there anymore; it had shot up above them.

His replica regained its footing. It'd been a decent break, but Carlos was going to make a mistake soon, as he was still out of breath.

He had to take a chance.

As his replica swung its blade toward him, Carlos feigned and, despite his best judgment, pivoted in a series of moves taught to him by 1st LT Lucio. The replica was not expecting this and had no counter. Carlos *hated* touching the thing, but he felt out of options.

He grabbed at his replica's wrists and twisted the sword out of its hand. Miss Siannon had once gone over protocols were they ever to encounter extraterrestrial life, but those had gone completely out the window after Trisalyn had tried to suffocate herself. With all of his might, he spooled his leg up and swept the replica over.

The replica's sword felt similar, yet less solid than the one he'd created. He readied to behead it. Why not? Its ilk had killed Reeve. Now Carlos could return the favor. Then he'd rescue Lyda.

"Don't do that!" Oliver exclaimed. Carlos saw the man was fast approaching and for a second he was afraid it was Oliver's replica.

The man tackled Carlos and Carlos's replica. "What are you doing?" Carlos asked, dazed.

"Look, I overcame mine," Oliver said, quick to scramble up and away from the duo. "It's—look, you don't try to kill it, Carlos."

Carlos stared at his replica. His mirror image. This was how people saw him. He hated it. It deserved to die. For all the trials it had brought before him. And what was its reaction? It didn't struggle. If anything, it seemed resigned. Locking eyes with the thing became mesmerizing. Why didn't it fight back now?

Afraid he was being put into a trance, Carlos covered the thing's face with his hands. It felt like everything else in this place had. Not alive, but still powerful. Energetic. What would happen if he gouged its eyes out? Maybe then it wouldn't be able to follow him.

"Don't act on hostility," Oliver said. "Otherwise it won't stop. Let things go. Think of yourself. Think of everything you've ever done. Accept it." Oliver patted Carlos on the back and stepped away.

Carlos, still confused, parted his hands and made eye contact with it. He followed Oliver's directions as best as he could. He thought of his life. His flaws. His desires. He imbued the thing with unbridled acceptance. He told it, "I am where I am now." And it lay still.

He took a deep breath before going and helping the others, not looking at the defeated replica. It seemed like Eric was down. James had finished his off, also thanks to Oliver. All that remained was Trisalyn, who was exchanging fast hits with a cutlass in her hands.

The surrounding environment had calmed significantly, nearly back to how they'd originally found the region. The group rallied around Trisalyn and with their help, she too disposed of her replica.

Carlos and Oliver raced over to Reeve, completely unresponsive on the surface.

"Moron," Oliver said, checking Reeve's pulse. "If only we'd known sooner."

Carlos saw the remnant of the Reeve replica was now almost completely disintegrated. "Why do your replicas look different?" he asked the grieving man.

"That's him," Oliver explained. "Or at least, it was me. Whatever just happened, this place, I think, it took our DNA or a biologically accurate copy. Projected it. Reeve and I... we weren't always..."

"Oh, right. I understand." Now it made sense.

"Eric thought the solution to beating these things was to kill them," Oliver continued. "It was a fairly logical plan... but as soon as I saw Reeve's form... and that he'd lost his fight... I knew what to do. Maybe it was easier for me to see this little gimmick for what it was. A curveball. I dropped my weapon, and I thought really hard about my life and what this thing meant to me. It's a part of me I left behind. To not think about anymore. I thought about who I wanted to be, and how I would leave here alive. This wouldn't be it. Reeve must have reacted differently. This is like... how I was born, but not who I wanted to be. Of course I'd like to hurt it... to kill it. But that's not what they tell you... you're only hurting yourself." Oliver was sobbing. "It isn't the right way to move on. You've got to be better. We were always fighting about that. Lord, I'm going to miss him. This is a screwed up way to win an argument."

Trisalyn appeared to give Oliver a hug. "You did it! You saved us."

"Hey, hold on, we're not out of trouble yet!" James called out a ways from Carlos and the others.

"Look, that doesn't matter," Carlos said. "Why don't we go and get Lyda?"

"Lyda's a million miles away and Eric's right here!" James said. So Eric was still alive.

"What's the problem then?"

"I can't tell. Eric's acting weird. He says it's him but..."

"Great," said Oliver, who looked over to Eric. "First Reeve goes and dies on me, now this."

"Forget about him!" Carlos said bitterly. "I don't think we can cut it here without Lyda."

"Carlos," Trisalyn said, her voice strained. "She promised James he would be safe, did he not nearly just die? Don't you think she's the one who got us tangled up and fighting for our lives in the first place?"

2.

There were whispers of annihilation. Finality.

For years, Will had been living in his own little world. But now he knew he'd been useless there. Using his privilege to isolate himself. Working on his little project from a detached perspective. All that had changed now. He was where everyone else was: trapped by the L'rias and their machinations. And he had done nothing to fight them. The Sleeping Sickness should have mobilized him, and it had, but not in the proper way. Now that Gabriel had shown him that peek of infinity, Will was lost.

He left the pens on the walls alone.

If these were the last moments before the L'rias had their victory, he would have wanted to spend them with his Grammy. But he'd been shoved away from where she was in Central Command. If he had a second option, he would choose Miss Siannon. She was likewise unavailable.

Ultimately, he checked on Stephen again. The man answered the door.

"Hi," Will said. "It's me again. I'm sorry about Lyda. And earlier. People have accused me of being a bad listener. But I remember what you said. You said it's not a great time. You're so right about that. And so, I think, I think that neither of us should be alone right now."

"Oh, alright. I see."

Will saw the man had torn his quarters apart. "Want a hand cleaning?"

"Sure, bud. I'd hate for Lyda to see this place so trashed when she gets back."

Will played along. "Sure, then she'd think it'd be okay to mess it up even more."

"No more dog hair..." Stephen said, trailing off as he let Will inside.

"I'm really grateful. Your grandmother helped give us some great extra years."

That was the tone of the conversation. They did not discuss that Flight Division was gone. How that meant there was no longer anything standing between them and their enemies.

No, instead, they talked about animals. About bugs. Squids that could change their shape. A species of jellyfish that could reset its biological clock and (theoretically) repeat the process indefinitely.

"That sounds like it could have some drawbacks," Will said.

"I get that. One round is enough for some people."

"You've made yours count."

"Thanks, Will. I like to think so too." They had, at that point, concentrated the mess to one segment of the room. It was how Will liked to clean his room on the rare occasion that he did. "So, you finished that book, right?"

"No, I was waiting."

"For what?" Stephen asked.

"For a line that could help people accept all of this."

"Well, it was worth a try."

"Hey, what's that?" Will asked, gesturing to a thick purple binder resting precariously on a pile of clothing.

"That's *my* book! I haven't finished it yet either."

"I'd like to see!"

"Oh, you'd love it. But you've already seen some of it."

"How?"

Stephen scooped the binder up and opened it. He brought the unfamiliar object over to Will. "It's a photo album. This is me when I was about your age. The Grand Canyon! Just think of a chasm almost two thousand square miles long. Hardly any buildings or technology, just nature."

"Looking good," Will said, noticing a gorgeous brunette standing beside a younger Stephen. "Whose that lady?"

"My mom," Stephen said.

"Oh, gotcha. Hey, one of the pictures is missing," Will said, pointing to a gap in the page.

"Right, yeah, that's... Lyda has that. It's one of her mother. One her mother gave me. I wouldn't have let her have it normally, but after Dominique went missing, maybe I..." Stephen thought for a moment. "I should put it back."

"Where is it?"

"I hope she hasn't taken it with her. That girl, she'd probably lose it."

"This is incredible. Grammy has shown me pictures of Earth, but I can never get enough of it. This non-digital thing is something too. Really tangible."

Stephen left the room and Will continued sorting things. "Yeah, here it is, by her bed. Wait a second..."

"Hmm?"

"Will, there's something on here I've never noticed before. Come here, quick."

Will ran for where Stephen was. The man was leaning against the bed, his eyes burning into the photograph. No. Not the side with the picture. Stephen had it turned over.

"Let me see."

"Oh, what would it mean to you?"

"Sorry."

"No. What I meant to say was—Will, there's some writing here. Dominique's."

"Okay, and what does it say?" Will was too impatient to wait for the man's stupor to pass. He lowered himself to read the words. "Let me see?"

Stephen dug his fingers into the picture. "I don't know. I don't understand it. I should be able to. I don't want to scare you because I don't know what it means."

"Does it say where she is?"

"No. Fine. See for yourself." He handed Will the photograph. "But be careful, Will. I think we're going to have to show that to Callum or your grandmother."

Though he wanted to, Will did not flip the picture over to see the other side. He only read the words that had affected Stephen so. In small print, there was a date circled, with a line connecting to a single sentence.

The line read: *My daughter will find me.*

The date was today.

Chapter Six

1.

Lyda became as it was. It seeped through her pores. Filled her lungs. Breathing was not an issue. There was light in motion. And it did not feel as if anything was around her. She felt inward.

There was no turning back. Even as she knew the speed she was traveling was altering her perceived time. Lyda's form drew beyond itself. Josie, who she held on fast to, also seemed to blur in her palm. They were soaring now to the heights of B3, but she did not know why. Was that where the aliens were? Her mother? She hoped so. This was much more jarring than she'd anticipated. Her thoughts were losing cohesion, getting harder to form. It didn't feel like she was inside of her body anymore.

It was challenging, but she managed to ask, *Where is my mommy?* to the oval.

All motion was halted. Josie was changing, enlarging. Turning into a dragon before her eyes. With skin like the material of B3, but much, much, brighter.

Flying, not falling, she thought once more. She climbed onto the dragon.

"Are you there, Josie?"

But it was just a vessel that housed energy. A beast.

"Take me to my mommy!"

The dragon did not comply. Instead, it granted Lyda more dazzling vistas of B3. She saw the others, fighting projections.

"Eric's acting weird," she heard James say. Then she was elsewhere. There was no preventing their unfolding ordeal. B3 had many things to show her. It was all only the beginning. At least she felt she had *some* control of Josie, for Josie was her doll.

Was it Josie though? It certainly seemed a far cry from anything hostile that the group had experienced. A being of light, but Lyda could not know what it wanted. They only went up, higher and higher. There it was dark. Dark dark. Darker than space. Darker than the darkest thing she could imagine.

Then it took Lyda through one of B3's boundaries, into space. She saw B3 as a whole. The entire area they occupied. There was Arqa, atomic compared to B3, but still flying on its own.

Miss Siannon had shown the ship to her in pictures. Lyda understood how the ion engines worked and how exterior belts generated the pseugra, but she'd never been outside of it. Able to see its pearly hull. Everything had happened for her within those walls. Arqa's front end was rounded, with two rectangular fins jutting out like a V to form the outer section. Between the two fins was a cubic center, slanting into the front end. Lyda saw it and knew love.

"Josie, this is incredible. But are you saying my mommy and Congo are still there?" She forgot it was futile to ask it questions. None of this was getting her what she needed.

Wait a second. Her home was under attack! Not a single ship from Flight Division guarded Arqa as the enemy buzzed around it.

A new thought came to her. But Lyda was not the one who had created it. *To know is to kill.* A woman's voice. One Lyda didn't initially recognize. Josie? No...

You! You're the voice from when I got that hair. After the bug. I don't know who you are, but I've come all this way. I did everything I was supposed to.

Knowledge mutilates ignorance wherever it goes, the voice proceeded, disregarding Lyda's words. *It is savage against ignorance and its manifestation, chaos... for chaos far outweighs knowledge and its manifestation, order. Chaos is indifferent to order's attacks, for chaos has no chance of being eliminated, only further reinforced as* unstoppable.

I don't understand what you're talking about! Lyda said.

Knowledge of chaos is the only necessary paradox.

Tell me where my mommy is.

Not here.

Lyda wasn't sure, based on context, what the voice meant by *here.* Sometimes it looked like she was back in B3, sometimes she was still in space. Lyda thought of an oscillating wave. Patterns at the source of flowers and galaxies and life and love and—

What?! Don't lie. You took her! You're hiding her. Give her back so she can do something. My daddy is on that ship! Will and his Grammy! Everyone I've ever known is going to be finished.

The self is constantly eroded. It is never there at all. What comes in its place is falsely labeled. What if what is lost... is all there is to a self?

Lyda's rage subsided. The voice wouldn't distract her from her goal. Aware of that, the oval showed her only herself.

Your people are in danger, the woman's voice observed. *Do you not wish to save them?*

Lyda felt herself less and less, merging deeper into this miasma of... it wasn't another consciousness... or was it? It hadn't been responsive at first. Now it was roused. *Who is this? Why aren't you helping me?* It wasn't Josie. It was posing.

Not that, no. But also only through you. Danger. Things are in danger that don't need to be. And the universe doesn't care.

What have you shown me? Lyda asked. *Battles on Earth, that ocean. These visions, they all came from B3. But what do they mean?*

One thing at a time.

I want my mommy. It feels like she would know!

She cannot help now, the voice informed. *You can. Time is short. Your home will be gone.*

And for the first time in a long time, Lyda felt something greater than the loss of her mother. The tragedy that would be Arqa's downfall. She realized just how urgent that was. She couldn't have stopped her mommy from going away, but she thought she could stop this.

Can't I just stop time and think about this for a second? Lyda asked.

The other voice coalesced beyond her. Lyda saw herself. Faint like an outline. *They'll kill your father. Your teacher. Your rule-makers. But you are in charge of this now.*

I can... stop the fighting? Really?

You need only to... want to.

The view of herself turned into a view of the Gaze Room. She was *outside* of it, floating alone, no longer on Josie. Looking through the window, she saw Gabriel. They were alone, but it still felt like somebody was watching them. Like Felicia, even though Lyda knew the girl wasn't there.

Gabriel was frowning. "Lyda. Do you realize how this is all happening?"

"How?"

"Think about it. This wasn't all a coincidence, you were guided. B3 unleashed the Sleeping Sickness onto Arqa... with certain assistance. It put the others under, sapped them. I could feel it happening. That's what it was. It took from us... to give to you."

"Me?"

"Yes. For this moment. But... have you thought of what it would mean to stop the enemy?"

"It's asking me if I want to save Arqa. I do! You'll die if I don't. But I didn't think—didn't know. I didn't come here to do that."

"I know. Even though we're little, we still have to think about what we're doing. Sadly, if you don't do something now, there won't be anything you *can* do. But doing something, that's going to be bad too."

"What do you mean?"

"It's a weapon of unimaginable power," Gabriel said. "It has already changed you." Lyda couldn't pinpoint how, but he was right. "Using it against them may seem like the only solution... but just think it over. If you do this, never forget: we're under this thing's control. Right now it's ours to use, but what about tomorrow?"

"I don't want to make this decision. I know it's doing things to me. I want to use it to find my mommy!"

"I'm just here to tell you the pros and cons. The L'rias will destroy Arqa if you don't think of anything else."

"Why does part of me think B3 and the L'rias are the same thing?" Lyda asked.

Gabriel frowned. "They're not. At the same time, every thing is one thing. I just wish... I don't know."

"Well, nobody listened. And now we're here."

"I... understand Lyda."

"I don't!" Lyda spat. "I hate the L'rias. Look at what they did to us. Maybe they're the ones that have my mommy now!"

"You'll have to be precise in crafting your intention if you suspect that," Gabriel said. "It doesn't seem like you are fully prepared to tell it what you want to happen. You better figure it out, fast."

Gabriel was right. Arqa was taking damage, losing the battle.

"Lyda, remember, if you aren't careful, you're going to kill the wrong people."

Gabriel and Arqa faded away. She was back in B3 again.

"You have Gabriel talk to me to tell me I shouldn't use you? What is this?"

Whatever voice had reached out to her would not heed her. Josie, that dragon of pure light, was still there. It wasn't exactly built with her interests in mind, she realized. Had she thought so? Lyda had walked around B3 like she owned the place. Maybe she could.

Lyda forged her decision. She thought hard and rose once more, joining Josie and entering space. The dormant and ancient power of B3 concentrated. From Lyda's mind, Josie grew. Arqa needed this. But what exactly? Well, light was good, right? B3 had helped her see what she already knew: Arqa was outmatched. Lyda just needed to turn the tables. Keep them alive by using the light.

Light was good.

At least, that's what she thought. But Lyda made the same mistake she'd been making this entire time; she couldn't help it. She felt all the life there was, as a new energy gathered. It would soon be unstoppable. It felt good. Like she was coming back together. The goodness was cut off by a brand new pain. An unusual sensation. In her abdomen. Her lower parts. No time to worry about that now. At least she was in her body again. Time moved faster.

"Get away from my ship," Lyda proclaimed.

And like that, dozens of lives were ended. Ships were pulverized in their tracks. Extinguished. Boundaries were broached. She had saved Arqa, but

(*fly by*)

one second a sum of life was there, the next it went missing. Not all of it, but Lyda still felt the full consequences of her actions. The last moments of each of those minds she'd commanded to end reached her. Sharp emotions and regret were all assimilated into the well of her consciousness. The enemy, they were not the monsters she'd thought they were. The adults had only told them a little part of the big truth...

2.

The oval spit Lyda out. There was no more flight. Josie was only a plush thing again. She cradled her stuffed animal tightly in her arms.

Those she'd silenced went helplessly, with no hope of surviving.

And she experienced their chasm into death long enough to forever feel it as it approached her.

...to be continued.

THE ARQA DOSSIER

To a Free Mind

"There was once a gravity, both spiritual and physical... made to set all in place, and keep them there. This grounding was briefly shattered by a species of innovators, who saw no alternative from the signs of an expiring planet. Just as in primordial times, when the first life-form made for shore.

All life is a mirror. Upon the summit of a mountain, we realize just how far down from the top of every actual thing we are, bound in Sisyphean condemnation. For the boulder to be rolled up the hill, it must be circular by design. Full rotations and closed loops trigger in us little satisfaction. And no position, no bastion, will provide us with the transcendence. For countering every desire and thought is this higher plane. Upon crossing it, we may never know."

-Nicholai Heron

Centuries of foolish debate have sealed the fate of our world. We had the option to listen, to see the cascading effects of greed. Fighting over territories like primates. Battles fought upon subsequently abused land. Even as the perils of the future outweighed the promises, the majority had fallen into digital landscapes with impenetrable and synthetic truths.

After it was too late, people never took responsibility. They blamed. Anyone who wasn't them.

We are a growing organization of autonomous minds who seek to sever ties with this doomed Earth. To pledge never again to pass the buck or let bureaucracy dictate evolution. Humanity has cut itself off from nature, endeavoring to elevate itself. But don't we still need oxygen? Don't we still need food? Why have we complicated our access to those needs when technology makes it easier than ever to distribute all we need?

Wars and gods have brought us to the worst stage in known history. We believe without severe measures and extreme consciousness change, soon we shall be no more.

The development of artificial general intelligence, long heralded as our only hope, has been stymied and prohibited by the powers that be. In that, they have banned our future. Under their values, the banners of blind consumption and faith, they have increased the probability of our extinction.

But some of us know a secret.

That life here is not an isolated incident in the universe. There are others, and they have reached heights well past our patterns of diminishing returns.

A human must either be free or *freed*. Free to disobey unjust laws. Free to save their species. That's why you are reading this now. We plan to do just that. To gather a vessel with Earth's greatest minds. For a new future. Where we can conduct the research Earth does not condone. To freely experiment and declare independence from every standing government.

We are confident that biological immortality, artificial general intelligence, and other forbidden discoveries are on the other side of this dire maneuver. We may fail, but if we do, it will be because of our conviction. To outlast our world. And fill the universe with compassion, intelligence, and love.

You have been selected out of millions to join our cause. To save our race.

Enclosed are Arqa's specs. Your new home, assuming you agree: There is no safe quarter. No chance left to do the work required to sustain life as we know it. No free inch left on Earth, the moon, or its other settlements. There is only the space beyond.

Our last chance to define what becomes of Homo sapiens.

ARQA

Arqa is an S^4 (self-sustaining spaceship). Originally, it was meant to house a team of scientists for a six-year expedition to Enceladus. When that mission was canceled because of changing circumstances on Earth, Arqa was left dangling in orbit (where it was initially constructed). This ship's estimated population threshold is 634, with a large section carved out to hold people in stasis, on a rotating basis. Its potential for other, more urgent purposes is clear. We intend to acquire this ship to preserve humanity and conduct research that will make Earth unnecessary.

DIMENSIONS

Length: 484m
Width: 122m
Height: 120m

PROPULSION

Arqa's primary means of propulsion is its ion thrusters. The ship can collect light gases abundant in space for indefinite fuel supply.

VECTOR

Our aim is to distance ourselves from Earth (a decision somewhat contingent upon the eventual trajectory and outcomes of future peoples and innovations), out past the Solar System.

PSEUGRA

Arqa's structure supports pseugra, in its living and working spaces. Exterior belts rotating around the hull provide the force. The artificial gravity available is not as strong as on Earth, and so one must be willing to accept potential hazards and alteration's to the difference.

INTERNAL CONNECTOR

Every person accepted onto Arqa will be given a procedure to install an Internal Connector. This device, while commonplace among most of the population, is specialized and distinct to Arqa. It allows for instantaneous communication through the ship and some VR capabilities. Holo-screens can be shared and conjured through this network. The device is connected to key points of the brain. Implicit in this agreement to board also means access to your saved memories and thought emissions upon the event of your death or otherwise life-threatening event.

UNFETTERED RESEARCH

Our top priority is the ability to conduct research discouraged on Earth. Self-replicating nanotechnology, artificial general intelligence, and genetic research all are on the table. We need to develop non-biological, sentient life with which to assimilate with if Arqa is to last more than a few generations. With strong AI, humanity's problems will be much easier to solve. Without it, we stand to go extinct. This leads some objectors to say strong AI may lead to human extinction, regardless. We are consciously developing artificial intelligence to encounter, not eliminate us.

SUBSTITUTING EARTH

Earth provides our body with a myriad of things. A life in space will never suffice as well as a terrestrial lifestyle. That being said, Arqa boasts some interesting adaptations to the challenges. For one, each space is designed with movement and exercise in mind. Fitness will be a constant requirement. There is a UV chamber, and more importantly, Siranis Fluid. Siranis Fluid is a distilled blend of vitamins, amino acids, calories, and other chemically yielded materials that provide the body with ample nutrition (through entirely plant-based means). Siranis Fluid has been developed to act as more than supplementation, and in fact makes solid food redundant (from a nutritional perspective). Current nanotechnology will allow for streamers, which will be administered intravenously and be able to monitor bodies for issues, including but not limited to: cancer, thyroid problems, blood sugar, cholesterol, excess radiation, and even improper muscular-skeletal motion. Death has symptoms, and by tracking them, we can extend life spans to a certain extent. Though limited, Arqa has livestock muscle cells and crops grown for the occasional meal. Meal passes will be distributed as available. Any waste from all of this consumption is in turn recycled effectively into drinking water.

SUSTAINABILITY

Arqa was not designed with *our* mission in mind. There have been many concerned voices regarding the generations further and further out from Earth. Fuel and food for the ship is easily produced and immediately available with the proper measures. Arqa also has collected 100,000 genetic samples future women can choose from.

EDUCATION

Arqa's mission hinges on the proper rearing and conditioning of its children. They cannot be made to know of certain things, and so we shall teach them with a clean slate attitude. Aptitudes will be honed in on to fill essential roles. These kids must have an understanding of general medicine, engineering, and communication.

PSYCHS

Arqa needs a staff of highly trained psychologists to attend to the population's mental health.

REGULATORS

Arqa also needs people who can assist in enforcing the rules. Regulators are not police, and they must understand deescalation techniques and the ability to employ tactical empathy.

BAY LINE

We have acquired a few Spaero ships, which, in optimistic scenarios, will be used for recreation to get people out of the ship. They will also be retrofitted with weaponry in the event of hostile confrontations.

FINANCIAL CONSIDERATIONS

Once we leave Earth, Arqa will operate without currency. Beforehand, however, the fulfillment of Arqa's mission will require capital. This is why we are also offering positions in our cryo chamber to those who can afford it. Your chances of benefiting from our research may very well seem better than what Earth has waiting for you. However, we cannot offer any guarantees that you will ever wake up again, and if you do, it may be years or even centuries after our initial departure. Our hope is that by that time, we have perfected the art of indefinite life extension, consciousness uploading, or other methods for assimilating with non-biological intelligence.

CONCLUSION

As you can see, this task we face is immense and we cannot do it alone. We have many positions open, but there is a long vetting process. After all, the position is permanent. If you are interested in learning more, please contact us. You know where we are. But don't wait too long. If Arqa is ever going to leave, it will be soon.

Dear Evalia,

Everyone I meet is stifled and jaded. I pity them and relish in you. At times it feels as if we are the last lovers in the world. I misplace most all of my joy when I think of the slim chances of us ever reuniting and ... I just have to say I love you. This time apart as left me uncommonly morose.

You are no doubt wondering how this letter has reached you without interference. I didn't say anything, but I had installed a tunnel for the express purposes of reaching you in the event civilization went the way it has. The truth is, you are not safe, even where you are. And I'm followed by death. But for all that, there is hope. Look at our species' failures as information. I write you now at great personal risk, and I am doing everything I can to make it back to you.

The rumors of Arqa are true. I don't know about you, but that makes me blissful. The initiative, it's just what we need, Evalia. I don't want to feel like love will die with us. And I need to do more than just survive.

We cannot do this on Earth.

I understand your misgivings. I respect your efforts to preserve what you can of the lives we had before, it's why I married you. I mean that. My words from our last talk have cursed me while I am bound to my duties here. And even now I say much less than I feel. I'm taking all the steps I need to so I might breathe you in again. If I go much longer without you, I'll be useless.

Attached to this letter are sections of a report detailing their plan. I've never felt better about something in my life. I look at the work the scientists are doing and see there is *real* results, not the unceasing disappointments we've been going through.

Evalia, they've asked us to join. To leave Earth with no assurance of returning. I would be charged with keeping the population focused and happy. I'm sure you realize what an opportunity this is...

Listen so, space is less dangerous than Earth now. You know it, I know it. And this could be our only chance to escape while there's still time. Could you do this with me? Could you let it all go? I await your response. Tell me what you think. What objections you might have. There's a life for us... but I see it only in the stars. That does not have to be depressing. Nothing is, so long as we're together. But I want years with you. I want them without conditions and crimes and blood.

I must emphasize something. Arqa's capacity is under seven hundred. To be selected, it's a distinction. They imagine I'm the best of the best. Critical to the future of life itself.

So remember that when you look these things over again. And... sorry I hid the letter at the bottom of the pile.

In the meantime, my heart yearns for you. And all I do is done to see you happy again.

With immense love,
Callum Benito

To stay updated on when the next book of *The Felled* get released, you can sign up for my mailing list. As a thank you, you'll get a free ebook to take home.

Sound good?

Sign up at:
Ryansleavitt.com

Check out my YouTube channel!

In addition to writing books, I also make videos on consciousness expansion and philosophy. It's a great way to see what I'm up to week to week. Search Ryan S. Leavitt on YouTube.

About the Author

Ryan S. Leavitt is a fiction author, primarily writing thrillers and science fiction with philosophical undertones. His books have been featured on BookBub and he has also appeared on the briefly televised reality sitcom *Quiet Desperation*. He currently lives in New Orleans.

Epilogue

Time passed...

Light was a good thing.

Too much of it though...

There was light that burned

then flickering darkness.

Torture... highly complex torture. A great big thing in the sky. Glowing and opalescent.

Where was Gabriel in all of this now?

Where was the end?

There was t
    u
   m
    b

      l
       i
        n
         g

& NOISE!

& pain.

The scent of chemicals. She still had a nose? Or was that a memory?

Scents. And then, nothing. But it never lasted, that nothingness. She always returned.

It seemed to be an impossibility that Kalyna was not dead.

Scorching abrasions. Unceasing distress. Is this what Miss Siannon dealt with? Kalyna had not charged the enemy vessel to know this level of regret.

```
                         t           n                   o
That had not been her i                     t                   n.
            n         e                 i
```

Her ship had to be gone, for she felt herself able to venture out and stretch, no longer confined to a cockpit. It was in that way the fried cells forced her to curl up;

it was her skin, that was not skin, but unfiltered agony.

The black void was gone again. Breathing was a raspy, challenging affair, but it was unstoppable all the same. For her maneuver had been impressive.

Zero gravity. Utter awareness. The pain diminished slightly as the intense light assailed her. Kalyna's head was tilted upside down. She needed to adjust herself or she would get woozy, but there would be pain whether she moved or not.

The light penetrated her eyes, the ones she still had. The ones she'd pried shut. But there was no shielding them even as she dared to move, gripping her arms against her face to block it out. Where was this coming from? It was as if that light came from within.

How long had she been kept here in this bubble, unable to remain still? Skin prickling and crisp, ripping and stabbing. The chamber she was housed in moved to make her dizzy if she was not careful.

Kalyna was not fully able to brace herself when the thing she was in whipped forward. New kinds of pain. They were traveling somewhere. The velocity was the worst sensation yet. Kalyna's life had not ended, no. Quite the opposite. And she was not pleased with that gift. Not even if it meant that she may one day return home. To sing her auntie's songs and build on her intelligence and love. Because she had been completed.

Content.

She had charged forth and faced her fate. Met it head-on. But that made no difference. Kalyna fought to accept that information. That no matter what action she had taken, she would have always ended up bound in this recurring pattern of radical bodily signals she could not control. Warning her that something was very wrong, but not moving fast enough to shut down. Yes, it was utterly confusing. But no more so than usual, she wagered. She had been given a mind, and it was for her to face its temporality. It was just a near-death experience. Those things happen.

She kept thinking about Arqa, and eventually, her surroundings morphed from that mysterious spherical glow into a more concrete physical plane. She found herself conjured into the Bay Line.

Her g-suit was gone. As was her hair and ability to speak. Ever since she'd collided with whatever it was she hit that made her like this. She grew to understand that that time was over.

As she fell hard under the force of the pseugra, people and their faces looked up at her. She was alive! They were alive! But wait...

Hadn't she been here before?

www.ingramcontent.com/pod-product-compliance
Lightning Source LLC
Chambersburg PA
CBHW060856250626
47159CB00008B/2762